THE MARIONETTE

A NOVEL

TERRY FALLIS

McClelland & Stewart

Original trade paperback edition published 2025

The authorized representative in the EU for product safety and compliance is Penguin Random House Ireland, Morrison Chambers, 32 Nassau Street, Dublin D02 YH68, Ireland, https://eu-contact.penguin.ie

Library and Archives Canada Cataloguing in Publication

Title: The marionette / Terry Fallis.
Names: Fallis, Terry, author
Identifiers: Canadiana (print) 2025011822X | Canadiana (ebook) 20250118238 | ISBN 9780771021114 (softcover) | ISBN 9780771021138 (EPUB)
Subjects: LCGFT: Thrillers (Fiction) | LCGFT: Novels.
Classification: LCC PS8611.A515 M37 2025 | DDC C813/.6—dc23

This is a work of fiction. Names, characters, places, and incidents either are the product of the author's imagination or are used fictitiously. Any resemblance to actual persons, living or dead, events, or locales is entirely coincidental.

Cover design by Matthew Flute
Cover art: Aan / stock.adobe.com
Interior art: Flatman vector 24 / stock.adobe.com
Typeset in Electra LT by Daniella Zanchetta
Printed in Canada

McClelland & Stewart
A division of Penguin Random House Canada
320 Front Street West, Suite 1400
Toronto, Ontario, M5V 3B6, Canada
penguinrandomhouse.ca

2 3 4 5 29 28 27 26 25

Penguin Random House
McCLELLAND & STEWART

ADVANCE PRAISE FOR *THE MARIONETTE*

"Canada's favourite humourist returns with a high-stakes comic thriller that managed to make me both laugh out loud and gasp in suspense. Bright, savvy, and dangerously funny, *The Marionette* delivers from start to finish. Terry Fallis is a legend." **—Ali Bryan, author of *Coq*, and two-time finalist for the Leacock Medal for Humour**

"In a world shrouded in darkness and shadow, Fallis remains a shining light of decency and big-hearted humour. In his latest novel *The Marionette*, a fast-paced, feel-good thriller, he combines laughter and suspense to weave a masterful tale of international intrigue and Canadian ingenuity." **—Rod Carley, award-winning author of *RUFF***

"Narrative surprises are a constant and the humour bubbles along as a Canadian thriller writer is conscripted into palace intrigue in a foreign land, then accepts a rescue mission that sends him on a daring high-wire escape to freedom in Terry Fallis's rousing novel, *The Marionette*. A great yarn." **—Trevor Ferguson, aka John Farrow, author of *City of Ice***

"Terry Fallis's *The Marionette* is a welcome reminder that fiction can be both artful and engaging. It's a comic thriller that teems with Fallis's trademark wit. He pulls off the feat of blending genres with elan, aplomb, and pure pizazz!" **—Wayne Johnston, author of *Jennie's Boy*, winner of the 2023 Leacock Medal for Humour**

"*The Marionette* is a funny, fast-paced romp of a thriller. Terry Fallis has given us an unforgettable new action hero in James Norval—a bestselling thriller writer and aspiring spy who finally gets his chance to go undercover. I loved every page. More Norval, please!" **—Susan Juby, bestselling author of *Contemplation of a Crime***

"Seldom has a Canadian spy mission to the West African country of Mali been this much fun. Just like what Terry Fallis did with Canadian politics in his first novel, *The Best Laid Plans*, he does the impossible once again, making something inherently unfunny into an amazingly delightful adventure. Someday I want to grow up and write like Terry Fallis." **—Drew Hayden Taylor, author of *Cold***

Also by Terry Fallis

The Best Laid Plans

The High Road

Up and Down

No Relation

Poles Apart

One Brother Shy

Albatross

Operation Angus

A New Season

Norval Hunter (1905–1986)
Gwen Hunter (1910–2014)

PART
1

CHAPTER 1

I WAS in one of the lesser "Stans" when it all started. In fact, it was the least of the Stans—the smallest, to be precise. Tajikistan is not exactly a vacationer's dream destination, but I wasn't there on holiday. Most of the foreigners in the nation's capital, Dushanbe, were mercenaries—not tourists—and a few were spies. Oh, and at least one was a writer.

When they dragged me into the interrogation cell for the third day in a row, something was different. Something had changed. There was an unwelcome addition to the room's furnishings. The handcart bearing three stacked car batteries, complete with wire leads and alligator clips, still threatened from one corner. Also still there, along the far wall, was what looked like a water-boarding station. (Well, the reclined chair bolted to the wet floor and the seven full buckets weren't there so I could re-enact that famous sultry dance scene from *Flashdance*.) On Day One, I had thought the battery cart and waterboarding station were just provocative but benign props—you know, strictly to intimidate. By Day Three, I wasn't so sure. But I digress.

That third morning, the new feature of my interrogation suite left me—and my stomach, for that matter—unsettled, and wishing I was anywhere else. And I do mean *anywhere* else. Right next to the chair to which I'd been secured for the previous two days was a small table on wheels, upon which rested a stainless-steel tray, its contents shrouded by a green surgical drape. That was not good news. Not good at all.

My lead interrogator—I called him Yuri because I was simply unable to pronounce his real Russian name—held a rolled-up magazine in his hand. Not exactly the most intimidating arrow in the interrogator's quiver. Across the room, a man I hadn't seen before cowered in a chair. He did not seem happy. Then Yuri pulled the drape off the surgical tray.

"No, no, no! That is not happening!" I heard someone shout. Turned out I was the one hollering.

"Please, Mr. Norval," Yuri said in thickly Russian-accented English.

He made a show of unrolling the magazine so I could see it. Uh-oh.

"Nope, not today, Yuri! Not today!" I screamed, thrashing around as much as my restraints permitted. To the casual observer I probably looked as if I were merely vibrating, but that's what thrashing in a good restraint chair looks like.

"Try to be calm, Mr. Norval," Yuri said, patting my arm. "I recently read an interesting piece in *The New Yorker* by . . . now, who wrote this article again? Oh yes, here it is. What a strange coincidence. It was written by none other than the famous thriller writer James Norval. And here you are as my guest. It is . . . how do you say it . . . uncanny. That's a strange new word I learned only this morning. 'Uncanny.'"

I would have been happy to spend the day discussing Yuri's etymological exploration of the richness and diversity of the English language, but he seemed to find himself and returned to the magazine.

"Sorry, new words sometimes *distract* me.. I learned what 'distract' means just last week. Anyways, in your article, you described, with your usual commitment to detail, your most unfortunate encounter with gum surgery."

I could feel myself shaking my head violently without meaning to.

"Let me quote from your article. Here we go. 'I don't know why interrogators the world over haven't added gum surgery, or even just the threat of gum surgery, to their persuasion protocols. I'd be singing like a bird at the first sight of an approaching periodontist.' I really liked that last part," he said, his tone upbeat.

"Look, I'm a novelist. That piece was just more fiction. It's what I do. I make stuff up. You can't believe everything you read in *The New Yorker*."

Yuri ignored me and beckoned to the nervous man across the room.

"Okay, I think it is time," he said. "Mr. James Norval, may I introduce you to Tajikistan's leading periodontist, Dr. Aziz Saidov."

I didn't fully catch the doctor's surname as I had resumed my senseless shouting at the word "periodontist," but it sounded like Sadist. Great.

I know what you're all thinking. What the hell is going on? Okay, okay, I understand. You're confused. I get it. All right, let me catch you up.

Three days earlier, I'd arrived alone—as usual—in Tajikistan's capital city, Dushanbe, to research my twenty-eighth novel. I've been a thriller-a-year writer for the last, well, twenty-eight years—see, the math works. I must say, I've been very lucky. I know that and try never to take it for granted. Somehow, my novels seem to have struck a chord with readers—not just in Canada, but around the world—and have kept me more than solvent all these years, largely thanks to the seven Hollywood blockbuster films based on my humble little tales, with several more in the pipeline.

Some have suggested that I'm living vicariously through the exploits of my recurring hero, Hunter Chase, a legendary lone-wolf CIA agent who saves the world, novel after novel. Yes, I know, Hunter Chase is a very Hollywood name. Well, perhaps that was my plan. Okay, I'll cop to that. It *was* my plan. I do regret not making Hunter a Canadian working for CSIS—the Canadian Security Intelligence Service—but the reality is, a Canadian intelligence agent would not have appealed as much to foreign publishers, and certainly not to Hollywood. So, yes, I sold out, you might say. But as to living vicariously through my fictional hero's exploits, well, the jury is out on that question.

To be honest, writing a wildly successful thriller series was my second career choice—my Plan B, as it were—after what I really wanted to do just didn't pan out. But that's another story . . . or is it?

I don't fully understand why the books have done so well, but I do have a theory. I think it's because I've always been a bit obsessive about getting the details right—hence my arrival in Tajikistan, the setting for my next novel. After all, Google Earth can only tell you so much.

After arriving at Dushanbe International Airport and making it through Tajik customs, where the officials took barely a glance at my passport and visa, I found my driver, Zafar. He held a sign bearing my first name only—I like to keep a low profile on research trips. Then we drove into the city in his fifteen-year-old Lada. I didn't think a Lada's lifespan reached beyond about six years. It didn't take me long to realize that this car should have been junked at least five years earlier. To put it politely, the suspension was, shall we say, compromised—or non-existent, if you prefer. I doubt Zafar would have known a shock absorber if, like a miracle, one had fallen from the sky. I felt every stone, pebble, and crack in the pavement as he navigated the crumbling roads of Dushanbe. Fortunately, he was a great driver and managed to avoid the hundreds of deep potholes, which, had he driven into any one of them, could have left me with a broken tailbone.

Zafar, a local Tajik, had come recommended by a good friend of mine who may or may not have been active in the intelligence world. In short, I trusted Zafar. I had to trust him. I really had no choice. No surname was provided, and I didn't ask. While he waited in the parking circle outside, I checked into Hotel Sharq, the highest-rated accommodations in the capital. Based on the Tripadvisor scores and my shabby room, I confess I was expecting more from the hotel. On the other hand, with corruption rampant in Tajikistan, I suppose the online ratings could have been gamed, like just about everything else in the least of the Stans.

I didn't want to spend more time in the Tajik capital than necessary, so Zafar and I headed out immediately to scout the locations I'd researched. My new novel had Hunter Chase secretly entering Tajikistan to liberate a British nuclear scientist abducted after presenting a paper at a symposium in neighbouring Kazakhstan. Her captors were interested in her research on small-scale, cost-effective nuclear power—and whether its innovative process might be adapted to develop a weapons program. And when I say "captors," it's likely I mean the corrupt Tajik government, always looking for ways to strengthen its geopolitical standing in the region. So, I set out to visit two of the eight universities in Dushanbe, Ayni Air Force Base (jointly run by the Indian and Tajik air forces), the Russian 201st Military Base, and several local restaurants and hot spots—and I use the term "hot spots" loosely, very, very loosely. I wanted my readers to believe the story I was inventing. And I've found that adding specific details, that some readers will actually cross-check, helps the novel ring true. The feeling that a made-up story just might be real is something for which I, and most other novelists, constantly strive.

It all ran smoothly until the afternoon of Day Two, when, from quite a distance away, I was surveying the aforementioned Russian military base and taking photographs, as was my habit.

Why rely on the pixelated photos on Wikipedia when I could shoot my own high-res shots right on location? Anyway, as luck would have it—in my case, bad luck—it seemed I wasn't quite far enough away from the base.

I'd left Zafar in the car and scrambled down a steep embankment to a secondary road to get a little closer to the base. But, I hasten to add, I was still quite far away. I walked about a half-mile along that secondary road and discreetly snapped some photos. Clearly, I needed a bit more practice on the *discreetly* part.

I concede that discretion is hard to achieve when you're using a ginormous telephoto lens that makes your Nikon look like a small howitzer. As I said, I always want to get the details right in the story, and quality photos help. As I watched, the gates to the base suddenly opened and two vehicles sped my way. Given how fast they were moving, I knew there was no way I could make it back to the car—besides, with a top speed of thirty miles per hour, our Lada would not have fared well in a chase. It could barely outrun a bicycle. I didn't really have any escape options. The terrain was so open, so desolate and barren, my pursuers could have parked on the side of the road and watched me flee the scene . . . for at least an hour, maybe two.

Knowing I was being watched, I was careful not to look back up the embankment from whence I'd come, hoping my new friends from the base had only seen *me* and not Zafar and his beautiful, finely tuned, Russian high-performance sports car. I turned my back slightly to the approaching vehicles and slipped the SD card from my camera. I slid it into a small slit in my wide leather belt and pushed a different SD card into the camera. Finally, I pulled a battered Helm field guide called *Birds of Central Asia* from my pocket—surely you've read it—and held it in my hand. The two vehicles approached, slowed, and stopped. I smiled and gave a friendly wave. No one waved back.

The first vehicle was, as you might expect, Russian military. The second was an unmarked van. Excellent, an unmarked van. It's never a good sign in my novels when an unmarked van shows up, and I suspected it was not a good sign on that lonely Tajik road—the one running past a restricted Russian military base.

Now, this kind of thing had happened to me before in other countries, but never in a place quite as lawless and dangerous as Tajikistan. I tried to appear as calm on the outside as my rampant fear and anxiety on the inside permitted. The three Russian soldiers who emerged from the military vehicle, weapons drawn, well, they were not calm at all. I raised my hands and the bird guide above me and kept smiling. The scruffy three men who piled out of the unmarked van—civilians, it seemed—looked almost gleeful.

I knew what Hunter Chase would have done in such a situation. In fact, he'd done it more than once in my novels. But I was fifty-three years old, about twenty-three years older than Hunter Chase, and I wasn't in quite as good shape. So, I just stood there as one of the men from the van roughly searched me. His powers of observation were not taxed, as the camera and its big honking telephoto lens were hanging around my neck. He took my wallet, passport, and eventually my iPhone when he found it shoved in my hiking boot. That perhaps wasn't a great hiding spot. Hunter Chase would never have done that. The guy holding my camera had turned it on and was scrolling through the photos on the digital screen. He looked puzzled as he watched images of birds slide across the camera's LCD screen. I waved the field guide still in my hand as at least a partial explanation for the avian shots on my camera.

"I'm a birder from Canada. I'm adding as many Tajik birds to my life list as I can before I fly out tomorrow."

He stopped at one photo and showed it to his colleagues. They laughed.

"This not Tajikistan," he said, pointing to the screen.

He turned the camera so I could see the image of a red-winged blackbird standing on a bulrush, with the CN Tower and Toronto's harbour in the background. Okay, so decoy shots of birds was a good idea on paper, just not in Tajikistan. Five minutes later I was sitting in the middle of the road wearing only handcuffs and my underwear. Fortunately, it was only about thirty-seven degrees Celsius in the unforgiving, blistering sun, and I had neglected to sunscreen up before leaving my hotel. Ten minutes later they found the SD card I'd secreted in my belt. The whole SD card switcheroo gambit had worked really well for Hunter Chase in my fourteenth novel. It had worked less well for me in Tajikistan.

My three civilian friends hauled me to my feet and dragged me towards their malevolent unmarked van. It was bad enough just seeing an unmarked van on the scene. You never want to be inside one.

"Perhaps you could just drop me off at the Tajik tourist bureau?" I said, just as a foul-smelling black sack was pulled down over my head from behind. I'd seen the old black-hood-over-the-head manoeuvre in countless movies and had even written it into a few of my novels. I just hadn't expected to experience it myself. My head covered by the hood, I could see nothing, though I could smell plenty—I just wasn't sure what. With a guy on each of my arms, my escorts attempted to throw me into the back of the unmarked van. The second time they tried, they kindly opened the doors first. I landed on my tailbone, which was already sensitive from the Lada's rough ride, but luckily, the corrugated steel–plated floor cushioned the blow.

Someone secured my handcuffs to a metal eye hook in the van's ceiling with just enough chain links to prevent me from sitting on the floor or on the metal benches on either side. Nor could I stand fully upright. So, I was forced to crouch in the back on the balls of my bare feet, neither standing nor sitting, for the entire drive. But how long was the drive? I'm glad you asked. It's tough to make tracking time a high priority when you're semi-suspended by chains in the back of a moving unmarked van with a smelly black hood over your head. But I knew it was important, so I did my best. I didn't count steamboats or anything like that. I just tried to be aware—in a crude and primitive sense—of the passage of time. When we finally stopped and the engine died away, it felt like we'd only been driving for half an hour or so.

If I listened carefully, I could hear the sounds of the city. So, by my reckoning, we were in downtown Dushanbe. I really hadn't been hanging in cuffs in the back of a van for long enough to be anywhere else. I mean, if we'd driven for an hour, surely someone would have offered me a sandwich or an apple or some other less-nutritious car snacks. But there'd been nothing to relieve the monotony of the journey, other than an occasional well-aimed truncheon strike whenever I cleared my throat or jangled my chains. It was only slightly less terrifying than my flight in on Tajik Air had been, though not a single flight attendant had hit me with a nightstick.

My first two days in the interrogation cell had not actually been too bad. I was threatened but never struck. My legs and shoulders still ached from my rough journey in the back of that van. But since arriving at the luxurious Chateau Correctional Colony No. 7, my hosts hadn't yet raised a hand to me. They were mean but seemed to be following an interrogation protocol that left the rough stuff for later. Instead, I was physically restrained and forced to spend two days stressing about that battery cart and waterboarding table in the room with me. And I think I forgot to mention that all this time, nearly three days, I was still wearing just my underwear. I'd actually gotten quite used to it. And it was always stifling hot anyway, so I stopped caring. Yes, you are correct, dignity was in short supply. To make matters worse, Yuri kept asking me the same slate of questions, and I kept responding with the same slate of answers. I had the advantage of continuously telling the truth, though Yuri's growing agitation made my honesty seem somehow ill-advised.

"Who are you?"

"I'm James Norval, a Canadian thriller writer. Check out JamesNorval.com or any bookstore in the world and you will see I'm telling the truth."

"Who do you work for?"

"I'm a novelist. I work for myself and under contract for Penguin Random House. I'm just a thriller writer."

"Why you take photos of Russian military base?"

"My next novel is set in Tajikistan, and I was just doing research to make sure I get the details right. It's what I always do. It's what I'm known for. I get the details right."

"So, you're not a birdwatcher?"

"Oh, that. No, not really. I didn't know what I was doing. I was just, um, grasping at straws. My bad."

"What does it mean, this 'grasping at straws' expression?"

"Oh, it just means I kind of panicked and made up the birdwatching story. Though I would like to learn about birds someday."

"Okay, okay, enough about the birds," Yuri said. "How did you get out to the base?"

"I took a cab from the street that runs in front of Hotel Sharq, something Muhammad Street, I think it's called. My cabbie drove me out to the base, and I guess he took off when I was searched, stripped, handcuffed, beaten, and thrown into the back of an unmarked van—or what you call 'being arrested.' I can't really blame him, but I'm rethinking his tip."

"What's his name?"

"Whose name?"

"The taxi driver!"

"Oh. How should I know? I never asked his name. Why would I? When you climb into a cab, do you really start by asking the driver's name? I don't know who he was. But I do remember his car was very uncomfortable. It was black, I think, and it really needs new shock absorbers, or at least thicker seat cushions."

"Most Tajik cars are black and need new shock absorbers," Yuri said. "You're not making my search easy."

Yuri and I performed this little choreographed dance over and over for hours on end, until I was eventually returned to my cell. My concrete cubicle boasted a single cot with a thin sleeping pad as soft and plush as plywood. A hole in the floor in one corner rounded out the decor, which was in a style I had dubbed "Early Siberian Gulag." Oh, and that hole in the corner did not flush. There was no pillow, no blanket, and the air conditioning was somewhat deficient. Now I know how it feels to sleep in a blast furnace.

Day Two was much the same as Day One, except the battery cart was pushed a little closer to me. When Yuri finally finished his barrage of questions and I finally finished my barrage of consistently truthful answers, he came up behind me and put his hands on my shoulders.

"Tomorrow we're going to try something a little bit different," he said. "I'm a small bit excited because we go to next stage."

"Look, Yuri—sorry I can't pronounce your real name—just go to Amazon.com and type in my name. You'll find all my books and plenty of author photos. Or just plug my name into Google."

Yuri looked over at the battery cart.

"Yes, I think it will soon be time to plug something in."

Here endeth Day Two. And did I mention my meal plan? I was served the same food at every meal, once in the morning and once in the evening. Well, I think it was food. If I had to guess, I'd say it was cold boiled cabbage with a few mouthfuls of goat meat. After all, I needed my protein to sustain me through my interrogations.

—

So, there you have it. You're all caught up. We now return you to our regularly scheduled periodontist programming already in progress.

"Get him away from me!" I shouted. "He probably has a busy day of gum surgery appointments back in his office. We don't need him. Let him go back and help his own patients. No! No!"

Dr. Perry O. Dontist—I'd already forgotten his name—backed away again, unprepared for the ferocity of my reaction. I mean, I doubt his other patients welcomed him with a smile, a hug, and a Werther's Original, but still, he seemed taken aback by my crazed rejection of his services. I changed course, or perhaps returned to my earlier practice of grasping at straws.

"Look, Yuri, why not roll over that battery cart and we'll start there? I'm even up for trying out the waterboarding table. What do you say?"

Yuri was smiling now, knowing he'd found my kryptonite. Damn that *New Yorker* piece. Yuri was right. I was not a fan of gum surgery, particularly the kind they had in store for me that morning—to be blunt, sans anaesthetic. But what worried me most was that for the preceding two days I had told Yuri nothing but the truth. I really was in Tajikistan just to research my next novel. So how much gum surgery was I in for if Yuri continued to doubt my wholly truthful story? Who was I kidding—Yuri didn't just doubt my story, he dismissed it outright. My gums started swelling and aching in anticipation.

At Yuri's insistence, the doctor was once again tentatively approaching his tray of instruments when the wall-mounted phone near the door rang. I had never heard a more welcome sound and prayed it wasn't a wrong number or a spammer. How about a forty-minute telephone survey? Yuri was annoyed but eventually answered the phone. Then he was even more annoyed. I only know a little Russian, but I did not need the translation app on my iPhone to understand what was happening. The pulsating vein on Yuri's forehead made matters quite clear. He slammed the receiver into its cradle, shoved the frightened periodontist out of the way, and barrelled towards me. Uh-oh. He veered at the last moment and circled behind me. He released the restraints on my forearms and ankles and loosened the three fabric straps across my chest, stomach, and thighs that had so effectively kept my butt in the chair for so many hours. He hauled me up and secured a fresh black plastic zip-tie around my wrists before leading me out the door and down the corridor. It all happened so fast. I just hoped it wasn't one of those *out of the frying pan into the fire* scenarios. I'd had quite a bit of experience with those.

We were not headed for my cell but in the opposite direction, towards the front of the prison. This was looking more promising. My heart—and perhaps even my gums—slowly returned to normal sinus rhythm.

The man in the tailored dark-blue suit looked out of place on the far side of the sliding metal gate. It wasn't just his fashionable attire that helped him stand out. He also didn't look Russian. There was not even the slightest suggestion of Slavic heritage in his face. When Yuri and I had passed through the gate and it had closed behind us, New Blue Suit Guy pointed in my direction and said something to the guard sitting in her protective plexiglass pod. She nodded, opened a big drawer, pulled out what looked like my clothes, shoved them onto a metal tray, and slid it into the security pass-through in the side of her station. I retrieved the tray and, throwing decorum to the wind, somehow managed to pull on my pants. But my tie-wrapped wrists made donning my shirt somewhat of a challenge. I finally turned to Yuri and held out my arms in surrender. Still fuming, he snipped my zip-tie with a pair of sharp nippers he pulled from his pocket. I slipped into the shirt and managed to do up the buttons, matching each one with its correct buttonhole—not easy with trembling fingers. The guard had failed to produce my shoes, socks, belt, camera, SD cards—either of them—or jacket, but I decided against lodging a formal complaint. My iPhone was there, but out of juice. Just before I was released, Yuri handed me a padded envelope he'd produced from somewhere containing my passport and wallet.

Without even saying goodbye or exchanging contact information, Yuri turned on his heel and headed back into the prison, presumably to meet his next new friend.

"Norval, I'm Etienne Rosseau from the Canadian embassy in Kazakhstan," the blue suit said once I'd been formally released into his custody. "Let's go."

He did not shake my hand but executed an about-face and walked out through the four sets of sequentially sliding metal gates of Correctional Colony No. 7 as I tried to keep up. It wasn't exactly the sympathetic and concerned demeanour I'd expected from a Canadian diplomat helping a fellow citizen in need.

"Did it ever occur to you that taking photos of a Russian military installation in a remote area of Tajikistan in broad daylight might not be a great idea?"

And here we go.

"Well, in hindsight . . ." I said.

"You're lucky to be alive," he snapped. "Come on, keep up. We gotta get out of here."

I trotted behind him, wincing with every step. I don't recommend rocking bare feet on gravel. I opened the front passenger door of the black Chevy Traverse SUV parked in front. My suitcase and computer backpack from Hotel Sharq were on the floor. That was a relief. I grabbed both and slid into the back seat. An instant after I closed the door, my surly saviour and chauffeur fishtailed out of the parking lot and through the security checkpoint that had opened for us.

As we drove, I quickly changed into clean clothes and stuffed my abduction outfit into the plastic laundry bag I never travelled without. I'd burn it later. I put on fresh socks and tied up my running shoes, the only other footwear I'd packed. They were pseudo-fashionable skater shoes that had never seen the deck of a skateboard. I checked my backpack and found my MacBook Air laptop and two portable hard drives for photo storage, just where I'd left them. Etienne drove in silence and looked about as happy as Yuri had back in my interrogation cell.

"Um, thanks so much for rescuing me, I am truly grateful. But how did you know I was there?"

"You can thank Zafar. He called us shortly after you were taken. You should have heeded your driver's advice."

It was true that Zafar had strongly recommended that I not roam around a remote Tajik road taking photos of a Russian military base. He'd said it would not end well. And he was right.

"Yes, well, I now have a better understanding of the consequences and won't be doing that again anytime soon."

"Zafar called and gave us a complete briefing on what had happened. The diplomatic overtures began almost immediately. We got it sorted and I flew down this morning. You're very lucky. If my ambassador had not been such a big fan of your books, you might still be in there."

I made a mental note to pay Zafar a big bonus when I was safely beyond the reach of Tajik authorities.

I was about to ask where we were going when I began to recognize my surroundings. We turned onto the road that led into Dushanbe International Airport. We drove right past the Arrivals and Departures ramps and instead turned into a driveway marked with a sign clearly representing a private jet. As we approached a security checkpoint, the gate suddenly and magically lifted, and we were waved through. Much to my surprise, Etienne drove directly onto the tarmac. I don't mean he drove onto the runway, but rather onto the asphalt off to the side, away from the planes that were landing and taking off with impressive frequency. Who knew Tajikistan had such a busy airport?

Etienne slowed and then stopped beside an unmarked private jet as its front hatch, just aft of the cockpit, swung open and down, revealing steps and a handrail. A clever design.

"Please board the jet and do not come back to Tajikistan. We've given certain assurances that you will never return here."

"Thank you again for your timely intervention. And believe me, I have no plans to return here," I said, as the whole frying pan and fire thing returned to my addled thoughts. "But who's on the plane? What am I walking into?"

Etienne's sigh was so mighty the windshield briefly fogged up.

"I'm not at liberty to say, but trust me, when you board that plane, you'll be in safe hands. Now, get out of my car!"

I quickly grabbed all my stuff and hopped out. It occurred to me that I may have enjoyed Yuri's company more than Etienne's, but I realized I wasn't yet in the best frame of mind to make that call.

"Thanks again!" I shouted as the car peeled away.

I climbed the steps and entered the jet. I had no time to take in the luxurious compartment because I was startled to recognize the man standing before me, his hand extended.

"Ahhh, we've been looking for you, Mr. Norval," said the man with the distinct Scottish brogue, scraggly grey beard, and the most chaotic hair I'd seen in a very long time. "I'm Angus McLintock, and they tell me I'm the Minister of Public Safety. Oh, and do not let my wee accent confuse you. I serve the Government of Canada."

Oh, I knew who he was. So did nearly every Canadian. It hadn't been that long ago when McLintock, along with his trusty sidekick and executive assistant, Daniel—I forget his last name—bravely thwarted an attempt on the Russian president's life during a brief Ottawa stopover. It played out like the finale of a Hunter Chase movie, with the notable difference that it actually happened. But that's another story.[1]

Several thoughts collided in my brainpan at the same time. This was not a Canadian government jet but obviously a private charter. Ministers of the Crown don't tend to fly to inhospitable, far-off places to pick up stray Canadians in trouble. Angus McLintock had a reputation for doing things his own way, letting honour and his conscience guide him. His hair seemed to defy gravity and a few of Newton's other laws. And suddenly I was ravenous and could quite happily have eaten a horse between two mattresses.

"Yes, Minister, I know who you are and I'm very, very pleased—let me reiterate, *very pleased*—to see you," I said. "I cannot begin to tell you how grateful I am that you somehow managed to find me."

"Well, laddie, we'll come to just how grateful you are in a wee bit, but just to confirm our embassy's report, you don't require the services of a doctor, do you?"

I shook my head.

"I'm merely hungry and sleep-deprived, though it looked like that would have changed for the worse had the Canadian cavalry not galloped into Dushanbe."

"Excellent. I'm relieved to hear it," the minister replied, before turning to the woman seated behind him. "May I present Ms. Vivian Kent, my advisor on all intelligence matters—including

---

1 *Operation Angus*, McClelland & Stewart, 2021

the operations of the Canadian Security Intelligence Service—that now seem to fall within my ministerial domain."

My ears perked up at the mention of CSIS. Ms. Kent was already seated and buckled up. Black, older, grey hair swept up on her head, with what looked to me to be kind eyes. She followed my gaze to the wheelchair secured behind her seat.

"Arthritis, Mr. Norval," Vivian said. "A rather nasty and early-onset case. It does make locomotion a challenge, but my brain is not restrained in the least. Delighted to meet you at long last."

I detected a faint accent, likely from somewhere in the Caribbean. "Nice to meet you, Ms. Kent."

"Vivian, please," she said. "Call me Vivian."

"Only if you call me James."

"Have a seat now, laddie," interjected the minister. "We're about to depart."

I stowed my luggage in the overhead compartment and happily buckled up in the luxurious and expansive leather seat. A younger woman—our flight attendant, I believe—appeared from a different section behind us to close and secure the hatch through which I'd boarded the plane. The minister then knocked on and opened the cockpit door and said something I couldn't hear to the pilot. Immediately, the plane's idling twin jets roared to life, and we began taxiing to the runway. On his way back from the front of the plane, the minister grabbed a tray of sandwiches and a couple of water bottles from the galley. He plunked them down on the table before me.

"Thank you from the bottom of my empty stomach," I said.

The minister dropped into the seat next to Vivian, both of them facing me, as the jet accelerated down the runway and lifted into the air.

"Apologies for the rush, but I'm reliably informed that the sooner we're all out of Tajik airspace, the better."

"You'll hear no argument from me."

"No, I imagine not," he said.

While we were still in our climb, I ate my way through nearly the entire plastic platter of sandwiches and polished off the two bottles of water in record time. To be fair, "ate" inadequately captures what I did to those sandwiches. In fact, "devoured" is hardly up to the task. I hoped I was not meant to share them with Vivian and the minister.

"We're bound for Madrid—about eight and a half hours in the air, with a quick stop for a splash of fuel somewhere in Croatia, I'm told—and then you will determine where we fly after that," noted the minister.

"I don't understand," I said. "I figured we'd just head back to Toronto, or Ottawa, even New York, whichever is most convenient for you."

"Well, understanding is coming your way very shortly," the minister replied. "Without descending into melodrama, Mr. Norval, let me just say that your country is calling, and we're desperately hoping you'll answer."

CHAPTER 2

"SIR, WHILE I'm still in the dark, I do know that a minister of the Crown wouldn't normally fly into Tajikistan to rescue a thriller writer who has arguably behaved recklessly in an unstable country. But in my current compromised state, I still can't fathom how I can possibly be of service."

"Well, Mr. Norval, you'll not have long to wait," the minister replied. "Let us reach what I believe they call our cruising altitude, and all will be made clear."

I looked out the window as we flew due west for Spain. The sky was clear, and the terrain below looked just as bleak from on high as it had from the ground.

"Mr. Norval, you must be knackered after what you've endured," said the minister. "Would you like a wee kip before we get started? We've a long flight and plenty of time."

"My curiosity has overtaken my fatigue. I think I'd rather be in the know before I fall into the coma that surely awaits me."

"You are certainly a writer, Mr. Norval. I like your way with words," he said.

About fifteen minutes later, the pilot extinguished the seat belt sign. The minister reached up into an overhead compartment and pulled down a zippered sports bag.

"It feels as if we've now levelled off, but before we begin, we weren't sure you'd still be in possession of your luggage, so we packed a few things we thought you might want on the plane," he said, handing me the bag. "I know you brought a suitcase on board, but we were reliably informed that the Tajik prison system is not known for its laundry services."

"Thank you. Very thoughtful," I said. "Mr. Rosseau did manage to salvage my bag from the hotel. But I failed to pack a jacket, and given the extreme efficacy of this jet's air conditioning, I wonder if there's a sweater in here."

"I do believe there's a jumper in there," he said.

"When I hear the word 'jumper,' I find myself looking for a bridge or a subway platform," I said, only half joking. "I'm not used to the British definition."

I unzipped the bag and quickly laid my hands on a navy-blue pullover.

"Eureka," I said, pulling it on. "It fits perfectly and looks just like something I'd wear. I'm impressed."

"Mr. Norval—James, I mean—we are a national intelligence agency," Vivian began. "Procuring clothes that fit you and your personal style is not the most challenging problem we've had to solve today."

"Point taken. Thank you."

"Well then, if you're comfortable and ready, I propose we get started," the minister said.

He turned to Vivian, who nodded her assent.

"Right, then, perhaps we should start with how we ultimately tracked you down, before moving on to why we're gathered here in this unlikely location."

"I am in your hands," was all I said in reply.

"Then off we go," started the minister. "You see, laddie, Global Affairs Canada can, of course, trace the whereabouts of Canadians when they formally enter foreign countries through the use of our passports."

"Understood."

"Now, not to tell tales out of school—CSIS and Global Affairs don't always play well together—but we were able to find out you landed in Tajikistan, of all places, four days ago. Then, in one of those coincidences that defies expectation, yet keeps happening it seems, we also became aware that you'd been detained by Tajik authorities. It was your enterprising driver who contacted the Canadian embassy in Kazakhstan. You probably know that we have no diplomatic mission in Tajikistan. So, to shorten the story, our need to find you, and your need for, shall we say, diplomatic intervention, have put us on this plane together."

"That all makes sense and nicely explains how I find myself here with you," I said, starting to grow a little impatient. "While

I am grateful for your timely rescue, and I say this with all due respect and gratitude, I keep waiting for the other shoe to drop."

"I'm unlacing it now," the minister began. "So, let's get to it. What do you know about Mali?" he asked.

Now, that was a question I'd not anticipated.

"Well, I've never been, but I believe it's an unstable country in northwest Africa—capital city is Bamako, if I'm not mistaken. I recall reading that there has recently been yet another in a long series of coups, merely adding to the country's already abysmal reputation on a host of fronts. But I gather this coup was bloodless, where the threat alone was sufficient to precipitate a leadership change. Brazen and illegal, but very efficient and definitely more humane. I know the new regime seems set on nationalizing various resource industries, much to the dismay of foreign corporations with heavy investments in the region," I said, trying to spin my flimsy knowledge of the country into something that appeared a little more substantial. "Oh yes, and to complete the less-than-rosy outlook, poverty runs rampant, outstripped only by corruption, crime, terrorism, kidnapping, and the institutional abrogation of human rights. Even I would think twice before visiting Mali," I concluded. "Why do you ask?"

The minister paused and exchanged a look with Vivian before proceeding.

"Well, Mr. Norval, we'd like you to visit Mali at the earliest opportunity."

If Tajikistan had been the frying pan, Mali sure sounded like the fire. But I said nothing and waited for him to elaborate. The minister nodded at Vivian, and she tagged in.

"You're essentially right in your assessment of Mali," Vivian began. "And I'm impressed with your knowledge of a country you've never visited."

"Occupational hazard. Who knows when I might set a novel there?"

"Perhaps you will, and sooner than you planned," she replied. "So, to bring you into our little situation, Tardif Resources is a Canadian mining company based in Montreal with a significant investment in gold mining in Mali's Kéniéba region, about three hundred miles northwest of Bamako. The Tardif mine is quite productive and profitable, employing some two hundred and fifty locals and with a senior executive and operations team of fifteen Canadians, led by CEO Monique Tardif. She took over the company when her father died. In short, the Tardif mine has been seized by the new regime. You're right, the new dictator has nationalized the mining sector, claiming ownership and the profits for the new government."

I figured I knew what was coming, but still couldn't understand what I had to do with any of it.

"Each night, the fifteen Canadian expats are detained in their compound under guard. And each day, they are escorted by Malian security personnel to the mine site to keep the operations going and the money flowing into the new regime's coffers. James, we are well aware that this is a lot to ask of a civilian, but we'd like your help in exfiltrating the fifteen Canadians."

"Exfiltrating? Well, I don't really see how a new skin-care regimen helps in this situation," I said.

Neither of them even cracked a smile. Some have accused me

of being a smartass now and then. There may be some truth lurking in the allegation.

"We both know that I did not say exfoliating. I said exfiltrating. And we also both know you're familiar with the term, because you use it frequently in your books."

"Touché, Vivian. Forgive me, I'm not quite myself right now," I explained. "Regardless of my vocabulary, and I am, of course, sympathetic to my fellow Canadians stuck in Mali, but what can a late-middle-aged thriller writer possibly contribute to such an operation?"

"Ahhh, we thought you'd never ask," the minister replied. "The fact of the matter is, Mr. Norval, for reasons that we'll shortly share, you are better positioned to help in this noble endeavour than anyone else on the planet."

"That is a bold claim, Minister," I said.

"Please, laddie, I cannae get used to the formal moniker you've been employing. Would you mind just calling me Angus? Even Vivian does when no one else is around."

"Oh, of course, um, Angus. I'll do my best. And please call me James."

"Aye," Angus said. "And I'll remind you when you lapse."

"And I, you," I replied.

He then opened the laptop that sat on the table between us and executed a few two-fingered keystrokes. He spun the laptop and positioned it so all three of us could see the YouTube video on the screen.

"This is newly installed president Adama Camara's inaugural news conference, convened in the presidential palace just a few weeks ago," Vivian explained, as Angus hit the Play button.

President Camara was not exactly what you'd call charismatic. Quite the opposite, in fact. He looked uncomfortable, not just seated at the oversized desk, but in his own skin. His eyes darted from left to right. He was perspiring. His voice was soft, quieter than you'd expect from a man who had just taken over the government by threat of overwhelming force. He seemed shy, almost timid. Vivian and Angus just watched, waited, and said nothing. Eventually, I stopped focusing on the president and let my eyes wander a tad to take in the rest of the scene. That's when I saw them.

On the middle shelf of the bookcase behind President Camara, lined up like soldiers awaiting inspection, was an entire hardcover set of my novels. I should have noticed them earlier, as they were the only books inhabiting the shelves. I assumed, since he'd just moved into the palace, he might not have had time to spruce up his new office before addressing the nation. But still, it was an odd sight. I didn't exactly know how to feel about a ruthless dictator who was so clearly a fan of my novels. I guess I admired his taste in literature, even if I rejected his megalomaniacal and hegemonic tendencies. Okay, the former hardly outweighs the latter, but I can't deny there was a slight uptick on my pride-o-meter when I saw all my novels lined up on one shelf. That never gets old.

I looked more closely at my books as President Camara kept droning on about his plans. Something wasn't quite right. I reached over and pressed the laptop's space bar to pause the video.

"Look," I said, pointing, "all of my novels, except for the last two, are in chronological order. Not only are the final two out of order, but if you look closely, they're slightly pushed forward from the rest. It's subtle but it's there. That almost seems too random to be random."

"Ahhh, now we're getting somewhere," Vivian said, nodding.

"Hmmmm, okay, okay," I started, thinking as I spoke. "That second-last book is my fifth novel, *The Prisoner*. And the one next to it is my eleventh novel, *Extraction*. Hmmm. I think it's possible that someone—probably Camara—just might be trying to send a message of some kind."

"Yes, I see where you're going with this," said Vivian, leaning forward to stare at the laptop screen.

"Well, pray enlighten me, for I'm new to this game and cannae see what you're drivin' at," Angus said.

"If those books are the president's, and he has arranged them on the shelf . . ." I said.

"They are his books," interrupted Vivian. "Later in the news conference, he's asked about them and proudly admits that you are his favourite writer."

"Oh, well, isn't that nice to hear," I replied.

"Aye, but back to the matter at hand . . ." Angus interjected.

"Yes, right. Of course," I said. "If we assume the president arranged the books, it makes matters clearer. There just may be more going on here than appears at first glance. I'm wondering if Camara, in his role as president, might not be acting entirely of his own free will. Perhaps he's the 'prisoner' of the book title, sending a signal, asking for help, seeking 'extraction.'"

"Good pickup, Mr. Norval," said Vivian.

"James, please," I said.

"Right, James," Vivian replied. "I confess, we had not recognized the chronological discrepancy in the display of your novels. It's an option to keep in mind, but at this early stage we ought to make no assumptions, though it's certainly one plausible working theory."

"It may be slightly more than plausible. He's actually using a plot point from *Extraction*. In that story, a writer's books were arranged chronologically in public view, but with the first four out of order and just slightly pushed forward from the rest of the lineup. This is likely where the president got the idea," I suggested. "Those four out-of-order book titles were *Hegemony*, *Escape*, *Langley*, and *Peril*."

"'HELP,'" said Vivian.

"Exactly."

"Help? Well, I could use some," said Angus. "You've gone and lost me again in the heather."

"Taking the first letter of each book title yields the word 'HELP,'" I explained. "So, in the case of our Malian dictator, it seems even more explicit."

"I'm catching up, but it still lies just slightly beyond my ken," Angus said.

"Angus, if we're on the right track in how we're interpreting the book display, it may well be that President Camara holds no real authority in the new regime despite enjoying the trappings of the presidency," I said. "It's quite possible that he is merely a pawn doing the bidding of someone else who actually wields the power."

"I see. Yes, I see it now. Well, that may complicate matters a wee bit," Angus said, his brow furrowed.

"Perhaps," I said. "But it doesn't change the need to move the Canadians safely out of the country. It arguably makes it even more urgent."

Angus nodded to Vivian again.

"All right, then, let's shift our focus to the exfiltration," Vivian said. "In the broadest terms, the idea, James, is for you to orchestrate a visit to Mali on the pretense of interviewing the new president as you research your next novel, which, in your cover story, just happens to be set in an African country in the immediate aftermath of a coup d'état. We want you to invite yourself to visit President Camara. And we think he'll be delighted to meet his favourite author and will roll out the red carpet for you."

She took a breath to let her words sink in, then continued.

"James, you should know that Angus and I don't strictly think of you as a civilian, though technically, that is exactly what you are. We are both aware that you applied to CSIS when you were a much younger man but didn't quite make it across the recruitment finish line," Vivian said. "I'm sorry you weren't accepted. I hope it wasn't too disappointing a blow. On the other hand, had you joined CSIS in your twenties, you wouldn't have twenty-seven novels under your belt today and be in line for this potential opportunity to revisit your past."

"Furthermore," Angus said, "the novels you write, while arguably portraying covert operations a wee bit more sensationally than they might typically unfold in reality, still move you to a much higher position on the intelligence learning curve—certainly higher than the average citizen. Now, we do not ask this of you blithely. And the safe, prudent, and sensible response would surely be for you to decline our invitation."

Vivian jumped back in before Angus could talk me out of this little adventure—faint hope of that.

"I should add that you'll not be on your own. A young but experienced CSIS operative, Lauren Cooper, would accompany you on the visit to Mali, playing the role of your research assistant. While there, the two of you would need to assess the situation and develop a plan for exfiltrating the fifteen Canadian mining execs. We have some initial options, but it really demands on-the-ground reconnaissance, analysis, and risk assessment before any plan is finalized and executed. Does that make our operation a little clearer?"

As she waited, she raised her bottle of water for a sip.

This was awesome. This was precisely why I'd wanted to join CSIS in the first place. This was fantastic. I'd been nodding my head throughout Vivian's overview. I was trying to be cool about it all. You know, not tip my hand. Leave the impression that I was reluctant, that I was weighing my options, thinking it through, balancing the pros and cons, playing hard to get, dragging it out, etc., etc. So I just sat there impassively for a good two, maybe three, nanoseconds before pumping my fist and shouting, "Yes! I'm in! I! Am! In! Where do I sign?"

Oh yes, I was the very epitome of cool. I'd finally made it to the show, the clandestine operations show. It had been nearly thirty years since I'd somehow botched it. But now I'd made it—albeit as a civilian—but I'd finally made it.

Vivian was caught a little off guard by my enthusiasm. I could tell because she flinched at my boisterous outburst and spilled water everywhere except in her mouth. Angus smiled as she wiped her tweedy jacket with a napkin. Eventually, she turned back to me.

"Just to be clear, James, involving a civilian in a CSIS operation is extraordinarily rare and a step we'd of course prefer not to take. But in this particular situation, we simply can't ignore just how uniquely qualified you are to serve in this unusual and very useful way."

"I understand the singular opportunity President Camara's literary preferences have given me. And I'm happy to serve," I said, settling back down in my seat. "At least his favourite writer isn't Agatha Christie or Ruth Rendell. I think I'm in a stronger position to help than they might be."

"I'm quite certain neither of them still walks the earth," Angus said.

"Yes, my point exactly, sir," I said.

Vivian pulled an official-looking document from a leather folder and placed it face down on the table in front of her.

"Thank you for agreeing in principle to support this effort, but to be absolutely clear, it is possible, perhaps even likely, that you will find yourself in some potentially dangerous situations that we simply cannot yet predict."

I nodded.

"You may be comfortable joining this operation as you sit in the relative safety of a private jet flying to Madrid. But when you land in Bamako, we cannot assure your safety. Do you understand what I'm saying?"

"I understand and will sign any liability waiver you put in front of me."

"James, you're not signing up to bungee jump," said Vivian. "We don't do liability waivers. This document outlines your commitment to observe the strictest secrecy standards at all times, and the potential sanctions the law provides should you abrogate your responsibilities in this connection."

She flipped over the document and slid it across the table in front of me, along with a cheap ballpoint pen.

"You may not tell anyone any of this unless or until at some point, perhaps years, even decades in the future, this operation is declassified—though I doubt it ever will be," she said. "As well, this mission is, as you often say in your novels, 'off the books.' Even though you are sitting with a minister of the Crown, this is a secret operation with no official ties to, or public sanction by, the Canadian government. Currently, only a handful of people know of this operation's existence, and they are the ones who will help keep you safe while you're on the ground in an extremely volatile country. If you have any reservations at all, I strongly suggest you declare them now and leave that pen capped on the table."

Throughout Vivian's remarks, the minister was quiet but fully engaged, and focused on me.

"I understand," I replied. "I really do."

I uncapped the pen and signed the document.

"Excellent," Angus said, before rising and shaking my hand. "On behalf of the Government of Canada and her citizens, we thank you."

Then he walked towards the rear of the plane and opened a door, revealing a second, smaller seating area A young, lean Black woman, dressed casually, followed Angus back to our more luxurious section of the jet. He motioned with his hand to turn the floor over to Vivian, who was beaming as she looked at the young woman.

"James Norval, meet Lauren Cooper. She is an experienced CSIS analyst with solid field work on her resumé as well. She has risen quickly in CSIS on the strength of her quick mind and dedication to completing whatever operation to which she is assigned. She is an outstanding intelligence operative."

Lauren had been beaming right back at Vivian through all of this. But when she turned to face me after Vivian had finished singing her praises, any traces of her smile had vanished.

"Cooper," I said, extending my hand.

"Norval," she replied. Then she squeezed my hand hard, and I mean really hard.

"Whoa, that is some grip you've got there, Coop," I said, wincing and shaking my hand to restore the blood flow.

"I'm sorry," she replied. "I've been told I have a firm handshake."

"Firm? Felt more like an attempted amputation." I paused until my throbbing hand returned to its normal size. "So, Coop, you and your vice-like hands are supporting this mission, eh?"

"No, Norval. I'm leading this operation. You are actually the support."

CHAPTER 3

WE LANDED at Madrid–Barajas Airport in the late afternoon. After an expedited customs review conducted on the plane by two Spanish uniformed officials, a member of our local embassy staff met us on the tarmac in a black Cadillac Escalade. He drove us into the city and dropped me off at Morrison's, a five-star hotel I'd been lucky enough to enjoy on some of my book tours. Coop, Angus, and Vivian carried on to the embassy for more briefings, but I was given the evening off to recover from my Tajik ordeal. The hotel seemed a tad lavish and expensive given that Canadian taxpayers were footing the bill, but I was told its proximity to the embassy made it the logical choice. Google Maps told me the two buildings were separated by a mere three hundred and six yards. I couldn't very well blame the traffic if I were late for my briefings the next morning.

My mind was flitting back and forth between Tajikistan and what lay ahead in, of all places, Mali. I was starting to get a headache, so I consciously tried to think of other, less important, less daunting, less dangerous, topics. As I had feared, that effort proved a colossal failure.

I was tempted to walk the streets of Madrid but that would have involved, well, walking. I was physically and mentally drained from two days of interrogations and three nights of not sleeping. And did I mention having to consume "food" that would never be free of quotation marks? Anyway, it turns out that sustaining a near-constant state of fear, hunger, and fatigue for sixty-one hours straight can leave one feeling a little rundown. I took a long and luxurious shower and even nodded off standing under the water jets. I know I was asleep because at one point I jerked awake and bumped my head on the tiled wall in the process. Hunter Chase would never have done that.

During the time when I was actually awake in the shower, my mind returned briefly to the delicious irony that I was now working with CSIS on a bona fide covert mission nearly thirty years after I'd crashed and burned in the agency's recruitment program. "Crashed and burned" might have been an overstatement. I didn't know for sure. All I knew was that as I was rounding the clubhouse turn and heading for the tape after nearly six months in the competition, I was suddenly informed that my race was over, that I wouldn't be joining Canada's spy agency. No explanation. No *Great job, but we're not taking on any new recruits right now*. No *You were so close but just not close enough*. Not even a *You're really not cut out for this. Perhaps try accounting, or fast-food franchise work, or beekeeping, instead*. Nothing. That's likely when I fell asleep standing up in the shower.

I felt more like a real human being after towelling off. Beyond the bag of emergency clothes that Angus had given me on the plane, yet another bag had been waiting for me on the bed when I entered my hotel room. Unsure of what I might need in Mali, Vivian and her team had acquired a suitcase and filled it with clothes, all in my size and fashion sensibility, not that I actually have one. They seemed to have thought of everything. It included all that the aging thriller writer might need to wear on his first undercover operation, even though I wouldn't exactly be undercover. There were two pairs of shorts, two pairs of long cargo pants with lots of pockets for whatever advanced secret gadgets I might be given to aid in a successful mission—or they could just be for snacks—one pair of hiking shoes, one pair of formal lace-up brown leather shoes, four T-shirts, a rain jacket, business-casual blue chinos, a light-blue button-up shirt, and one navy-blue blazer in a really light material. Not bad. Finally, I'd been informed that a formal blue suit was hastily being altered in a reputable Madrid men's shop so that I'd have something to wear in case a state dinner was held in my honour. Unlikely, but we wanted to be prepared.

To address my hunger, I ordered a room-service club sandwich—and it was better than any hotel club sandwich I'd ever had. And believe me, over years of book tours, I've ordered a boatload of club sandwiches. It just seems harder to mess up a club sandwich than, say, mushroom risotto or beef bourguignon. It is possible it was just another run-of-the-mill club sandwich, but in my depleted state, it was heavenly. I then proceeded to free-fall into a deep sleep, despite it being only eight thirty in the evening. I didn't open my eyes until the front desk called the next morning at nine o'clock to say an embassy official was waiting for me in the lobby.

"I could have made my way to the embassy without an escort," I said, after recognizing the staffer who had driven us from the airport the day before.

"It's no problem, sir, this is right on my way in to the office," he said. "And we just didn't want to leave anything to chance."

When we arrived at the Canadian embassy, the lineup of tourists at the counter was already long and, judging by the many forlorn facial expressions, likely populated by Canadians who were no longer in possession of their passports, whether through carelessness or crime.

Minister McLintock—Angus—was waiting for me in the reception area. He didn't exactly blend in. He cut a, shall we say, unique figure. He was wearing a suit. It just didn't look like it was *his* suit. His hair was really something, each strand acting utterly independently of all the others. And his beard. Wow. I'm not sure I can actually put it into words, and I'm apparently a professional wordsmith. If I had created a character like the Honourable Angus McLintock in one of my novels, my long-suffering editor would have told me he was far too outlandish to be believable. She would have made me tone down his look considerably. I can hear her saying, *Okay, James, you can keep his wild hair or his crazy beard. But you can't have both.* Yet here was Angus standing before me in all his physically anarchic glory. However, his unintentionally antic appearance belied a clear mind and a sense of honour and integrity carried by few politicians. He nodded to my escort, who then faded away.

"Good morning, laddie. I hope you slept well after what you've been through."

"Well, I have a vague memory of lying down and I remember waking up twelve hours later, but of that long stretch of time in between, I recall nothing. I guess that's a good sign."

As long as I was with the minister, passing through the security protocols and gaining access to the embassy's inner sanctum was a breeze. A young woman hovered on the periphery, keeping Angus in her field of view. I figured it was standard operating procedure not to allow him to wander around the embassy unescorted.

"Mr. Norval—James, I ought to say—may I present Ms. Meredith Atkins, who has the difficult task of keeping me on the straight and narrow when I'm lumbering through these precincts." I nodded to her; she nodded back. Then we were walking.

"While I'm travelling abroad on CSIS business, I'm not permitted to use my infernal mobile phone, the very bane of my existence," Angus said. "So, I must come here to communicate with my staff in Ottawa through the embassy's secure network."

"Yes, foreign embassies often play into my novels," I replied. "I think they give readers a false sense of security when the hero is supposedly safely ensconced in his nation's embassy. So, I promptly subvert their expectations by turning the allegedly safe and secure embassy into a very dangerous place."

Ms. Atkins looked a little alarmed.

"Fear not, Ms. Atkins," I soothed, "it's fiction, and a tad far-fetched at that." She didn't look particularly relieved. Angus tilted his head towards me as we walked.

"I'm to take you for your briefings with Vivian and Lauren, but unfortunately, I'll not be partaking myself, though I'd dearly love to. You see, I've learned as a minister of the Crown that my time, even my priorities, are seldom my own. My days are scripted and scheduled in bleedin' six-minute increments from dawn till dark, and often before and beyond. I had more control over my own affairs when I was a toddler," he lamented. "The upshot is, I'm afraid I must fly back to Ottawa for pressing matters there. Forgive me, my schedule is not your problem, but it surely is mine. Aye, it surely is mine."

We walked in silence down a long corridor. I could see heavy wooden double doors at the end. *Secure Boardroom*, read the sign, which also featured two built-in lights, one green and one red. The red light was illuminated. Next to it was mounted a button pad with a digital screen. We stopped at the door, with Ms. Atkins holding station a discreet distance behind us.

"James, I've read a few of your books, and I've read a dossier about you compiled by my staff. As I said yesterday, you are uniquely positioned to get our boots on the ground in Mali. But you dinnae have to do this. You can back out now and not disrupt what seems to be the lovely life you're leadin'," the minister said, his hand on the doorknob. "But if you walk into this briefing, you'll be well and truly into this little affair, right up to your peepers. It could lead to a spate of trouble, or worse, so no one would begrudge a decision to withdraw after passing a night of sober second thought."

I smiled but said nothing, leaving the floor to him.

"So, am I escorting you through these doors, or is Ms. Atkins here seeing you back to your hotel?"

"Minister, Angus, I appreciate the final gut check, but beyond my gratitude for rescuing me from, at the very least, an unpleasant situation in Dushanbe, you said yesterday without even the slightest hint of hyperbole that my country was calling. And here I am, answering," I said, my arms spread open before me.

Angus smiled and shook his head, his hair and beard flying off in all directions.

"Aye, 'tis what I expected you'd say. I am grateful, and I know Canadians would be, too, but regrettably, they will never know."

He punched in a code on the button pad and waited. Two beats later, the red light was extinguished, the green light illuminated, and the heavy double doors buzzed and swung open. It reminded me of the opening sequence of the old *Get Smart* TV series, a spy spoof that always made me laugh. Angus led me into the boardroom.

Vivian, in her wheelchair, and Coop were seated around the board table. Maps and papers were strewn about its sprawling surface. A large screen at one end of the room displayed what I cleverly deduced were satellite images showing the mine site in Mali, the Canadian compound, and the surrounding area. I swiftly reached this conclusion courtesy of the white digital labels on the maps explaining exactly what I was looking at. Yes, I know. I am a quick study.

"You've started without me," I said.

"Good morning, James," Vivian said. "Yes, we convened a couple hours ago. We figured you could use the sleep." Coop said nothing. She just stared at me with a cold and hardened look on her face. Coop either didn't like me or was in the throes of severe heartburn, perhaps even angina.

"I will leave you in Vivian and Ms. Cooper's experienced and capable hands," Angus said, as he hovered near the door. "They know of my close interest in this operation and have pledged to keep me informed as the story unfolds, and even if it's stalled."

He looked at them as he said this, and they nodded.

"Good. Thank you, all three of you, for taking on this wee spot of bother. I know, and we can surely assume the families of the detained Canadians know, this is important. And we will spare no effort to see our citizens safely reunited with their loved ones," he said. "Ms. Cooper and Mr. Norval in particular, you may be walking into the lion's den, or worse. Godspeed and a hearty 'O Canada.' We are all in your debt."

With that, the doors buzzed open and Angus left the room. Behind him, the doors swung closed once more.

I could tell that Vivian and Coop wanted to get started, so, with the pleasantries over, I sat down.

"Did you bring your laptop?" Coop asked.

"I did," I replied, pulling it out of my backpack.

"Turn it on and log in as you normally would."

I did as I was told.

"Now, give it here, please," she said.

I slid it over to her and she searched for a port for her memory stick.

"Hang on," I said, as I pulled an adaptor from my backpack and plugged it into my MacBook Air. "You'll need this."

She inserted her USB stick into the adaptor, then started clacking away on the keyboard.

"Don't worry, I'm just upgrading your security and installing our top-grade encryption. Having your own six-year-old computer in Mali will strengthen your cover, rather than bringing a brand-spanking-new CSIS-issued laptop that you obviously don't know your way around. So, we'll go with yours, but it has to be Fort Knox. This'll just take a sec."

Made sense to me, but I wasn't sure how she knew my laptop was six years old.

With Coop hunched over my computer, Vivian took over.

"James, if you're well and truly on the team, time is exceedingly short. Even before we get into the formal operational briefing, our first priority is to punch your ticket to Bamako. Without that, we have nothing," she said. "We need you to draft an email to President Camara inviting yourself for a visit, ostensibly to research your next novel. He needs to know that due to other commitments, you have a very small window within which to visit. It would have to be in the next week, preferably later this week."

I nodded.

"Okay, your security is updated," Coop said, as she pushed my laptop back over to me. "Just use it as you always do. The beefed-up security software runs in the background."

It took me about fifteen minutes to craft the email while Vivian and Coop watched over my shoulder. I wasn't accustomed to having scrutineers standing over me while I wrote. Then again, I wasn't used to much of anything in the world I now inhabited. So, I just tried to roll with it.

President Camara,

May I be among the first to offer my congratulations on your new position as president and head of state of Mali in the wake of your successful and bloodless coup d'état. I found it impressive that you toppled your corrupt predecessor without a single shot fired in anger. A rare and humane achievement that we all hope helps secure a prosperous and stable future for the people of Mali.

I watched your inaugural news conference with interest and was so pleased to learn that you have enjoyed my humble novels. That is very gratifying. As it happens, I am in the middle of writing a new novel, coincidentally set somewhere in Africa in a nation that has just weathered a coup d'état of its own. You may know that research is extremely important to me and, I believe, to the success of my novels. I'm a stickler when it comes to getting the details right. With this in mind, your recent and timely ascension presents me with an extraordinary research opportunity that I simply cannot ignore, though you obviously have the final say on this question—and I guess on most any question, now that you're president.

I know you must have a great deal on your plate right now, but I would be forever in your debt if you might be able to spare some time for me and my research assistant in the next week to help me get the details right in my new novel, tentatively entitled *Coup*. After all, you have just lived through the very scenario I am writing about. And I'm determined to get it right.

I'm afraid I only have the next week or so open before I am overcome with competing commitments having to do with a Hollywood film in production based on one of my earlier novels. So, Mr. President, could I impose briefly on your time and good will for a visit? Could I interview you in the coming days? Could you help me understand what the life of a new president, post-coup, is like?

I eagerly await your response. I can depart for Bamako immediately if you agree.

Respectfully,
James Norval

Coop provided the email address that had appeared at the bottom of President Camara's first news release. I didn't want my missive to slip by unnoticed, so for the email's subject line I typed *Urgent Message for President Camara from the Novelist James Norval*.

"I like it," Vivian said. "You're fast on the keyboard."

"Well, I have had some typing experience," I replied.

"Is the tone a little too familiar?" asked Coop.

"I wouldn't think so," said Vivian, before I could say anything. "It opens formally enough, and remember, Camara is a real fan. Such a conversational email should make him feel even better about James. It gives the sense that they're already friends. I think it's more likely to elicit the response we're looking for."

They both looked at me.

I just pointed to Vivian and replied, "Um, what she said. That's exactly what I was going for."

"Okay, I get it," Coop said. "It's strategic familiarity, calculated familiarity."

I nodded.

We collectively wordsmithed a few minor tweaks to finalize the email.

"Are we ready?" I asked, my index figure poised to do its thing.

"Off it goes," Vivian directed.

I hit Send, and it was gone. My heart rate ticked up a notch as I visualized my message winging its way through cyberspace towards its final destination some eighteen hundred miles to the south.

Just then, a quiet chime sounded. Vivian turned to a small monitor on the credenza and tapped the screen. The scene just outside the boardroom door flickered to life. Two young women—one wore a lab coat and held a small bag, and the other I recognized as the redoubtable Ms. Atkins—stood there waiting. Vivian touched the green button on the monitor and the doors buzzed and opened automatically.

"Come in, please," said Vivian as she waved the newcomers in. The doors closed again behind them. "Welcome back, Ms. Atkins."

"Thank you, Ms. Kent."

"I assume the minister has now departed?"

"Yes, he left for the airport just a few minutes ago," Ms. Atkins replied. "This is Dr. Rampala, who provides medical support to embassy staff and operations."

Ms. Atkins yielded the floor to Dr. Rampala.

Coop and I were not introduced. I guess that was logical and prudent under the circumstances.

"Hello, all," the good doctor started, then turned to address Coop and me. "Am I correct in assuming neither of you has been vaccinated for yellow fever?"

"I've already been inoculated for it, and I packed the documents to confirm it," Coop said.

Dr. Rampala nodded and turned to me.

"I don't even know what yellow fever is, and don't believe I've ever been jabbed for it," I said. "But I did have a tetanus shot last year, if that gives me any bonus points."

"Mali requires confirmation that you've been immunized for yellow fever before granting you entry to the country," she explained. "Please roll up your sleeve."

She opened her bag and started prepping a syringe.

"What, now?" I asked.

"Yes, sir. I gather a visit to Mali is imminent, so we can give you the shot right here, right now."

"Are you not a fan of needles, Norval?" Coop asked, smiling at me for the very first time.

"I don't love them," I conceded. "I mean, let's just say that experiencing needle pain is not a cherished pastime."

But I did as I was told and presented my bare left arm. Dr. Rampala swabbed my bicep, then gave me the shot while

I looked at Coop. For her benefit, I put on my stoic face, at least until the needle pierced my skin.

"Yow!" I said in a louder voice than I'd intended. "That feels more like a dock spike than a needle."

Coop was smiling even more and shaking her head. It looked like Vivian was doing her best not to smile.

"Sorry about that," the doctor replied. "Yellow fever is one of the more painful shots, but in my experience, warning the recipient tends to exacerbate the situation."

"Well, if there's ever a referendum on that question, or even just a telephone survey, I'd vote in favour of warning the patient."

"Duly noted," Dr. Rampala said, as she applied a small circular Band-Aid to the site of the dock spike's recent entry. She then signed and formally handed me the official vaccination certificate like I was receiving an honorary degree.

Ms. Atkins handed us more paperwork.

"And here are your visas. Keep them with your passports and vaccine certs, as you'll need all of them to enter Mali," she said.

"Thank you, Meredith and Dr. Rampala," Vivian said. "We appreciate the quick turnaround."

Vivian triggered the automatic double doors once again, and our two visitors took their leave. With that done, Vivian began to lead what would turn out to be hours of briefings and planning.

"First of all, while your covers will be an acclaimed thriller writer and his research assistant, let me be clear that the reporting relationship for the operation is the reverse," Vivian explained. "Lauren is in command and has final say on all mission decisions. She's experienced and has been in the field multiple times since

July of 2021, when that wise federal judge ruled CSIS could operate in other countries. So, James, on all operational questions, Lauren's word is final. And that could save your life if things go off the rails."

I nodded dutifully but thought she might be making too big a deal of it.

"I need to hear from you, James, that you understand and will honour that chain of command."

"I understand," I said.

". . . and I will . . ." Vivian prompted.

"I understand and I will honour that chain of command," I said. "Honest. Cross my heart."

"Good," she said. "I also strongly recommend that you stick together to the greatest extent possible. This will ensure two sets of eyes and two brains are deployed in analyzing whatever you find."

Coop and I nodded at one another but said nothing. She was back to displaying a cold countenance, not unlike a UFC fighter staring down her opponent at the pre-fight news conference—minus the trash talk, though the day was young.

Vivian's voice brought us back to her.

"Here's what we know about Adama Camara and his principal advisor, Demba Dembele," she said. "These dossiers of information and insight were largely prepared by Kiran Hassan in our Bamako embassy. She is smart and capable. She will be your CSIS contact in Mali, but her role at the embassy means that she'll be out of the play when it comes to executing the escape plan. As well, we know at least something about the Camara–Dembele relationship because they both studied at Harvard, and in the last several days we've been able to speak discreetly with some of those who knew them in those days. I'm afraid we have almost no data at all about any of the other players in the new regime. But we're working on it."

She paused to make sure we were still listening.

"Okay, I suggest you not take notes, on paper or computer. It would be too dangerous to have any incriminating files with you in the field, so you might as well get used to memorizing the key points. All right. Camara, forty-three years old, and Dembele, who is forty-two, have known each other since they were young boys growing up in the same Bamako orphanage. They are both smart, and in particular gifted in languages. While French is more commonly spoken in Mali, they both learned English in school in Bamako, but it really took hold when they were at Harvard. They both speak English very well.

"After leading their respective classes at Mandé Bukari University in Bamako, and through the financial support of a wealthy American mining executive and several aid agencies, they were both given the chance to study governance, public policy, and economics at Harvard. A rare and welcome opportunity."

Vivian stopped to scan the briefing note before her, then continued.

"The idea was that after Harvard, they would return to Mali to improve the quality of government and civic leadership—arguably the best kind of foreign aid developed nations can provide. They are obviously close, given their history. It's also important to note that Adama Camara has a ten-year-old daughter, Amina. Her mother died of Lassa fever when Amina was only five—a sad fate not uncommon in Mali. Adama also contracted Lassa fever but survived to raise Amina on his own. Are we okay so far?" Vivian asked.

Coop and I were taking it all in. Both of us nodded.

"As a person, we understand Camara to be happy, optimistic, impressionable, perhaps too trusting, committed to his country, and hungry for knowledge that might help lift Mali out of poverty and yield a stable and just government, not to mention sound economic policies."

"He didn't exactly carry himself that way during his news conference," I said. "He seemed anxious, nervous."

"Which is exactly how he might look if he were not really the one in charge," Coop replied. "It plays into our working hypothesis."

"So, what happened after Harvard?" I asked.

"Camara returned to Mali and joined the faculty of Mandé Bukari University, in the economics department. He also completed his mandatory military service. Despite, or perhaps because of, the relative instability of the government, he came to believe that democracy, along with universal education and health care, represented the only way forward. And that's the book on Camara, at least as much as we currently know."

"He doesn't sound like a power-hungry dictator," Coop said.

"No, he doesn't, which also lends credence to our working theory that he may be a pawn in someone else's power play," replied Vivian. "But let's not be too seduced by that notion. It is only a theory that you will soon confirm or dispel."

"Okay, then what about Dembele?" I asked.

Vivian opened a second dossier and gathered her thoughts before beginning.

"Right. Dembele, a year younger, is Camara's chief of staff. He controls the president's agenda and is obviously a powerful voice in the new government. According to our interviews with some of his Harvard classmates, Demba Dembele is not quite the open book Camara seems to be. He's quieter, more closed down, apparently more serious and cynical. 'Machiavellian' was the word one classmate used to describe him. We've also had several reports about a nasty temper, but all indicators point to a very shrewd and smart guy."

"They sound like mirror images of one another," I said.

"Yes, they are quite different, but opposites often attract," Coop suggested. "They could both be looking for qualities and assets in the other that they themselves don't possess. It becomes a bit of a symbiotic relationship."

"Well, based on what little we know about Dembele, it's hard to imagine that he hangs around with Camara just to try to gain a sunnier and more optimistic disposition for himself," I observed. "He doesn't strike me as a guy who reads self-help books. I think it's more likely that Camara can prove useful to Dembele—like, for instance, pushing Camara out in front of the new regime so Dembele can lurk in the shadows, perhaps even pulling the strings."

"Again, we don't have enough data or evidence to draw that conclusion," Coop argued. "It's way too early to lock in our assessment. We need to get on the ground with open minds."

"Absolutely right, Lauren," Vivian said. "Right now, all we have are theories, hearsay, and intuition. But before we leave Dembele, there's one more interesting point that came to us from a former classmate. She said over his time at Harvard, she noticed a change in him. When he arrived on campus, she remembered him in class debates as very much pro-democracy. He supported left-leaning social contract ideas, where you work to close the gap between the rich and the poor, help those who can't help themselves, share and share alike, et cetera. But by the time Dembele finished at Harvard, he seemed to have . . . now, how did she put it? Yes, here we are. She said he seemed to have fallen under the spell of the American Dream. She claimed to have seen subtle signs that he'd been overtaken by an ideology of greed. It manifested as a fascination with Wall Street, easy money, junk bonds, and pyramid schemes. He still kept pretty much to himself, but she was worried by what she'd seen."

"But haven't we just circled back to hearsay?" Coop asked. "We still have no corroboration of this one person's view. Maybe they had a fight? Maybe he was mean to her in class? Maybe they dated and he broke up with her? We have no idea."

"All true, Lauren," agreed Vivian. "But it doesn't mean we shouldn't keep this idea on the table and be on the lookout for behaviour that either supports or contradicts this information. As gossamer-thin as Dembele's dossier is, it's all we have."

"I know we don't have much hard-core evidence," I said. "But there seems to be a pattern emerging, if we follow what little of the story we know. And it points to Demba Dembele as a key player who may well be calling the shots. I understand we can't yet accept it as the truth, but it does give us some signposts to guide our sitrep when we get there."

"'Sitrep'? Look at you and your fancy spy words," Coop said. "But just so you know, intelligence agencies don't really use that word. Sitrep is more of a military term. Nice try, but we know what you meant."

Just as I was mobilizing a witty retort, my email dinged with a fresh arrival in my inbox. There was silence in the room as I clicked into my email program. Bingo! I looked up at them both.

"I don't know what one says at a moment like this," I said. "Hallelujah? The eagle has landed? He shoots, he scores?"

"You can start by telling us whether Camara replied," Vivian said.

"Sorry, yes, he did," I said.

I opened the newly arrived email and started reading it out loud. My heart was pounding more than I'd expected.

> Dear Mr. Norval,
>
> I hope I may call you James at some point, but that will be your decision. I was beyond the moon when I read your message. To think that you, my very most favourite author, had seen my news conference from the presidential palace. The thought left me feeling a little giddy and overwhelmed. And thank you for your good wishes for our new government. There is much to do, much to fix, and much to build.
>
> It was a thrill to hear that you are writing a new novel set in an African nation. I knew you would, one day, and now you are. Perhaps you will honour us by choosing Mali as the setting.

Looking at my schedule, I am certain that we can spare some time to talk about your book. Please do come to Bamako at your earliest convenience. You and your assistant will stay in the palace, and we will take care of any needs you might have while you are in our beautiful country.

I am so excited to host you and I am already anticipating your visit. I will now return to rereading yet again one of my favourites of your novels, *Darkest Before Dawn*.

Just tell me when you will be arriving, and I will greet you at Modibo Keita International Airport. Just so you know, Modibo Keita was our first president in 1960.

Until we meet, I remain your humble servant and very big fan,

President Adama Camara

I kept my cool, but the more I read, the more excited I became.

"Well, it sounds like you're in!" said Vivian. "That was just the outcome we sought. Well done."

I looked over at Coop, who was smiling and nodding.

"Well, Coop, looks like we're going on a trip. And we're going undercover!" I said, my clenched fists punching the air in front of me.

"Um, Norval, we don't usually celebrate as if we're heading off to Disneyland," Coop chided. "We're intelligence officers. We try to keep it a little more on the down-low, okay?"

"Got it," I replied, with both my hands held high in front of me. "I am officially dialling it back to *down-low*."

"Do you think his reference to a specific one of your novels is significant?" Vivian asked.

"Hmmm. *Darkest Before Dawn*. Good question," I said. "Citing that title could indicate that he's in a rough spot but that help is now on the way. We might actually be the dawn he's referring to."

After a quick discussion among the three of us, I crafted and sent a response to Camara telling him we'd land in Bamako the following afternoon on a private jet. I provided a touchdown time and the jet's tail number. Two minutes later, he confirmed: *All will be ready for your arrival.*

We were in. We were well and truly in.

CHAPTER 4

EXCEPT FOR a short break for sandwiches at lunch, we'd spent the entire day learning about Mali, Camara, and Dembele. I was already exhausted by the time we confirmed our flight to Bamako and our reservations at the presidential palace. Vivian gave us the evening off, but we'd be starting again first thing in the morning. It was five thirty by the time Ms. Atkins arrived to help Vivian down to the lobby and then drive her back to her hotel.

As Coop and I were packing up for the day, I said, "Um, look, we didn't really get off on the right foot today. I take full responsibility. Let me take you for dinner tonight."

She stopped loading up her bag and gave me a solid dose of side-eye. I barrelled ahead.

"We're going to have to help each other when we're on the ground. I know I'll need you more than you'll need me, but let's get back on the same page, starting tonight. Come on. It's important to the operation. It may even be 'mission critical,' if that's a term CSIS uses."

She sighed. "Okay, okay. But we're not staying out late. We've got lots to cover in the morning."

"Done. We'll just go to the hotel restaurant. I hear it's amazing. Early night."

I felt better after taking another shower, and I'm pleased to report that I remained fully conscious for the entire twenty minutes I spent under the water jets. I wore a casual but presentable outfit—though "outfit" is not a word I often use—and waited for Coop in the lobby. For what it's worth, I'd pulled on a nice pair of jeans, brown leather lace-up shoes—think desert boots minus the suede and weird crepe soles—the light-blue collared shirt, and the new blue blazer. In short, it was an ensemble entirely composed of items Vivian's team had chosen for me. I thought it looked great. Then again, I really knew nothing about fashion. But I felt good wearing it.

Coop cut a fine figure when she walked out of the elevator. She wore grey dress pants with a floppy dark-green knit sweater, and dressy sandal-like shoes with chunky, lowish heels. (Okay, so I know even less about womenswear, and I'm certainly not up to speed on women's fashion terminology.) She had put on some makeup and was actually smiling as she headed my way.

The restaurant was busy, but we managed to secure a quiet spot in a corner of the small mezzanine level, looking down over the bar and tables below. Coop ordered a rum and Coke and I a Balvenie DoubleWood twelve-year-old single-malt scotch.

"So, here's my thinking," I said. "We have to get to know each other if we're going to work together as well as we can. It could save our lives out there in the wilds of Mali."

"Isn't that a line Hunter Chase tries on a young CSIS agent in one of your books before going on to seduce her?"

"Absolutely not. I would never write a line like that. But it is possible it's a line from one of the films. I don't write my own screenplays and they never let me near the script. Regardless, I maintain that knowing each other a little will help us a lot in the field. So, I'll go first. Ask me anything and I pledge to respond truthfully."

She nodded, playing along, and started.

"Married?"

"Ahhhhh, no."

"It sounds like there's a story there," she prompted. "I'm going to need a little bit more."

I finished my first single malt and ordered another. She called for a Negroni. I assumed that was a drink, but I'd wait to see.

"Okay, I can do this," I said. "This is the very short version of an aborted engagement. She was an engineer who worked for the National Research Council in Ottawa. As far as I was concerned, she was the one. I fell hard. We were together for two years before I proposed. She said yes and seemed excited, until a few months later when she suddenly wasn't. She couldn't even talk to me about it beyond breaking off the engagement. Two months after that, she landed a new job and fled to Europe with someone else. As far as I know, she still lives with him in Italy. That happened twenty-two years ago, and I've had zero contact with her since."

"Ouch. Sorry about that," she said. "I thought stuff like that only happened in movies."

"Well, it does happen in movies, but they're usually rom-coms, so they get together in the end and everyone's happy. I don't see that happening in my case. But I'm okay with it. I poured my pain and renewed focus into my writing, and that's when things really started to happen for me as a writer."

"Believe it or not, I've actually read quite a few of your books," Coop said. "Not that they reflect the real life of intelligence operatives, but they can be entertaining at times. And I've liked some of the movies, too. You've definitely hit the big time."

"Yeah well, I can't complain, but it's a bit of a grind. I guess I'm a little fanatical when it comes to getting the stories right, and that takes time and more research than I'd like."

"At least it pays well."

"I suppose, but I really don't care about the money."

"Spoken by one who now has more than he'll ever need."

I paused.

"Well, you may be on to something there," I admitted. "I used to care about the money, only because the writing and research always felt like work to me."

"My heart bleeds for you," she replied. "You write a novel a year, travel the world, live in luxury, drive a nice car, walk the red carpet at movie premieres, and are interviewed on television a lot more than most writers. But wait, there's more! Let's not forget that you're also relatively easy on the eyes. You basically have it all. So, it does seem a bit churlish to complain about it."

This line of thinking always irritated me.

"Good use of the word 'churlish.' But hang on a sec. I'm definitely not complaining. I know how lucky I am," I said, trying and failing to stop my mouth from running any further. "But more importantly, maybe writing novels wasn't my first choice. Did you ever think of that?"

Damn, I hadn't wanted to go there. And I noticed a little more edge to my voice than I'd intended.

"Well, well. Nerve struck. Now we're getting somewhere," she said. "I need another drink."

We took a little break while waiting for our refills. I calmed down and loosened up a bit. My third single malt helped, and Coop was keeping up with me. She was quicker to smile with a few drinks under her belt.

"Okay, you were about to tell me what your first career choice was, what you'd rather be doing than raking in millions of dollars in book sales, Hollywood blockbusters, and streaming series."

"Well, now that you've lured me into a corner, if you must know, I wanted to be who you are."

"I don't know why anyone would want to be a young Black woman of Jamaican origin working for CSIS," she said, looking a little wistful. "I wouldn't wish it on anybody."

"I was particularly focused on the last part."

"Wait, you applied to CSIS?" she said with elevated eyebrows.

"No laughing at me. This is a schadenfreude-free zone."

"I'm not laughing at you, and you can't baffle me with your highbrow literary terms. I know what 'schadenfreude' means."

"So, yes, when I was twenty-five or so, I did go through the CSIS application and recruitment program."

"So that's what Vivian meant the other day when she said 'now you can finally get in the game'?"

I nodded.

"And by the way," I said, "congratulations on making it through. I know what a tough road it is."

"Thank you. But I didn't find it too bad."

"Not too bad? Come on. When I tried out, there was a rigorous four-step process of exams, strategy development, field simulations, and countless interviews. It was exhausting, and it took six months for them to say no."

"Well, when I did it, the process was nine steps, and it took a year for them to say yes."

"Right, and that's why I'm congratulating you. I've been through at least four of your nine steps, so I at least have a sense of how tough it is."

"So why did they wash you out?"

"What makes you think I washed out?"

"Well, because I believed you when you just said it took them six months to say no. I just assumed you were telling me the truth."

"Right. I guess I did say that. Okay, okay, yes, I washed out, but I really hate that term."

"Well, it's better than 'flamed out,' which was all the rage when I went through."

I paused again.

"You know, it isn't the washing out part that still hurts—it's more that I never found out why. They just said no and broke off all communications. You know, all I really wanted to do was field work, covert and outside of the country if possible. I did not want a junior analyst's job pushing paper all day in a cubicle until it was time to drive my four-door Toyota Corolla home to the suburbs. Not what I was signing up for, so maybe it was all for the best."

"Norval, lots of good people wash out. Besides, CSIS had no legal authority back then to operate on foreign soil anyway."

"Believe me, I remember," I replied. "But there was a strong feeling we'd be granted that ability soon enough, even though it ended up taking much longer."

We both sipped our drinks. I could feel the Scotch loosening every sinew in my body and sending a wave of warmth across my abdomen and chest.

"Anyway, back to me," I quipped. "I really felt as if I'd aced the exams and the scenarios, and my interviews all seemed to go well. I thought I was on fire, but I guess I was just—as you said—flaming out. I just wanted to know why. I got no response to my Access to Information request."

"Probably because national security and intelligence matters are exempted from the Access to Information Act."

"Well, I'm glad that wasn't a question on my CSIS exam."

Coop laughed. She actually laughed. Her face took on a completely different look when she laughed. I guess that's true for most people, but for Coop, it was particularly pronounced.

"But back to your second career choice. You're a famous thriller writer with umpteen bestsellers and action films to your credit. I bet you're not driving a Toyota now. It looks like your backup plan worked out pretty well."

I sighed.

"No complaints, but it was still my second choice. It was always my second choice."

I didn't tell her that I still held a grudge against CSIS for rejecting me when I was certain I'd be accepted. That rejection had been in my head for nearly thirty years, and I still couldn't shake it. It had even led to a brief crisis of confidence back then, and it took me a while to get back on track. The success of my first novel—by any measure an international blockbuster—had cemented my new-found career as a novelist. It, and the many books that followed, brought—or rather bought—me some contentment, but it wasn't quite the happiness and fulfillment I'd been seeking.

Sure, I had none of the financial worries that plagued so many of my contemporaries, writers in particular. But those common concerns had been replaced by a nagging, niggling, persistent malaise that weighed me down and never entirely let me enjoy the fruits of my literary labour. And yes, many would balk at my use of the term "literary" when describing the books I write. I suppose I'd be hard pressed to argue. But the alluring alliteration got the better of me. My point is, even those who appear on the surface to have the world by the tail, to have been blessed beyond all reasonable measure, may still have something hollowing out their insides and robbing them of some of the joy in their lives. (And this will draw today's episode of *Armchair Analysis* to a close.)

"Okay, enough about me. I think I've done my part and laid my soul bare on this table. Now it's my turn to interrogate," I said. "What about you? Where did you come from, and how were you able to become a fully fledged CSIS operative?"

"Hold that thought," said Coop, as she swallowed the last of her second Negroni and ordered a Paper Plane. For those of you wondering, that's also a cocktail. We took that opportunity to order dinner, too. I opted for the strip loin while Coop chose the shrimp risotto.

"Okay, so I grew up in Jamaica. My parents sent me to Toronto to live with my aunt when I was fourteen. It's just another immigrant story. I did well in high school, and without really trying lost most of my accent."

"I think I can still detect a slight Jamaican lilt."

"You should have heard me in grade nine. I sounded like a deejay at a Montego Bay reggae station. I managed to get a scholarship to the University of Toronto, where I got a B.A. and a master's in clinical psychology. I didn't feel like doing more research or starting my own practice, so I joined the RCMP for a while, and that's when CSIS said they were looking for recruits with various backgrounds, including psych. And here I am."

"Amazing. You somehow made what I'm sure was an interesting, even exciting, origin story sound rather pedestrian. There must be more to the tale than that."

Coop smiled.

"Okay, I've glossed over the negative stuff. I'd already spent a harrowing three years in the RCMP. Being a woman, let alone a Black woman, in the RCMP back then—well, let's just say it wasn't exactly a warm and welcoming environment. Law enforcement in general isn't what you would call the most enlightened sector, and the RCMP was known as a particularly regressive organization where women were concerned."

I nodded.

"I have some sense of what you're talking about. I once interviewed several women in the RCMP for a novel I was writing. It was around the time those high-profile harassment court cases were in the news. It was rough enough just hearing about what went down. I can't imagine being a victim, right there in the middle of it."

"I read that book you're talking about. You got it close to right."

"Thanks," I said. "So, what about your relationship with Vivian?"

"Vivian was in charge of CSIS when I first joined up," she said. "Anyway, you know all those clichés about women, particularly women like me, never 'seeing themselves' in books, films, careers, and organizations, particularly law enforcement and intelligence agencies? Well, I'd met so very few Black women in the RCMP, and I didn't have much hope it would be any different in CSIS. But I just had to get out of where I was. So, I applied for CSIS and somehow got the green light. I'd gotten used to feeling pretty much alone in my career. But then I met Vivian. She was running the whole shop back then. One day early on, she called me in to her office to welcome me."

"I'm just guessing here, but I doubt she invited all the young, up-and-coming white men recruits in for a little chat in her office," I said.

Coop paused and looked through me for a few seconds.

"Vivian saw me, and I saw her," she replied. "We stayed in touch even after her arthritis cut short her career and forced her into retirement. She's been looking out for me ever since."

"But how is Vivian now back in the game?" I asked.

"Technically, she doesn't work for CSIS," Coop explained. "She's on the minister's personal staff as his intelligence advisor. I'm told they bonded while working together on the whole Russian president assassination affair that went down a while ago. I'm so glad she's back in play."

"Right," I said. "Okay, that was a redemptive story, well told. But we're not done yet. You didn't marry, move to the suburbs with your own Toyota Corolla?"

"Not interested. CSIS and relationships don't easily coexist, and field work makes it even tougher."

"I remember Vivian saying you had experience on the ground. What have you done and where have you been? I want all the spine-tingling details."

"Ha! You're funny. You know I'm not permitted to share anything from past operations even with CSIS colleagues, let alone famous civilian thriller writers, but none of my field work would make for exciting reading. We got the job done, but tense, dangerous, and exciting? Not so much."

I downed another single malt.

We talked for a long time, often ignoring our meals, despite how great they were. I felt good about our evening—alcohol-assisted or not—and I thought we understood each other a little better than we had before we ordered. And that had been the whole point.

I figured Coop was a bit tipsy when we parted paths at the hotel elevator. I definitely was.

CHAPTER 5

THE THREE of us—Vivian, Coop, and I—reconvened at the embassy the next morning for our final briefing and planning session. Later that afternoon, as hard as it was for me to believe, we'd be landing in Bamako to stay with the newly installed President Adama Camara in his swanky palace. Oh, and we also had that other minor task of figuring out how to spirit fifteen Canadians out of the country safely and then actually doing it, while always bearing in mind the all-important *safely* part.

Strangely, I didn't feel anxious, nervous, worried, concerned, or scared about what lay ahead. Figure that one out, if you can. I sure can't. I should have had all of those feelings, and many more. But I really didn't. For some reason, Vivian, Coop, and even the minister made me feel like we could do this. That we could pull it off, even though we couldn't develop a plan until we were actually in Mali and had gathered more information. But we had an ace up our sleeve. I just happened to be the president's favourite writer. That gave us an edge. At least, I thought it did.

Despite our boozy late night in the hotel restaurant, Coop seemed to have returned to her normal icy demeanour by the time we met again in the morning. I thought we'd broken through some barriers at dinner. We'd both shared stories—some of them quite personal—and even had a few laughs, usually at my expense. But I didn't mind. I figured if we knew each other better and ended up working more effectively together when we reached the critical phase of the operation, it would be well worth it. But the Coop who, the previous evening, definitely did not walk in a straight line from the restaurant to the elevator was not the Coop who was all business that next morning.

"We're running out of time," Vivian said, after we'd all sat down. "Let's talk about possible options for getting the Tardif team out."

"I had an idea last night that I think might work," I said.

"Well, we've had a team of analysts looking at this problem, so I think we should probably start there," Vivian said.

"Vivian's right," Coop agreed. "But I'd be curious to hear what Norval has in mind. Then we could return to the analysts' recommendation."

Coop seemed to be enjoying this, which did set off a few alarm bells in my head. Then again, I'm quite good at silencing alarm bells echoing in my own skull.

"Okay, James. With Lauren's blessing, what have you got?" asked Vivian.

"I'll keep it short," I said. "Okay, picture this. A Black Hawk chopper lands at the Tardif compound in the early hours of the morning. We rush the execs on and escape with them over the border to Senegal before anyone is the wiser?"

Coop burst out laughing, but quickly gathered herself.

"That's it?" she asked. "A quick in-and-out Black Hawk airlift?"

"Well, that's the basic idea," I said. It was a little hard to hear her, as those alarm bells had suddenly grown much louder.

"Well, you'd need at least two Black Hawks, because there are fifteen Canadians, plus the two of us makes seventeen, and that heli can only carry twelve," Coop said. "Frankly, we'd also likely need an Apache attack helicopter to provide air cover in case the troops on the ground start firing. Oh, yes, and there's the other minor matter that Canada has no Black Hawk assault helicopters and no Apache attack helis. Those are American birds. Instead of Black Hawks, we'd have to use a couple of our Griffons, and they are now nearly thirty years old."

"But . . ." I started to say. Coop raised her hand to stop me before barrelling on herself.

"And since Canada doesn't really have any attack helicopters, getting in and out of Mali safely with fifteen civilians using only Griffons is just too dangerous and risky. It's out of the question. But wait, there's more. If I haven't already shot down the Black Hawk stratagem, let me remind you that we're in Mali secretly operating on our own with no overt, official ties to our government. So we can't just send in the Canadian Air Force rescue team. That is the very definition of a non-starter. This is an intelligence operation, a CSIS operation, not a military exercise."

Coop stopped to take a breath. I wasn't sure she was finished blowing my Black Hawk out of the sky, but I didn't wait to find out.

"Okay, well, clearly we'll need to rethink certain aspects of the plan. But I'm very glad you're not taking the idea off the table. We can tweak it."

Coop just shook her head and looked at Vivian before turning back to me.

"Um, Norval, there'll be no tweaking. Your idea was never anywhere near the table. It's not even in the room. It's not happening. It's never happening."

"Okay, okay, let's just settle down a bit," Vivian said. "I think we're getting a little ahead of ourselves. James, thanks for the idea, but I still think our first step is to consider what our own team of experts believes to be the safest, easiest, and fastest way to bring fifteen Canadians home. Can we start there?"

"Of course," I said. "I was just brainstorming, you know, just spitballing."

I didn't dare look directly at Coop but I'm pretty sure she rolled her eyes. My peripheral vision definitely picked up some motion in the vicinity of her face. Okay, so that hadn't gone well. I really had nothing to counter Coop's well-reasoned dismembering of my little plan. I just hoped neither Coop nor Vivian had read my third novel, in which Hunter Chase had piloted a Black Hawk in just such an operation. It had worked well in the book.

Vivian opened a file marked *Top Secret*. (I know that sounds like a cliché, but Top Secret is in fact the official designation for documents earning the highest level of secrecy within CSIS and the broader Canadian government. And those words were in fact written in a stark red font on the front of the file folder.)

"Bearing in mind the location of the Tardif mine and compound, we believe the easiest escape route will be across the border into Senegal, due west of Kéniéba, but not through either of the two heavily guarded border crossings in the area. And remember, Kéniéba is a long way from Bamako, so you'll have to figure out how to get up there."

She clicked the remote in her hand, and a map of Mali appeared on the big screen with the key locations marked.

"We think your best shot will be via an old and seldom-used Kéniéba mining road, preferably under cover of twilight or, even better, darkness. The road dead-ends at the Falémé River, which marks your crossing point. You'll signal across the water with a flashlight in a pre-arranged pattern, in response to which you should see a return signal from the Senegal side of the river."

At this point, Vivian clicked a new slide onto the screen, showing what I assumed was the Falémé River. It did look manageable. It was more like a stream than a river, with Senegal beckoning a mere ninety feet away, according to the measurements displayed on the screen.

"At the crossing point, the river is narrow, very shallow, and slow moving."

Coop was nodding. I was nodding. It wasn't a flashy stratagem. There was little chance of this escape plan finding its way into a future novel of mine. But it did seem to be the easiest and safest way out of Mali.

"You'll need to wade across the Falémé, where Senegal officials and a CSIS field team will meet you on the far side of the river. But how you get the fifteen Canadians to the crossing point remains an open question. That'll be up to you. We just don't have enough intelligence even to point you in the right direction, beyond this proposed optimal escape route."

I reviewed the plan in my mind to get it straight. The whole wade-across-the-river part seemed quite simple, doable, easy to pull off. As Vivian had pointed out, the tougher nut to crack would be how to get the fifteen Canadians to the crossing point undetected, at a time when they were supposed to be somewhere else and under guard. That would be the challenging part, the dangerous part, the *How the hell are we going to pull that off?* part. Okay, got it.

Vivian's voice brought me back to her.

"You may want to consider planting some disinformation, like a map with a phony route marked along Trans-African Highway 5 up through Kayes, to throw off any pursuers and buy you some more time."

"Well, assault helicopters would be more fun, but I guess crossing the river into Senegal might also work," I said. "But the movie won't be nearly as exciting."

"We're not looking for excitement," cut in Coop. "Again, this is not an action film or one of your thriller novels. We're just looking for success, and that means a safe and uneventful exfiltration."

"Um, Coop, I was kidding," I said, a little annoyed. "I like the river-crossing plan. It makes sense. But that's the easy part. We still need to get them to the river."

"I'm afraid that's on both of you," Vivian said. "That's why you're there on the ground. So, it's time to set aside the petty friction that is apparent between you two this morning, and start acting like a team, supporting one another, helping one another, learning from one another. You both have certain skills, and I think we're going to need all of them working in concert if you are going to pull this off. And I do mean *you*. Because when you land in Mali late this afternoon, it will be just you two who will have to push this operation from the starting blocks all the way to the finish line. Are you hearing the message I'm sending? Otherwise, we'll just pull the plug right now, close up shop, and go home."

Coop looked at me and I looked at her. It felt like we were sitting in the principal's office being disciplined for disrupting class.

"Sorry, Vivian," Coop said. "I'm not used to working with a civilian. We'll turn it around."

"Right," I added. "And I'm not used to working with facts and reality and doing things in the real world. I do fiction. I just make stuff up. So, I'm still adjusting. But, yeah, we'll get there. We'll turn it around."

"Good," Vivian said. "Some other points. You know this already, Lauren, but for your benefit, James, please remember, you can only speak freely to one another outside the palace, in the open air. And not in any official cars, either. If the president is in fact just a puppet, many rooms in the palace, perhaps all of them, will be bugged. We also expect that the offices of Tardif Resources and their living compound will have their fair share of listening devices. Nothing will blow your cover and have you arrested faster than talking out of turn to one another anywhere but outside with the sky above you and a breeze blowing. Clear?"

We both nodded as the door chime sounded. On the digital monitor, another woman in a lab coat appeared holding a small cardboard box. Vivian buzzed her in.

"What have you got for us?" Vivian asked as the woman entered.

"Nothing too fancy," the woman replied, placing two black, robust-looking phones on the table. "We don't have a lot of tech in this embassy. But here are your encrypted satphones. They are safe and secure to use."

"Hi, I'm James, and you must be Q," I said. *Why did I say that?*

The woman looked very annoyed.

"Wow. Never heard that one before," she said, also sounding very annoyed. "What an utterly original line."

Coop glared at me, so I gave her my patented exaggerated *What did I do?* shrug that I've been perfecting since I was twelve years old.

"What are you, twelve years old?" Coop asked.

"Well, now that you mention it . . ." I replied.

"It was a rhetorical question," she clarified. "I wasn't seeking a response."

"I know what a rhetorical question is," I counter-clarified.

"Thank you, Sandy," said Vivian. "These two are just getting to know each other. Now, how about a quick refresher on satphone use?"

"It's quite straightforward," the woman apparently named Sandy replied as she picked up one of the phones to demonstrate.

"Ideally, you go outside and find a spot with a wide-open view of the sky. Pull up the antenna like so, and then turn on the power with this button. Enter the PIN that you will need to commit to memory and then wait until it connects to a satellite. The red light will turn green when it has. Finally, you dial zero-zero, then the country code, then the phone number, and press the green Call button. That's it. Easy, safe, and secure."

"Thank you, um, Sandy," I said. "Very helpful."

Coop nodded her thanks. Then Sandy left the room after handing Vivian a small card bearing the PINs for the two satphones.

I found all this a bit odd, but I gathered that when working on a clandestine op, few embassy officials introduced themselves or sought the names of those they were meeting. We didn't need to know their names, and they certainly didn't need or want to know ours. Secrecy, discretion, and even anonymity were almost universally observed, I guessed for good reason. It might just save lives. I made a mental note to include this idea in future novels to make my stories a little more realistic. I also made a mental note to stop being a jerk and trying to be funny.

I confess I was worried about Coop being able to play her role as my assistant convincingly and sustain it for however long we'd be in Mali. I wasn't about to mention it right then, given the dagger eyes she was still firing my way. But as my research assistant, Camara would expect her to be deferential, dedicated, tirelessly helpful, congenial, and quiet. I only knew Coop as cold, calculating, terse, and by-the-book, while valiantly and humourlessly overcoming all the obstacles life had thrown in her path as a young Black woman in CSIS. I commended her. I applauded her. But carrying off a chipper, optimistic, and devoted researcher type might just be a stretch. Whereas for me, my cover as a celebrated thriller writer who was confident, knowledgeable about tradecraft, affable, brave, smart, and an all-round nice person was right in my wheelhouse. I could play that guy. That was who I was already, right? *Right?*

Just before we wrapped up and headed for the airport, Vivian worked with us on simple and subtle physical signals—gestures, really—to help us communicate with one another amidst the cameras and listening devices and other people in the palace. I wasn't sure we'd need them, but they were good to have in our repertoire.

We agreed that casually rubbing one's right elbow meant there was something urgent to discuss. Clasping one's hands in front meant something to report, and that we should take a walk outside at the earliest opportunity without arousing suspicions. There were a couple more gestures that we committed to memory that could come in handy. When, at one point, I raked my hair with my right hand, Coop was confused.

"Sorry, Coop, that one's not part of our hand-signal arsenal. I was just trying to tame my messy hair that so desperately needs cutting."

I swear it was an innocent mistake—one that earned another eye roll from Coop.

After a final walk-through of our plan—incomplete though it would remain until we were on the ground in Mali—and a pep talk from Vivian, she hugged us both and sent us back to the hotel to rest for an hour, pack, and check out.

"And do not pack anything, anything at all, that could somehow link you to CSIS or reveal in any way that you might be there on false premises," was Vivian's final directive.

When we left her and headed back to the hotel, we didn't know if or when we'd see her again.

I spent the hour creating a set of computer files with the same names that I always used when writing a new novel—file names like *Characters*, *Story Arc*, *Timeline*, *Settings*, *Possible Titles*, *Relationships*, *Scenes and Narrative Exposition*, *Word Count Table*, and *Manuscript*. It would be odd if I turned up in Mali without some digital evidence that I was in fact working on a new novel. I went on to create some phony but convincing documents for most of the new files. I put nothing in the manuscript file, as I could simply say I was not yet at the manuscript stage of my writing.

Coop had been given a new, secure laptop to take in support of her cover as my research assistant. I'd work with her on our nearly five-hour flight to make her laptop files authentic.

I was excited about what lay ahead, but as I packed my suitcase, the smallest little knot formed in my stomach. I almost didn't notice it, but it was there.

At about twelve thirty, Coop and I boarded the same private jet we'd flown in from Dushanbe a few days earlier. But this time, there was no Vivian and no Angus. We were on our own. Our jet was actually registered in Los Angeles and belonged to a respected leasing firm. Courtesy of a shell-company intermediary, there was no paper trail linking the plane either to CSIS or to the Canadian government. I say again, Coop and I were on our own.

The lone flight attendant did not hover in our seating section towards the front, but discreetly popped in periodically to see that we had everything we needed. The pilot kept us informed, but the weather was clear, and we levelled off at our cruising altitude after twenty minutes or so.

Coop and I had not said much to each other since our less-than-harmonious briefing session that morning. I had thought that our dinner the previous evening had been a breakthrough of sorts in moving us closer together. Then I had proposed a possible escape idea on which Coop had mercilessly dumped from a very lofty height. In hindsight, I see now that I was thinking like a thriller writer looking for a movie deal rather than a seasoned and effective intelligence operative trying to get in and out of an unstable and dangerous country, quietly and with precious cargo. I understood. I did. But it's tough to shut down nearly thirty years of writing exciting, action-packed thrillers and begin to see the benefits of safe, boring, effective, and successful.

After a somewhat lengthy and awkward silence, Coop, in the seat next to mine, turned towards me.

"Look, if it weren't already obvious, I was opposed to a civilian taking part in what could be a dangerous mission. But it wasn't my call."

"I know you don't think I'm qualified for field work, but I do know a thing or two about clandestine operations, and millions of readers worldwide will back me up on that."

"Here we go again. I've read a few of your thrillers, and I can report that while they are entertaining, you have absolutely zero grasp of intelligence matters and in-field operations."

"Well, I appreciate your candour," I said. "And in the spirit of reciprocity and honesty, I feel compelled to tell you that my initial preference was for me to go in alone . . ."

Coop burst out laughing.

"You, alone, managing a field op? That's insane. Not only would that never happen, but if through some miracle it ever did, it would be a disaster, likely culminating in sixteen body bags."

"Are you done?" I asked.

"Well, yes, I guess I am," she replied. "At least for now."

"Good, because you didn't let me finish," I said. "I was going on to say that after our briefing sessions and after getting to know you at least a little bit, my view changed. I clearly see now that going it alone would not have been a good idea. In fact, it would have been folly—maybe not body bags bad, but definitely folly. I get that now. So, I'm learning something, right? And now I'm glad we're in this together. I would like to survive the operation to write a few more novels, and I figure you're my best shot to get out of Mali alive."

"Oh, I see," Coop replied. Sheepish is the word I'd use to describe her facial expression. But what do I know?

"Now, don't you feel bad for jumping the gun before I could finish?" I asked, smiling at her.

"A little bit," she conceded. "Sorry about the body bags crack."

"Yeah, you really went right for the jugular with that one."

"Okay, now that we've both fallen on our swords, why don't we use the time before we land to fine-tune our covers?" she suggested.

"Excellent idea."

"So, one more time, how did we meet?" Coop asked.

"You worked for my publisher as a publicist and responded to an internal posting for a research assistant to help me get the details right in the Africa book I'm writing," I said. "Then in the interview you gushed shamelessly, like an open fire hydrant, about my writing and my books and how they changed your life. Then you threw yourself onto my editor's desk and threatened to handcuff yourself to her chair if she didn't give you the job."

I had actually forced her to smile as she visualized my over-the-top version of the scene.

"I'd dial it back a notch if you ever have to tell that story in Mali."

"Obviously. I'd probably go with plastic zip-ties instead of handcuffs. Feels a little more believable."

She smiled again.

"Okay, what did you like about me?" she asked.

"You already had solid publishing experience, you knew the business, you demonstrated an advanced understanding of search engines, the researcher's primary source, and your master's in English literature didn't hurt, either. What was the focus of your M.A. again?" I asked.

"The novels of Toni Morrison and how they reflect the contemporary Black experience in America."

"Right. Plus, you're warm and friendly and open-minded, and care about other people and how you treat them."

Then she laughed. An unrestrained, uninhibited laugh. It was the first time I think I caught just a very brief glimpse of the real Lauren Cooper.

"Hang on," she said, shaking her head. "I know how to assume a different persona when I'm in the field, but I'm not a miracle worker."

I laughed. It felt like a bit of a breakthrough in our relationship, such as it was.

"So, what if Demba or somebody in Mali's intelligence agency digs into your background?" I asked.

"I'm glad you asked. I keep meaning to mention this," she said. "First of all, a CSIS team in Ottawa cleansed the internet of any evidence of my real life. You will not find the real me online anywhere, and certainly no photos. Every new CSIS recruit digitally disappears shortly after they join. Secondly, that same internal team has already created and seeded digital evidence to back up my cover story, including a LinkedIn profile and various social channel accounts, with just enough info to satisfy the curious internet surfer that Lauren Cooper the literary research assistant actually exists."

"Brilliant," I replied, impressed.

"Okay, you're up," she said. "Why are you in Mali?"

"If you know my writing and my reputation as a novelist, you'll know that I'm a meticulous researcher to ensure that my books ring true and feel like fact, not fiction. I'm working on my very first novel set at least partly in Africa, perhaps even in Mali. It's about the aftermath of a military coup and how intelligence agencies jockey for position under the new regime."

"Okay, so what happens in your story?"

"Well, as usual, my lead character, Hunter Chase, is in the middle of it all. As he opens communications and starts to build relationships with the various factions operating below the surface in Mali, and in Bamako in particular, he stumbles upon a plot by a lesser-known warlord to overthrow the new president even before he's fully settled in the palace. Hunter determines that it is not in his interests, nor in the interests of geopolitical stability in the region, for this upstart warlord to succeed. So, through various covert means, Hunter Chase undermines the uprising, allowing the new and quite smart president to stay one step ahead of his detractors and ultimately prevail."

"Sounds like you have it all figured out. But why put yourself at risk by visiting Mali when the story is already fully baked?"

"Ahhh, well, I have the storyline in good shape, but for the novel to work the way I want it to, I need to delve into the motivations of the characters themselves to understand, and then convincingly convey to the reader, what makes them tick. I can't do that from my condo in downtown Toronto. So here I am."

"Good," she replied. "The story holds, and you talk about it with real conviction. I'd even read that novel if you ever decide to write it."

"Well, that part is easy. This is actually how I write novels. It's nice when a big chunk of my cover is actually true."

"And the plot of your Africa novel should appeal to President Camara, given that it ends well for him."

"I think he'll like it," I said.

We sat in silence for a few minutes, until she put her hand on my armrest and turned towards me again.

"And we cannot forget that from the time we land to the time we're safely on Senegalese soil, we're likely to be watched, followed, scrutinized, and surveilled, by human assets and/or cameras and listening devices, so you can't so much as elevate your eyebrow in my direction without it being picked up and analyzed. We are strangers in a strange land, and we will be on a very short leash."

"You'll be happy to know that despite strenuous efforts over decades, I am still unable to raise one eyebrow independently of the other, so I think we're fine," I said. Then I raised my hands in surrender and put on my serious face for just a moment. "I understand and completely agree."

We then turned to setting up Coop's computer so that it resembled that of a researcher, with appropriate files and draft documents. It didn't take long, and that was good because we were nearly there.

As we were flying over the African continent, Coop looked over at me.

"Look, I know 'making friends' isn't exactly my strong suit," she said. "I haven't really had much experience with it."

"Coop, we don't have to be *besties*, as the cool kids say these days. But we do have to be colleagues. And I think that can work for us if we both make a little effort. I will certainly try. So, as a show of good faith, I'm prepared to admit that I have a lot to learn about what it's really like in the field," I said. "And I hope you'd be prepared to concede that sometimes the CSIS field operations manual isn't going to help us, and we may need to be a little more creative if we run into problems."

She paused, mulling it over.

"Okay, I can live with that. Agreed," she replied, and even offered her fist for a collegial bump. Just as we finished our awkward fist bump, the captain was on the mic.

"Buckle up, folks, we are on final approach to Modibo Keita International Airport."

The land below us was brown and scrubby. As we descended, I could see through the window that the area past the airport was a little more built up as the outskirts of Bamako came into view. From a few thousand feet in the air, it still looked like the developing country it clearly was. I saw no glass towers. In a way, it looked like Tajikistan. I shoved that thought from my mind, as well as the topic of gum surgery, which, for me, will forever be linked to Tajikistan.

PART 2

CHAPTER 6

Mali: Day 1

THE CAPTAIN made a smooth landing. As we touched down, we were surprised to see out the window a large military marching band just off the tarmac, waving to us. We whizzed by them and out to the end of the runway. Then we turned around and slowly taxied back. Next to the marching band, a five-vehicle motorcade was parked in formation, with uniformed military officials milling about. The front two and back two vehicles were shiny black examples of the ubiquitous Cadillac Escalade, the conveyance of choice for senior government officials and embassies the world over. But the middle car was much older, a classic black stretch limousine, perhaps from the early 1990s.

A red carpet led from the motorcade to the runway, where our skilled captain was carefully positioning the jet. It wasn't his first rodeo, and he nailed the parking job. As we'd been briefed to expect, when the flight attendant opened the door, two uniformed passport control officers were waiting to board. Coop and I were ready with our passports, visas, and vaccination documents. They spoke quite good English and went about their task quickly and efficiently. Given the crowd and festivities awaiting us just outside the plane, I didn't think they would strip-search us before allowing us to enter Mali. Happily, everything seemed to be in order. After applying a couple of stamps to our passports, the two officials disembarked.

I watched out the window as they crossed the tarmac to the main terminal. Just then, I noticed the back door of the old-school stretch limo open, and President Adama Camara stepped out, in full military regalia, grinning from ear to ear. He'd obviously been waiting until the customs team had done their thing. Then the door on the other side of the limo opened and Demba Dembele stepped out, wearing what looked like a very expensive tailored suit. Even I could see that.

As planned, our co-pilot had stepped down to the red carpet to make sure all was well and we could safely leave the plane. He stood there surveying the scene.

"You'd better get out here, some bigwig is walking this way," he said.

I stood up and faced Coop, extending my hand.

"Coop, looking forward to working with you and learning from you," I said with some solemnity.

She smiled and grasped my hand.

"Me, too, Norval. Me, too," she said.

"Easy on the hand, Coop."

She squeezed firmly, but not like the first time.

"Ready, Norval?"

"I have no idea. But we're here, so we might as well, you know . . ."

Coop inhaled deeply and then slowly released her breath.

"Okay, Norval, time to hit the field. Your top-notch research assistant will be right behind you," she said, guiding me to the door.

I stepped out of the plane and was hit by a blast of scorching, humid heat. At the same time, the band struck up—though "struck out" would perhaps be a more apt description. They sounded slightly worse than my grade nine band when I ill-advisedly and temporarily took up the French horn. Listening to them doing their very best from the tarmac, I could have sworn that half of them were playing one song while the other half played another. I managed to navigate the stairs without mishap. Coop was right behind me. It was a reception fit for a visiting head of state. On the far side of the red carpet, excited school kids in traditional Malian costumes were performing dances while beaming and waving to us. I waved back and turned up the wattage of my smile.

As I hit the red carpet, President Camara was waiting. He stepped forward, offering his hand in welcome. I met his hand with mine and he pulled me in tight, hugging me with his other arm. In mid-embrace, his mouth was quite close to my ear.

"I cannot tell you how happy I am that you are here," he whispered in my ear in only slightly accented English. "But my car, my office, and the entire palace are bugged. We can only speak freely outside under the sky. Laugh as I pull away from you." Then he drew back, smiling and laughing. I, too, laughed and nodded, patting his shoulder in what I hoped appeared to be a comradely fashion. At least, that's what I was going for.

Well, he sure hadn't wasted any time making his first move.

Still standing close to President Camara, I turned to wave Coop into our circle.

"President Camara, may I present Ms. Lauren Cooper, my outstanding research assistant."

She was smiling up a storm as she extended her hand. Settling into her role, she seemed completely different from the Coop I'd come to know in the previous few days—less confident, warmer, more curious, more open. As President Camara shook her hand, she even performed what loosely resembled a curtsy, accompanied by a shy smile. After all, he was the president of a bona fide nation-state. And she clearly hadn't given him the full Lauren Cooper handshake experience. He barely winced while their hands were linked.

"A pleasure to have you both in our wonderful country," he said, facing us. "Welcome to Mali."

An honour guard of soldiers lined the red carpet. President Camara took my arm and led me to the far end of the military lineup. We walked slowly down the line, ostensibly inspecting the soldiers. We both smiled and nodded at the stone-faced troops as they kept their eyes fixed on the horizon. Coop trailed a few steps behind. I concede I was a rookie at reviewing honour guards, but it sure didn't look like a particularly buttoned-down, spit-and-polish assembly. One soldier had forgotten his hat, while another had done up his tunic—if that's what you call the jacket part of the uniform—one buttonhole out of order, making him look askew, even slightly scoliotic. President Camara stopped and helped the soldier rebutton his uniform properly. Our smiling host certainly wasn't about to levy any wardrobe deficiency fines, and merely patted the young recruit's shoulder after assisting him. I just nodded, smiled, and kept on walking.

When we reached the other end of the honour guard, the band launched into a new song. President Camara suddenly stood at attention and held a salute. So, naturally, I stopped and stood ramrod straight, too, but resisted the temptation to salute. The song was half over before I was able to recognize our own national anthem, "O Canada." When it had started, it sounded more like a nursery rhyme, or maybe an early Bee Gees song. When our anthem died away, the president held his pose, so I held mine as yet another tune started up. How wonderful, more music. I assumed this was Mali's national anthem. Standing next to me, the new president was singing the French lyrics quietly. But towards the end, he switched to English, changed up the lyrics, and sang in my direction, "Remember, happy talk in the car. Only happy taaaaalk," holding the last note to close out the piece.

The military band finished their performance, signalling the end of the formal ceremonial welcome and putting a stop to the mercifully brief—but not brief enough—cacophony of musical dissonance. Our co-pilot passed our bags and backpacks through the front hatch to Coop, who followed President Camara and me along the red carpet back to the aging limo. Coop stowed our luggage in the trunk but brought the backpacks carrying our laptops and satphones into the car. We hadn't yet been introduced to Demba Dembele, but he didn't seem to be in any rush to meet us. He climbed into the front seat of the second Escalade, leaving the limo to us.

Coop and I were seated next to one another facing President Camara in the back, with the driver and a bodyguard seated up front. It seemed we were finally ready to start this parade. A moment later, the two Escalades in front of us slowly pulled away, followed by our limo and the two other Escalades trailing us. When we passed the security station and left the airport, two jeeps with high-calibre machine guns mounted behind the drivers joined our procession, one out front and one bringing up the rear, to round out the motorcade. The president was still beaming as he looked at me.

"I cannot believe you are here, sitting with me in my car," he said.

"Well, I can't believe we're in the presidential limousine, either," I replied.

"We should be at the palace in approximately twenty minutes."

"At this time of day, when I'm driving in Toronto, nothing is only twenty minutes away," I said.

"Well, it is helpful that my security team has cleared the route of any other vehicles," he explained. "There is normally heavy traffic on our roads, except when my motorcade is driving on them."

"One of the perks of power," I replied.

"Did you enjoy the children's dance at the ceremony?" he asked.

"I thought they were wonderful and full of energy and innocence," I said, looking at Coop for support.

"Yes, they were fantastic," Coop said, on cue.

"The children are from the school that I went to as a boy. I try to involve young kids whenever possible. It adds a sense of optimism and a look to the future. And we need both in our country."

"Well said, Mr. President."

"Do you know what my name, Camara, means?"

Coop and I shook our heads in unison.

"Teacher. Camara means teacher. Nothing is more important than educating our next generation, for they will one day be the leaders of our nation."

"That is a wise and forethoughtful focus for your government," I said, as Coop nodded vigorously beside me.

"I am so happy that you are here, and I very much look forward to showing you around the palace, the grounds, and other special sites in Mali. And I'm eager to hear about your new novel. Thank you for coming."

"Well, thank you for accommodating us on such short notice, and giving us some of your precious time to introduce us to your country and government. We're excited to be here."

What little of the city we could see through our tinted windows did not make me want to vacation in Bamako and visit its hot spots. Frankly, all the spots were hot. Temperatures were stifling and well on the way to searing.

And how was I feeling as we headed to our destination? Well, I think I felt fine. I was excited but not overly anxious, though distinguishing between the two is not my forte. On the other hand,

I knew how to play the role of a reasonably high-profile thriller writer and had dealt with hundreds of fans over the years. President Camara just seemed like another in a long line of fanboys fawning over their favourite writer. Sure, it gave me a bit of a buzz—it always did—but I could play this part in my sleep.

Though I had to admit, lurking beneath it all, I could still feel that little knot in my stomach—the one I'd first discerned before leaving Madrid—and it was tightening. After all, we still had a lot to do and plenty of unanswered questions to, well, answer. Our plan was full of holes that could only be filled with information, intelligence, and insight that we hadn't yet gathered but would need before pushing the button on our little exfiltration exercise. Not to mention that the Tardif mine and compound were a staggering 267 miles from the palace. In a country like Mali, with a somewhat primitive transportation infrastructure, 267 miles was very far away in both time and distance. How the hell were we going to pull this off? I felt my heart rate kick up a notch.

Okay, step back, calm down, take a breath. We had made it to Mali safely. We'd been welcomed with open arms and atonal music. We were sitting in a stretch limo—though it had seen better days—and we'd soon be checking in to the presidential palace. Not a bad day's work. So far, so good.

"James?" Coop asked, bringing me back.

"Um, yes?" I said, bringing me back.

"President Camara just asked if you were okay?" said Coop. "You drifted away for a moment."

I looked to our host and leaned forward towards him.

"Oh, so sorry, Mr. President. I guess I'm a little jet-lagged, and I don't think the heat is helping," I replied. "But I'm back now."

"More air conditioning, please!" Camara shouted towards the front seat.

"Oui, Monsieur le Président," the driver replied, cranking up the air.

With Coop sitting right next to me, I couldn't see her without turning my head towards her. I didn't want to be obvious about it, but I was curious as to how she was feeling. Luckily, when I peered out my side window as President Camara pointed out a few Bamako landmarks, I could see Coop's reflection in the glass. For the first time since we met, I could watch her without her knowing. She was smiling and gazing about with a happy, cheerful, almost vacant expression on her face. She certainly didn't look anything like the cool—sometimes cold—steely Coop I'd come to know over the last few days. When she slipped into her cover story, she fully inhabited it. She also spoke more freely, asked questions, and even laughed a few times, particularly when President Camara deployed a witty remark. I'd heard her laugh before—at me—but I'd never heard her full-throated guffaw until we were travelling in the presidential limo through the streets of the capital. I don't even remember the president's triggering lines, but they certainly weren't funny enough to warrant Coop's outbursts of hysterics. I liked the sound of her laugh, and the president seemed pleased to have sparked it. I thought it made her more human—like a real person and not a by-the-book CSIS operative. I wondered where her cover story ended and the real Lauren Cooper began.

"You will both enjoy our welcome dinner this evening," Adama said. "We will be introducing you to the very best of Mali's cuisine."

I'd meant to do some basic research on the food we would be encountering—some of which we might even have to eat—but I'd run out of time. Despite my research trips around the globe, I didn't exactly have a broad, international palate. I'm not big on spices beyond pepper, salt, and maybe oregano. I stick to the major food groups: steak, potatoes, pasta, pizza, bread, chicken, cereal, salt and vinegar potato chips, and steak. You get the idea. And, yes, I know I listed steak twice. I meant to. Adventurous in my taste for international cuisine? Ahhhh . . . no. So, I wasn't exactly itching to explore Mali's culinary delights. But when one has a job to do, one must make sacrifices.

We stuck to what the president had called, in his singsongy voice, "happy talk" for the duration of our drive to the palace. There were no knowing glances, no contrived facial expressions, no whispered or even mouthed comments, no meaningful looks. I surmised that beyond the listening devices in the limo, there were probably stealthy cameras, too. So the three of us carried on playing our roles for an audience we couldn't yet identify.

Not long thereafter, we pulled into the heavily guarded presidential property. Wow, it was quite something. There wasn't a moat, but the high white walls that encircled the palace, with guard stations placed along them at regular intervals, made it look impenetrable. The front gates, which came with armed sentries, closed behind us as we drove up the road to the palace's entrance. On the outside, a series of arches ran the length of the building on all three floors. Every inch of the exterior was bright white. It looked like stucco, but I couldn't be sure.

Uniformed palace employees were lined up to greet us. I hoped the president and I would not also be required to review this honour guard of domestic staff. As soon as I climbed from the limo, the assembly applauded. I'm not sure it was a legitimate standing ovation given that they'd already been upright when we pulled up, but it was still very nice of them. President Camara took my arm and escorted me up a few stairs and into what I dubbed the grand foyer of the palace. Coop, still smiling, refused any assistance as she hauled our luggage from the trunk. She hobbled into the palace lugging our bags before setting them down on the shiny marble floor.

After Coop's entrance, Demba Dembele walked in and approached the president. He didn't exactly look pleased. He took his friend's arm and led him a few steps away and out of earshot. I watched without staring and hoped any observers could see the difference. They spoke intently, with much brow-furrowing and some hand gestures, before Adama took Demba's arm and dragged him over to me.

"Mr. Norval, may I introduce you to my senior advisor, and an old friend since our days in the orphanage, Demba Dembele."

I reached out my hand to shake his, but then lost sight of it in Dembele's catcher's mitt of a paw. He squeezed almost as tightly as Coop had, which I had kind of expected given his reputation as Mali's new strongman. He leaned in and spoke through gritted teeth and a fixed—I would even call it paralytic—smile.

"Welcome to Mali for your very brief stay," he said. "When will you be leaving?"

"Well, thank you for having us," I replied, ever polite. "I shouldn't think my research will take much longer than six months."

He recoiled, utterly baffled. I didn't wait long before taking him off the hook.

"I'm kidding, Mr. Dembele. Just my Canadian sense of humour," I said, chuckling. "Depending on the president's schedule and how quickly we're able to visit some of the locations I'm considering in the novel, I think we'll only need a week, but no more than two."

"A week sounds like long enough to me," Dembele said. "You will have our full logistical and transportation support to ensure you conclude your work as quickly and efficiently as possible. President Camara is very busy with pressing affairs of state. I hope I have been clear."

"Demba, do not worry," President Camara cut in. "It will not take so long. Do not trouble yourself. These pressing affairs of state you cite will not suffer for Mr. Norval's visit. I promise."

Without another word—although there was a withering look—Demba Dembele retreated down the corridor and disappeared around a corner.

I craned my neck to take in the grand foyer much like a tourist might gawk in Versailles. There were paintings on the walls and an ornate moulding and ceiling design. I also noted several security cameras, none of which was hidden in the least. They seemed to be everywhere, including the long corridor down which Dembele had receded.

"Mr. Norval, I am so pleased to welcome you to the presidential palace," President Camara said. "Could I suggest that your assistant get you settled in the two rooms we have ready for you? Then Ms. Cooper can rest up while I take you on a tour of the presidential campus."

"I'd certainly love to join the tour, too, Mr. President," Coop replied, bowing slightly.

"That can be arranged, but at a later time," the president said. "I'd like very much to spend some time with my favourite living author. I have been dreaming of this for as long as I've been reading his novels."

"Yes, that would be very nice, Mr. President," I said, before turning to Coop. "Please sort out our accommodations and give some thought to our itinerary tomorrow, and I will meet you for the welcome dinner a little later on. Sounds like a dress-up occasion."

"Of course, James," Coop said again, plastering on her artificial smile.

Just then, a door to the left opened and two guards entered with a young girl between them.

"Papa!" the young girl said, rushing over and hugging President Camara.

Judging by the placid reaction of the guards already in the foyer, she was not an assassin. Given her salutation, I thought it more likely she was the president's daughter. I've always been good at putting two and two together.

She spoke to him in French, but he shook his head.

"En anglais, s'il te plaît, mon petit, pour nos visiteurs," he said, pointing our way.

He turned his daughter to face Coop and me, his hands on her shoulders.

"This is my precious daughter, Amina," he said. "Amina, this is the famous writer I was telling you about, Mr. James Norval, and his research assistant, Ms. Lauren Cooper."

Before I could say anything, Coop bent down with one knee on the floor in front of Amina. She beamed at her, and spoke slowly, not knowing the young girl's fluency in English.

"Hello, Amina. So nice to meet you," Coop said, shaking her hand. "You can call me Lauren."

"Hello, Lauren. Nice to meet you, too," Amina replied, demonstrating a strong grasp of the language.

I waved but could not compete with the warmth of Coop's greeting.

"Ma petite, I am taking Mr. Norval for a tour of the grounds before our big welcome dinner. I'll come for you after, and we'll go to the grand ballroom together."

She nodded, then waved to us and exited through the door she'd entered, the same two guards flanking her again.

Coop grabbed our bags and followed an older, uniformed woman up the sweeping staircase, presumably to our rooms. She did not look happy.

CHAPTER 7

I ACCOMPANIED President Camara and two bodyguards out a back door onto the landscaped presidential grounds. Again, the wall of heat hit me as I stepped across the threshold and into the open air. Concrete pathways criss-crossed the grounds, passing alongside lush gardens and diverse congregations of flowers, shrubs, and trees.

"My predecessor was an evil man, but he did create this wonderful presidential garden that features only flora that is native to Mali," he explained.

Then he turned to the two guards trailing closely behind us and asked them to give us a little more space so that he could enjoy getting to know his favourite writer without them hovering over us. They agreed and backed off until we were out of earshot.

He put his hand on my arm and chuckled while he spoke.

"Please keep smiling and following where I'm pointing, but listen very carefully. Why have you come to Mali?"

"Well, I, um, am working on a new novel that is set in West Africa, and it involves a coup . . ."

"Please, be honest with me," the president cut in. "I am a devoted subscriber to your monthly newsletter, so I know your new novel is not set in Africa. It's about a nuclear scientist abducted in Kazakhstan. What really brings you to Mali?"

Uh-oh. My mind raced as I tried to figure out how to respond. I hadn't anticipated this line of questioning. By his earlier comments at the airport, I had thought he believed we were there in response to the Bat-Signal he had displayed on his bookshelf. He was waiting, looking right at me, looking right into me. I had nothing, so I went with my gut, which at that moment was feeling a little queasy. And my gut was advocating for the truth, or at least some of it.

I pointed to various landmarks and nodded while I answered his question.

"Okay. Maybe I'm wrong, but I thought you might be in trouble when I saw how you had lined up my books behind you at your news conference," I said. "I thought you needed help."

His gaze bore into me once more and he said nothing for a time. Then he looked out across the palace grounds and pointed to the hills in the distance.

"Bless you, James Norval. You got my message, and you came. Bless you."

"Yes, but what exactly did you mean?" I replied, nodding and pointing in the same direction.

"I mean, this regime is not what it appears to be. It is a carefully crafted mirage. I am nothing but Demba's marionette," President Camara said, working hard to keep smiling and pointing. "He is twisted, rotten to his core, out to fill his pockets and wring as much wealth from our country for himself as he can."

I laughed, prompting him to laugh, too.

"I see," I chuckled. "Then, yes, Mr. President, we did receive your message."

"Please, when we are alone, you may simply call me Adama," he said. "That is my given name."

"Of course, and please call me James," I replied. "But what power does Demba have over you that you do not just have him arrested for corruption?"

"He has my most precious possession."

Then the penny dropped.

"He's threatening to harm your daughter?" I asked.

"You are a quick one, James Norval."

"But he's just one man," I replied. "You are the president."

"Yes, it is true. I have the presidency, but Demba has the power."

"I see. I suspected as much, thanks to your carefully contrived array of books," I said. "Very clever on your part."

Adama nodded and kept us moving down the path.

And very clever on my part, too, I figured. It was just as I had postulated. I confess it was satisfying to have figured out the coded message the president had sent at his news conference. We hadn't been in Mali for more than an hour and we already had a solid grasp on the power dynamic in the palace, and in the country for that matter. Not a bad start.

"Demba and I were close friends—the best of friends—until our years at Harvard, when he latched onto a more malignant version of the American ideal, driven by small government, individual liberty, naked greed, and personal aggrandizement regardless of the cost. Whereas I, on the other hand, maintained my optimistic outlook, a leftward ideological slant, and a commitment to bringing the new knowledge we were acquiring back to my birth country to improve the lives of Malians."

"A noble calling," I said.

"Now, many years after our return from the U.S., Demba orchestrated the coup that ousted our previous leader, and installed me in his place. I am but the reluctant and largely powerless face of the new regime. In reality, Demba is forcing me to do his bidding as he grows richer and richer through corruption, raking in ill-gotten gains that should be used to advance the government's social and economic goals."

"But why isn't Demba the president?" I asked. "Wouldn't that be simpler?"

He laughed again and pointed over in a different direction, turning me to face other structures on the site to at least appear to be explaining them to me.

"Demba is more at home in the shadows, free from public scrutiny. The lower his profile, the easier it is to do what he does best, line his pockets and strip this country bare for his own benefit. The presidency would constrain him and his greed."

"But that still doesn't explain his hold over you," I said. "Why do you play his game?"

"Demba's power stems from his control over the President's Personal Protection Force, PPPF, stationed at the palace. Demba personally recruited all of the PPPF, and they are loyal to him alone. They share in his illicit gains and perpetuate the corruption. Of course, on the surface, the PPPF is there to protect me and my daughter, Amina. But in fact, we are merely living as prisoners in their gilded cage. We are watched at all times and cannot leave the palace unaccompanied."

"To be clear, has Demba threatened to have the PPPF harm Amina?" I asked.

Adama threw his head back and howled with laughter, all the while nodding vigorously. Laughter is contagious, so I did my part, too.

"Does Amina know why she can't have friends over or go to a concert like a normal young girl?" I asked.

"No," Adama replied, shaking his head.

"But why not?"

"Because my daughter is only ten years old. She is too young to know that humans are capable of such evil."

I wasn't a parent, but his answer made me feel like one.

"I need to get her out of Mali. I need my daughter to be safe. She is all I have."

"I see that, but why does she think she is always accompanied by armed guards and can't leave the palace?" I ask while pointing at a distant tree.

"I simply told her it is because I am the president and that for her own protection, it must be this way, at least for a while."

Having heard all of this, I made a split-second decision right then and there. I doubted Coop would have agreed—scratch that, Coop definitely would not have agreed—but she wasn't there at the time, so I made the call and then acted on it. Being a CSIS operative in the field sometimes meant making decisions unilaterally. At least that's how I justified it in my own mind. Besides, Adama had just bared his soul. He'd given us the perfect opening to come to Mali and get our people out. Couldn't we help him in return?

"Mr. President," I said, talking with my hands in a way that suggested I was telling an exciting story with twists and turns, highs and lows . . . well, you get the idea. "I'm not here researching a new novel, Lauren Cooper is not my research assistant, and we're not really here to help you, but I'd like to if we can."

As I heard the words leave my mouth, I realized how bizarre it was to be blowing my own carefully contrived cover—Coop's too—and revealing all to the new dictator of Mali. That's not usually what happens in an undercover mission. But it felt right, and necessary for our mission to succeed. On the other hand, given my deep and varied experience in clandestine operations on foreign soil, it was also quite possible that I'd just destroyed our chances of exfiltrating the Canadian mining team into Senegal.

The president's eyes widened briefly before he quickly recovered and reinstalled the smile on his face.

"I hope you are not a CIA assassin, or I would feel rather foolish inviting you to my palace."

"Well, Mr. President—Adama—I'm Canadian, so I'm definitely not a CIA hitman," I explained. "And I'm quite sure our intelligence service does not employ assassins. But they do employ Lauren Cooper. She's a Canadian intelligence officer."

"And who are you, Mr. Norval?"

"I am in fact James Norval, and I still write novels, but right now I'm here trying to help the Canadian government bring fifteen Canadian mining executives safely home from the Tardif Resources operation in Kéniéba. That's why I'm here. That's why *we're* here."

"Why don't they just return home on their own?" President Camara asked. "Just because we nationalized mining doesn't mean they must stay here if they do not wish to. They are free to leave at any time."

"I'm afraid that's not true, Mr. President. Lauren and I are here because they are being detained at their compound and forced to continue operating the mine," I said. "I wondered if you knew."

Adama shook his head as understanding dawned. Then he caught himself and pointed something out to me on the northern horizon. He laughed.

"Demba must be behind this. I should have seen this coming. It explains why he has visited Kéniéba a few times recently. He is after the gold."

"Demba's interest in the Tardif operation may complicate our efforts," I said. "But we have to get to Kéniéba, connect with Monique Tardif, and get the Canadians out. We haven't dared reach out to her in case her phone is tapped. So, she doesn't even know we're coming."

Adama was deep in thought as we walked along the paths through the presidential gardens, the palace receding behind us.

I noticed automated irrigation systems that kept the plants and flowers well hydrated in the stifling heat. With these temperatures, I would have expected them to be wilted and withered, but then again, I didn't know much about gardening. Actually, I didn't know anything about gardening, except maybe how to grow a Chia Pet. My grandmother gave me one when I was a kid.

"So, if I understand our situation, you came to Mali in response to my signal, but just as a convenient ruse to enter my country and rescue your fifteen Canadians," he said, sounding dejected.

"Well, when you put it that way, I guess it does sound a little opportunistic, but . . ."

"We can help each other," he said, almost in a whisper.

I glanced back at our PPPF tails, but they didn't seem interested or engaged in what we were doing fifty yards ahead of them. Still, I put my hand on his shoulder to turn him around and we resumed walking, our backs once again to the trailing guards.

"I will provide all of the necessary assistance and logistical support to get you to Kéniéba. I'll do whatever I can to help you get your citizens out. But I will do all of this on one condition."

I knew what he was about to say before he said it.

"You must take Amina with you. You must get her out of Mali. If you do not agree, well, I'm sorry, I cannot help you."

I had a pretty good idea how Coop would react to this suggestion.

"Um, Adama, I'd like to say yes, I really would, but I'm not the one calling the shots." I pointed back to the palace to confuse our minders and make it clear to Adama that I was referring to Coop. "And I'm sure she's not going to be prepared to change our mission and add a ten-year-old foreign national to our escape plan—who also happens to be the president's daughter. That sounds like the very definition of a non-starter."

"You are a famous writer, known the world over. Without me, without my hidden message, and without my invitation, you and your secret-agent friend would not be here to rescue your fellow citizens. I brought you here. You must help me. If you can get Amina out, it takes away Demba's power, and maybe then we can do some good here."

I thought he made a rather persuasive argument. And I certainly felt like we owed him one. But to the best of my knowledge, that wasn't how CSIS operations normally worked.

"Adama—Mr. President—a foreign intelligence agency can't just arrive in Mali, secretly exfiltrate fifteen Canadians, breaking several Malian laws in the process, and then kidnap the president's daughter and whisk her out of the country, too. That would be a major international incident."

"I'm sorry, James, but it would also be a major international incident if the great James Norval and his research assistant, both confirmed as Canadian intelligence agents, were imprisoned in Bamako for espionage. And I can make that happen with a few whispered words to Demba, based on what you've already admitted to me."

I thought this new argument was even more persuasive. In fact, I thought it was virtually unbeatable. I was convinced.

"Okay, if you can get us to the Tardif mine, and help us as our plan comes together, I will do absolutely everything in my power to include Amina in our exit strategy. I'll need to convince Lauren, and that won't be easy, but I think I can make that happen."

I actually had no idea whether I could make that happen, but it felt like the right time to sound confident.

"Thank you, James," he said. "I know you will succeed. Hunter Chase always succeeds in the end against terrible odds. This time, do it for yourself, and for Amina, and for Mali."

"Hmmm, if we can get Amina out, maybe we can get you out, too. You'll be beyond Demba's reach if you're outside of the country," I said.

"No. Amina is my primary concern," he replied. "And I will not leave my country. I must stay and try to figure out how to, shall we say, neutralize Demba. I must try. But I will make no move unless and until Amina is safe. And you, James, are my, and her, best hope."

"Understood," I said, continuing my now habitual laughing and pointing at things. "Now, I must be seen to be doing some research on my next novel, or Demba's suspicion may be aroused."

"Of course. We can do interviews in my office. That will be convincing evidence of your so-called cover story. Everything in my suite is recorded. We will put on a good show. You can ask me about Monique Tardif. But there will be no mention of Amina."

"Right. And can you please arrange for Coop—sorry, Lauren, my 'research assistant'—and me to visit Monique Tardif?" I asked. "It would have to be at the mine site. It doesn't help us to meet her anywhere else. And it must be soon."

"I met her before I became president," he said. "She is a bit of a . . . how do you say it? Reptile lady?"

"Dragon lady?" I suggested.

"Of course, dragon lady. That is what I meant," he replied. "She is very tough, even difficult, but she has invested more in the community than any other mining company in Mali. She is setting a new standard. So, I like her for that. But to your question, the answer is yes. I am the president. I can arrange for you to meet with her to 'research' your new novel. I will make the arrangements, quickly, now. Then you can help Amina escape."

"Do you have any allies within your government who might be helpful?" I asked.

He thought for a moment, as he pointed out some strange-looking flowers in the garden we'd just reached.

"The Minister of Defence, Oumar Sissoko, is a close friend," Adama said. "He hates Demba but has fallen in line, probably to protect himself and his family. But in the right circumstances, I think he would rise to the occasion."

"It's not bad to have the defence minister in your corner," I said. "It's certainly better than having to count on, say, the Minister of Culture."

"Correct, James. Access to ribbon cuttings and movie premieres is not what we need. Military might, on the other hand—or even just the threat of it—could be quite useful," President Camara said, this time gesturing to the sky just to throw our escorts off the scent.

My heart was pounding. I feared I'd just botched our entire operation by revealing our true intentions, and then essentially agreeing that we'd bring Amina with us when we spirited our fellow Canadians out of the country. It sounded like a movie, and I didn't like the ending that flashed before my eyes.

Just before we completed our circumnavigation of the presidential property, an idea flitted into my cluttered and anxious mind.

"Can you somehow have Amina spend some time with Lauren?" I asked. "Maybe Amina would like the company of a young woman—a mentor, of sorts. I think it would be good for both of them."

"I see what you are doing, James. Excellent suggestion. Leave it to me."

A short time later, we stepped back into the air-conditioned splendour of the palace. It was such a relief. On the positive side of the ledger, through sweating alone, I'd probably lost a few pounds on our perambulation—and I could stand to lose a few more.

CHAPTER 8

COOP KNOCKED on my door when it was time to head down to the much-ballyhooed welcome dinner. She wore a long-sleeved black dress that fell below her knees, just in case the devout set had also been invited for dinner. I thought she looked great, although she wasn't exactly effervescent and ebullient. In fact, she glared at me when I opened my door. Her back was to the CCTV cams in the hallway so no harm, no foul. I assumed she was still peeved at being excluded from the presidential promenade I'd enjoyed earlier. Little did she know that was the least of her worries. To complete my fashion commentary—and trust me, I'm more enthused to complete it than anyone—I wore, for the first time, the new dark-blue suit that had been frantically made to measure for me in Madrid. I chose to complement the dark blue with a classic white shirt that had arrived with the suit, and a dignified red-and-blue striped tie. There, I'm done.

"You look nice," I said, smiling for the cameras as we moved towards the staircase.

Coop smiled.

"Thank you. So do you."

Scintillating dialogue, I know. But neither of us could risk saying what we wanted to say, at least not yet.

Naturally, I couldn't quite remember our agreed-upon hand signals and worried about sending the wrong wordless message. So at the top of the staircase I stopped, bent down, and tied my shoe. On my way back up to my feet, I whispered without moving my lips: "We need to talk." (If you try it, you'll discover that you can in fact say those words clearly enough without moving your lips. It's not just ventriloquists who have need of that skill.) Coop didn't acknowledge my comment, but I knew she'd heard me.

Dinner was served in the palace's grand ballroom. I'm not sure how many ballrooms there were in the palace, but this, apparently, was the grand one. The long wooden table could have accommodated two dozen guests for dinner, yet there were only five place settings awaiting us. I need not have worried about the devout set. Apparently, they weren't on the exclusive guest list.

I assumed President Camara would occupy the solo seat at the head of the table. After all, he was the head of state. I knew who was to be seated at the other end, because he was already there. Demba Dembele stood up when we arrived. He ignored Coop and addressed me.

"Mr. Norval, you are to sit there," he said, pointing to the lone chair at the president's right hand.

On the president's left hand were two place settings, both unoccupied.

Then he turned to Coop.

"You can sit in one of those chairs," he said as if it pained him to speak to her. "You can choose."

"Thank you, Mr. Dembele," Coop replied. "Or should I address you as Demba?"

His first response was to furrow his brow, and he was quite skilled at it. His eyebrows fairly plummeted to an altitude just above the bridge of his nose.

"I would prefer that you use Mr. Dembele."

"Okey-dokey," she replied.

"Pardon me, Ms. Cooper," I said, giving her the kind of stern look an employer might give an entitled underling.

"Sorry—I mean, of course, Mr. Dembele," a chastened Coop replied.

Then an awkward silence reigned as the three of us stood behind our respective chairs waiting for the two remaining guests to make their entrance. I scanned the room. It was your typical presidential grand ballroom. A large stone fireplace and mantel graced one wall, though given Mali's extreme heat, the grate was empty. It was clear that several large pieces of art had been removed from the walls, betrayed by the large rectangular empty spaces where the paint shone a little more brightly.

"What used to hang . . ." I started, before Demba cut me off.

"We removed the several extravagant portraits of our predecessor in power," Demba explained, anticipating my question.

"I assume President Camara will be soon sitting for portraits of his own," I replied.

"Indeed."

There was not much else in the room beyond two large sideboards and about a dozen extra chairs stacked in one corner, no doubt to be used when the table was booked to its full capacity. There were four large chandeliers made of bronze or copper, or maybe tarnished brass. I don't know. I'm a writer, not a metallurgist. They cast four large pools of light on the table and floor below.

Thankfully, the double doors at the far end of the ballroom finally opened, and two guards entered. Seeing no danger, they stood to the side and bowed their heads. I had expected a trumpet fanfare, but having heard the military band at the airport a few hours earlier, I was relieved that they seemed to have been given the night off. In strode President Camara, dressed in full military regalia, with Amina by his side. His shoulders were overburdened with geysers of gold braid, and his chestful of medals suggested at least a century of valorous military service. I was surprised he could even attempt locomotion weighed down by so much hardware. A sword dangled from his waist and occasionally clanged on the floor. I'm not even going to try to describe the hat he wore. I was getting a headache just looking at it. Amina wore a poofy bright-yellow dress, complemented by black patent-leather shoes with silver buckles. She looked very happy to be there.

Adama approached the table as regally as his weighty and unwieldy ensemble permitted. He was holding his daughter's hand and beaming down at her. Amina's eyes lit up when she saw Coop. Her eyes did not light up for me, but I was not offended in the least. In fact, this was part of my grand plan—well, more like a small slice of a plan that was circling my mind but had not yet been cleared to land.

Amina let go of her father's hand and rushed over to Coop's side and the last unclaimed chair. To her credit, Coop bent down to greet Amina and offered her hand to shake, presumably intending to dial back her standard squeeze index. But Amina ignored it and simply went in for the hug. This caught Coop a little off guard, but she recovered quickly and reciprocated.

President Camara ignored Demba and cut over to my side of the table.

"So glad you could join me for dinner. We don't often have guests," he said, his hand on my forearm. Then he leaned in. "Amina was very excited to sit with Ms. Cooper."

He took his place, as expected, at the head of the table. When seated, he raised his right hand and then lowered it back to the table. At that signal, another set of double doors opened and several of the house staff entered, bearing trays arrayed with a great variety of culinary offerings. Some of the dishes I could identify and some I most assuredly could not. It was those in the latter category that concerned me.

While the servers moved around the table doling out dinner, Adama rose. He clinked his glass with his fork.

"I am so glad to have such a distinguished guest with us in Mali. I know you have much work to do in the short time you are here with us, but still, you must eat. And tonight, you will experience a few of Mali's classic dishes."

As he sat down again, I nodded and mouthed a silent *thank you*. Courtesy of the early warning system of my nose, my stomach was already on high alert. I'd been worrying about the food at the welcome dinner. I was starving but hoped there'd be something on the menu for me—and my pedestrian palate. Despite my best efforts, I was unable to associate a few of the aromas swirling about the room with any foods—or even food groups—that I knew. That didn't bode well.

Yet I survived the meal, even after tasting everything. I wanted to make a good impression, so I loaded my plate with modest portions of every dish that came my way. I was certainly not about to imperil our mission by rejecting food I didn't recognize, offending my hosts, and requesting macaroni and cheese instead. We had a job to do.

As I learned from Adama and the servers, our welcome dinner comprised several popular dishes of Mali. Naturally, we started off with Tiguadege Na, considered to be Mali's national meal. Essentially, it is lamb or chicken or goat, along with large chunks of potatoes, carrots, and eggplant, immersed in peanut sauce. Served alongside it was Malian jollof rice. I didn't love it but didn't mind it, either, even after learning it was made with long-grain rice, grass, palava sauce, leaves, and banana peels, all cooked in the same pot. I would rather slip on a banana peel than eat one, but I kept that thought to myself.

Our next main-dish offering was called La Capitaine Sangha. As Adama explained, this was Nile perch served with whole fried bananas, rice, and spicy chili sauce. Now, I've never been a seafood fan and, as previously noted, I don't tolerate spices well. So putting these two food groups together was unlikely to end well. But I did my part and tasted several forkfuls. It was very, very spicy—think ghost pepper on steroids. In fact, while chewing, it felt like someone was arc welding in my mouth. Not quite as bad as gum surgery, but in the same hemisphere. No second helpings on that item.

The couscous that followed was a balm to my incinerated mouth and throat. While my taste buds were still offline from the perch, the couscous provided some gentle and welcome relief.

My favourite part of the meal was the dessert. I admit to a bit of a sweet tooth. Bouillie looks like pumpkin pie but is actually a smooth and delicious brown custard in a sugar cookie–like crust. Very good, and even more soothing and cooling comfort for my mouth. To demonstrate my enthusiasm and appreciation, I had three servings. Adama seemed pleased.

All through the dinner, Coop and Amina were giggling away while conversing quietly. I couldn't tell whether Coop was legitimately charmed by Amina or just playing the role her cover story dictated. Perhaps it was a little of both.

At the far end of the table, Demba was devouring his meal and demanding seconds and thirds. I would say that his table manners were abominable, but that would presuppose their existence in the first place. Let's just say he would have been kicked out of a post-raid Viking feast.

"Ms. Cooper," Demba said, in a rare moment when his mouth was only half full. "Where are you from?"

"I was raised in Scarborough, Ontario, Canada. It's really the eastern part of the city of Toronto."

"No, no, I don't mean where you ended up, but where are you from, your ancestors?"

"Oh, I see. Well, my family is from Jamaica, and before that Sierra Leone."

"Ah, a sister from the Lion Mountain," he said. "Will you visit your homeland on this trip?"

"I don't think we will have time, but I'd like to, in the future."

"You really should. The beaches are beautiful," he replied. "And what did you study at college to earn a spot on the esteemed research staff of the great James Norval?"

"Well, first of all, Mr. Dembele, I alone constitute the esteemed research staff of the great James Norval, and I have a B.A. and an M.A. in literature from the University of Toronto."

"And what was your specialty in your post-grad work?"

"The works of Toni Morrison."

I wondered where this was going but couldn't figure out how to intervene. Yet Coop looked calm and serene.

"Ahhh, yes, Toni Morrison," Demba said. "My favourite of hers is *I Know Why the Caged Bird Sings*."

"Mr. Dembele, I'm afraid you are mistaken. Maya Angelou wrote that book, and it is a memoir, not a novel. Morrison never wrote a memoir, though I'd have read it if she had."

"Yes, of course. My mistake," Demba replied, smiling. "Just a few more questions . . ."

"Demba," Adama interrupted.

"Yes, Mr. President?"

"Please. These are our guests."

"As you wish, Mr. President. But I was hoping to hear more about Mr. Norval's upcoming Mali novel."

Adama turned to me, and I gave him a *no problem* nod before turning to Demba.

"Well, it's early days, but I've long been interested in this part of Africa. I don't yet have the story fully cooked . . ."

"I'm sorry, cooked?" Demba said, leaning forward.

"My apology, a poor choice of words," I said. "Let's just say I'm still mapping out the story so that it holds together."

"Why Mali, specifically?" Demba persisted.

"Demba," Adama interjected again.

Demba ignored him and barrelled ahead.

"Mr. Norval? Why Mali?"

"You're right, Mr. Dembele. I said earlier that I'd long been interested in this part of Africa. I exaggerated. What I'm really interested in is how new regimes establish and maintain order after a coup. How they deal with foreign investment, and in particular the role of the national intelligence apparatus. You know, intelligence agencies often have a tough time adjusting when someone new takes up residence in the presidential palace."

Demba nodded and stared me down. I returned fire with my gaze and carried on.

"So, the story I'm working on is about competing factions in the country's intelligence agency. One faction is loyal to the ousted president and the other is loyal to the new president.

It's a delicate and dangerous situation. And compounding this infighting in the intelligence community, there is another storyline in the novel about the new regime's decision to nationalize the resource sector and basically kick out all foreign companies because they believe they are exploiting the country's resources. My hero, Hunter Chase, is dropped in the middle of it as tensions continue to rise."

"This is not a new story, Mr. Norval. Several other African nations have similar histories."

"I guess I could have gone to other countries to research this, but the most recent regime change has been here in Mali. I think it's the perfect fit. I know Malian state security spending has increased recently and that a private Russian security firm now has a presence here on the ground, because I always research the nations I visit. The details are important to my readers. So, having the Russians here makes for an interesting dynamic. I also know you're in essence nationalizing the mining sector here in Mali. So that all fits very nicely into the story I'm writing. I can learn a lot from what you're doing here."

"I am concerned that Mali will not be positioned in a favourable light in your book," Demba said.

"Demba." Adama stepped in again. "Mr. Norval is a novelist, not a reporter or a historian."

"Quite right, Mr. President," I said, seizing the opening. "Just to be clear, I'm not writing a non-fiction book about what's happening here in Mali. I will likely leave the country unnamed in the story. I write fiction, Mr. Dembele, I write novels. So, I'm just making up a story, as I always do, and trying to make it interesting and exciting and suspenseful and realistic. That's what I do, and Coop—sorry, Ms. Cooper—helps me do that."

Demba didn't say another word the rest of the evening and left the ballroom after inhaling his third slice of Bouillie—shortly before I inhaled my third slice.

"I'm sorry about Demba," Adama said after his childhood friend departed. "He is just looking out for my best interests, and Mali's."

"Of course, Mr. President. I kind of like his style," I replied.

"Amina," Adama said. "It is time."

Amina stood up and went around the table to give her father a hug.

"Bonne nuit, Papa."

"I will be in to say good night shortly," Adama said.

Then Amina waved to me and headed straight back to Coop. She hugged Coop and whispered something in her ear before walking to the double doors. One of the security guards escorted her out while the other one remained in the ballroom.

Coop and I expressed our thanks for the lovely welcome dinner.

"Oh, Mr. President, would it be all right if I walked Coop around the grounds before we turn in for the night?"

"Of course. You have free rein here. One of my guards will be nearby if you need anything."

Two minutes later, Coop and I were outside in the fading light of the day. The skies were clear, and it was that magical hour when there were stars in the eastern sky but the sunset's pink light lingering in the west. It was a beautiful night. Even the temperature had moderated to a comfortable level, though it promised to be blistering again the next day.

Coop and I followed the same general route that Adama and I had a few hours earlier. The paths were illuminated by solar lights, as were many of the gardens along the way. True to form, a sole guard trailed us but stayed far enough away that we could not be heard.

"My mouth is still burning and I'm not sure I'll ever taste again," I said.

"I've had spicier food at my mother's table," Coop said. "You get used to it."

"I don't want to get used to it. And I could sure use some mashed potatoes right about now."

"Okay, enough about the food and your white-bread ways," she said, looking up and pointing at something in the distance. "What have you got?"

"Well, don't be mad. When I tell you the whole story, I think you'll understand it was the right thing to do to get us across the finish line as quickly as possible. Anyway, I told Adama who we really are and why we're here."

She stopped and turned to face me, a big smile on her face as she eyed the guard over my shoulder. Then she laughed.

"That's not funny, James," she said through gritted teeth and an artificial smile. "We never joke about important operational matters. We just don't."

I looked at her and plastered my own kind of frantic, crazed smile on my face. I said nothing.

"Jesus, you weren't kidding," she said. "You actually revealed who we really are and then explained our covert operation?"

"Well, yes, I guess I did, but I did it so we can complete our mission efficiently and successfully."

"I cannot believe it," she said, turning her back to me. "Within an hour of landing, you've completely blown our carefully constructed cover story, thrown our mission into dire jeopardy, and risked our lives and those of the Tardif execs?"

"But . . ." I started.

"I'm not finished," she said. "You've put us in danger and imperilled the entire operation. We'll likely be arrested as soon as we walk back into the palace. And I hope you're up for some advanced interrogation techniques. We might have a long night ahead of us."

"Whoa, whoa, dial it back a notch or three," I replied. "I'm telling you, Adama is the victim here. He's on our side. He sent a distress signal in his news conference. He's admitted it. That's why we're here. Demba is the bad guy. Adama will not sell us out. I promise."

"You promise?" she mocked.

"Wait, I jumped the gun and skipped to the end before giving you the context. Bad form on my part," I said, pointing something out on the horizon in a different direction. "Adama confirmed my suspicion about who's really in charge. Demba is the power and is using Adama as the face of the regime because it's easier for Demba to fill his corrupt pockets if he keeps a lower profile, skulking in the shadows."

"Just out of academic interest, before we pack our bags and leave Mali forever, or perhaps are detained and tortured, what's Demba got on Adama to make him do his bidding?"

"Amina," I replied. "He's got Amina and has threatened to harm her if Adama doesn't comply and play his role as the caring president while Demba enriches himself on the backs of the people. Adama and Amina are basically both prisoners here in the palace."

I paused to take a breath and then remembered another important point.

"Oh, and Demba has recruited all of the guards in the President's Personal Protection Force, and they are only loyal to Demba. That's his power. That's how he can pull this off."

We were both looking at the sunset and the lovely clear sky. Coop was taking in everything I was saying but was clearly not yet ready to speak.

"It was only after he told me all of this that there no longer seemed any benefit to hiding the truth from him. He's willing to help us get up to Kéniéba, and he will even run interference for us. He can make it easier for us to get the Tardif team out, and he can make it all happen faster."

Coop held up her hand, cocked at the wrist so that only I could see. She was giving me the *stop* sign, so I shut up. Eventually she spoke through clenched teeth.

"That bastard," she seethed. "Threatening a child. A real class act."

I decided not to mention Adama's plea that we get Amina out of the country with the Tardif team. There would be a better time to drop that bombshell, so I kept my yap shut. It could wait.

"I am about a hair's breadth away from aborting this operation. The president of Mali knows who we are and why we're here. I'm fully expecting we'll be arrested when we set foot back in the palace. And if I thought we could pull it off, I'd steal a car right now and crash the closest border crossing. We are in deep, deep trouble, and you put us there."

"Please, Coop. Despite appearances, I'm not a complete moron. I made a judgment call that I still believe was the right one. Do not make any rash operational decisions tonight. Believe me, Adama is with us. He will help us do our job. You'll see. Just carry on. Situation normal."

She shook her head and walked away towards the palace.

As I'd promised, nothing seemed amiss when we returned to the palace—that is, except for a note under my door.

Meet me in my office at 9:00 a.m. tomorrow.

Demba Dembele

CHAPTER 9

Mali: Day 2

"I JUST wanted to follow up on our dinner conversation last night," Demba said the following morning when I settled into the chair across from him. "My job, and I take it very seriously, is to protect my president and the interests of the Malian people. I know the president loves your books and is delighted that you are here, but he has work to do. We're writing non-fiction here, Mr. Norval. We're writing Mali's future and making history in the process. To be honest, I don't care about your little novels. I care about my president and my country. So please do your precious research, but do it quickly. And I'm certain I can provide whatever information you need. I want the president's attention focused on Mali, not on your next bestseller. I hope I have been clear."

"Well, I can't imagine how you could be any clearer unless you were shouting and waving your arms around. But I still believe there are questions that only the president can help me with."

"I do not agree. I can answer your questions," Demba insisted. "No need to bother our head of state."

"But I like the president, and he seems to like me," I said, playing for time until I could figure out what to say.

"Yes, the president is, how do you say it, struck by a star . . . ?"

"You mean *star-struck*."

"Yes, star-struck, because his favourite author is here. But my responsibility is to keep him focused on our agenda. I don't want him wasting his time giving you the grand tour of Mali."

"I understand, but unless I'm mistaken, he is the president, so if he really insists on showing me around, I will be grateful and go along with it. I want my next novel to be as accurate and precise as my others."

"Mr. Norval, again, out of respect for the president and his affection for your fanciful books, we will try to accommodate your wishes, but we cannot have the real business of Mali grind to a halt so you can write a novel that may not cast my country in a positive light. Your book is fiction. Mali, the president, and our government are facts."

Then, with a casual flick of his hand, I was dismissed. I welcomed the exit opportunity and left his office without another word. I sure told him. Naturally, I thought of several pithy and clever responses I might have delivered just a few minutes after I was shown the door. 'Twas ever thus.

After leaving Demba's office, I went off in search of Coop, with one of my PPPF shadows not far behind. It's amazing how quickly having someone tail you everywhere you go becomes normalized. I half expected one of them to be seated at the foot of my bed waiting for me to open my eyes in the morning. Then again, assuming there were security cameras in every room, there'd be no point.

Coop wasn't in her room or floating around the sprawling reception rooms in the palace. So, I looked through a window in the corridor running along the rear of the palace and caught a glimpse of her walking the grounds again. By the time I'd slipped outside, Coop was heading towards the concrete, fenced-in play area where Amina was shooting baskets as two guards idled nearby. She was actually quite good, sinking about three-quarters of her practice free throws. I guess that stands to reason. Prison inmates are often stellar shots from the foul line, as basketball is among the few things they can do in "the yard" each day.

I was still a hundred yards behind Coop when she stopped to watch Amina taking shots. When Amina glanced up and saw Coop, she waved. Coop waved back.

"Bonjour, Amina," she shouted, before walking towards her.

One of the guards jumped up, darted out of the fenced-in half-court, and trotted up the path towards Coop. His hands were raised in front of him in the time-honoured gesture for *Stay back, you are not authorized to be here, so turn around and walk away right now*. When hand gestures alone didn't seem to deter Coop, he stopped in front of her and tried his words, though they were in French. By this time, I was close enough to hear them but not close enough to intervene without shouting.

"You are not permitted to interact with the president's daughter," he said. "You must walk somewhere else."

"Why can I not play basketball with her?" Coop demanded, also in French.

"You cannot. It is a security measure. Please walk somewhere else."

"I think your orders are a little out of date. I am a guest of President Camara, and at dinner last night, I sat next to Amina, and we interacted for over an hour," she explained. "I will go directly to President Camara if I have to, and when I do, I'll be shooting hoops with Amina, and you might be transferred to kitchen duty."

He smirked at her. He actually smirked.

"I do not report to President Camara. I protect him, and his daughter."

I finally reached the standoff and raised my hands in that time-honoured gesture for *Okay, everyone, calm down*. (It was actually similar to the *Turn around and walk away* hand motion the guard had employed minutes earlier, but context is everything.) Then I, too, tried out my French words.

"Sorry, sorry, we understand . . ."

I put my hands on Coop's shoulders, gently turned her 180 degrees, and walked her back down the path towards a different, less volatile part of the grounds. When we were some distance away, Coop stopped and turned around to watch Amina.

"Just look at her," she said. "Held captive. All alone. No friends. Armed guards watching her every move. That's no way for a little girl to grow up."

"Hmmm, this is a more humane side of you I haven't yet seen," I said. "I like it. And I'm glad to see it, because there's been a slight change in plans that I couldn't tell you about yesterday, what with all the microphones and cameras."

"What are you talking about?" she asked, looking simultaneously perplexed and annoyed.

"Well, um, at Adama's request—or really, insistence—we're taking Amina with us when we exfiltrate the Tardif team."

In a massive—well, more like colossal—understatement, I'll just report that this seemed to catch Coop a little off guard. She looked in pain. She scrunched up her face and used the palms of her hands to rub her temples. She used such force, I almost expected to see clumps of hair falling at her feet.

"Wait! I'm sorry. For a moment there I thought you said something about exfiltrating Amina as well," she said. "Now, I don't recall Vivian or the minister ever mentioning this part of our plan. I just don't remember it ever coming up. So, what did you say a second ago? I assume it only sounded like you wanted us to risk the entire operation, Amina's life, and political stability in the region by sneaking her out of a heavily fortified palace filled with cameras and listening devices and, oh yes, right under the noses of a highly trained, heavily armed, elite security force. And, if that weren't enough, then somehow getting her safely across the border into Senegal. So, clearly, I misheard you. What did you actually say?"

"I know that you majored in clinical psychology at U of T, but did you also minor in sarcasm?" I asked. "Coop, our plans haven't changed. We'll still cross over into Senegal with the Tardif executive team, but we'll just have one more small passenger to add to our roster."

"Absolutely not! That's crazy. That's insane. That's not our mission. No way."

"Look, getting Amina out removes Demba's leverage over Adama and may even clear the path to putting Demba out of business. Besides, Adama is helping us get the execs out. Without him, do you really think we could just make our way up to the Tardif mine and ask if Monique and her team can come out to play so we can then go wading in the Falémé River?"

"I don't care about taking out Demba. As I said, that's not our mission," she snapped. "We're not saving a country, or the president's daughter. We're saving fifteen Canadians who are being held against their will in a foreign land. Period. Full stop. End of story."

"But, Coop, we're going to find it hard to complete our job without Adama's support. He is committed to helping us get the Tardif crew out. And all he's asking of us in return is to take Amina with us. Adding one more to our head count on the Senegal Express seems a small price to pay. Without Adama, I don't see how we're going to get our people out."

"If we have to, we're going to grab a car from our embassy's motor pool, drive nine hours to Kéniéba, meet Monique Tardif, and start planning our escape. That's called field work."

"Coop, you can't deny that it'll be a whole lot safer, easier, and quicker to have Adama on our team helping us out," I pleaded. "We need his assistance. And, to be honest, I don't know how he's going to react, or what he's going to do, if I tell him we can't take Amina."

"And that's precisely why telling him was so wrong, and why not telling me was a betrayal that gives me more than enough grounds to abort this operation right now. Now, stop talking. I'm trying to think."

I clammed up. I'd shot my bolt anyway. I had nothing left. Coop walked on ahead, her head bowed, I hoped in thought and not prayer. Despite her fierce tirade, perhaps she had listened to me or, better still, given due consideration to what I'd said. A long shot, I knew. But long shots were all I had.

Fifteen minutes later, she seemed to have cooled down, and made her way back to where I stood.

"What a shitstorm," she said. "Completely hypothetically—I repeat, hypothetically—how would we ever get Amina from this very secure palace in Bamako all the way to Kéniéba, 250 miles away?"

"I'm still working on that, but I think Monique Tardif might help," I said, grasping at straws.

"You *think* she might help?" she snapped.

"Well, that's what I meant when I said I'm still working on that part."

We walked in silence for a bit. I was out of things to say and so, as a last resort, I left Coop to mull it all over. She then stopped again, turned, and looked at Amina in the distance, still taking shots. She watched her for a long time.

"Do you know what Amina whispered to me at dinner?" Coop asked without looking at me.

"Tell me."

"She said Adama seems sad, and she doesn't know why. But she senses something is wrong. She told me—and I'm quoting her now—'I miss who he was before. I miss my father.'"

I shook my head.

"For a ten-year-old, she is a very perceptive and sensitive young girl," I replied.

"Does she get any kind of schooling while she's held captive here?" Coop asked, her eyes still on the president's daughter.

"Adama told me she is taught every day online by a dedicated teacher based in Bamako. Apparently, she's already well ahead of students her age."

"I believe it," Coop replied. "She's a pistol, that one."

Another long pause reigned as Coop just kept staring at Amina, her eyes narrowed, her head bobbing slightly. I hoped that meant her brain was in overdrive. I waited. Then she heaved a heavy sigh. I wasn't sure that was a good sign.

"Okay, just to play it through as an intellectual exercise only, maybe Monique Tardif could invite the president to see the mine site and the great investments she's made in the local community?" Coop said. "And then, maybe Amina has a school research project assigned on mining in Mali and perhaps could join her father on the trip to Kéniéba? You know, two birds, one stone."

"Yes! Now you're talking, Coop. Great ploy. Love it. That puts everyone we're trying to get out just a short bus ride from the Falémé River and Senegal. We can work with that."

She glared at me. But I could see she was also thinking it all through.

Our shadow was still with us some distance back, looking supremely bored. We sustained our little charade of pointing at items of interest in each garden we passed, occasionally broadening our horizons to note the geography of the surrounding area, and even making some meteorological observations. Coop and I have very broad interests.

"There are still big, daunting, open questions that we need to answer before a real plan can be developed, let alone executed, and before we even consider the remote possibility that Amina might escape with us," Coop said. "We really need to get to the Tardif site."

"Understood," I said, trying to sound calm. "Adama will contact Monique Tardif—they've met before—and ask if you and I can visit her as soon as possible to research mining operations for my novel. If Adama's call goes well, we can be there in the next day or so."

"Fine," she replied.

"Then, when we're there, we can get away to check out the site of our little river crossing," I said. "Do you think the embassy will help us? We could sure use a nondescript car that would blend in parked in Kéniéba."

"Shouldn't be a problem," Coop said. "We'll likely be tailed either on foot or in a car if we leave the compound."

Coop was coming back online. She had slipped into planning mode, which was better than yelling mode.

"Right. But I doubt Malian intelligence operatives are skilled in tradecraft," I said. "I was thinking we could walk into Kéniéba from the compound, lose our tail, and then jump into our chariot parked on a side street."

"Hmmmm. Perhaps," Coop said, still thinking it through. "Whether our tail is walking or driving, we'll be gone before he figures it out. Is that what your guy, Hunter Chase, would do?"

"Well, it's probably a little too boring a tactic for Hunter," I said. "In a novel, there'd probably be a high-speed chase, some light artillery fire, and then a perilous car jump across the river after the bridge is blown. But I'm not going there. I'm really trying to think more like you and less like a thriller writer."

"Good. We're not looking for explosions. They attract too much attention," she said. "Okay, then we can orchestrate Monique's invitation to the president for a visit. He'll ask if he can bring Amina so she can research her mining project, and Monique will quickly agree. Okay, it's a start."

Coop turned her head one more time to watch Amina.

"Then we can start to figure out just how we're going to explain to Vivian and Minister McLintock why we've kidnapped a ten-year-old Malian national who also happens to be the president's daughter. Oh god, are we insane?"

"We've never been saner," I said. "I really think this plan is coming together. It's the right approach. Getting the Tardif team out might not be possible without Adama's support. But with his help, we'll soon be in Senegal. It's perfect."

"I'm not sure 'perfect' is the right word, but the idea does have some initial promise," Coop conceded. "So, let's get ourselves up to Kéniéba ASAP and start putting the right pieces in place."

"I'll take it," I replied. "Thank you."

"And as of this moment, you are to stop freelancing this mission on your own. No more behind-my-back planning sessions with Camara. If it happens again, I may sell you out to Demba myself and leave you in a Bamako prison," she said, poking my sternum with her index finger. "Am I coming in loud and clear?"

"Copy that. I promise."

"And adding Amina is not yet a done deal," Coop said. "I'm still on the fence."

I nodded, choosing not to risk saying anything. But half an hour earlier, Coop had been nowhere near the fence. She couldn't even see the fence in the distance. So, I took this as a big win. I knew there was a human being lurking somewhere beneath Coop's frosty exterior.

I found some time that afternoon to take another walk with Adama. I mean, what else did I have on my plate? With all this promenading I was doing, I figured I'd be in good shape by the end of the operation. Adama showed me a part of the grounds I hadn't yet seen just to avoid arousing any suspicion.

To complete the charade, I alternately held my iPhone up to my mouth and up to Adama's as we walked, perfectly simulating a recorded interview though my recording app wasn't even open.

"We're working on a plan but it's too early to share it at this stage, and the less you know the better, at least until it's finalized," I said, before moving my iPhone towards Adama.

"I am putting my confidence, my faith, my hope, and my trust in you, James."

No pressure, I thought to myself. *He seems to have more confidence in me than I do.*

"The first step is getting Coop and me to Kéniéba to do some reconnaissance just as soon as possible. Can you arrange that for us using our standard novel-research cover story? We have to do it quickly."

"Of course. It fits with why you're here, so I can do it right now, openly, from my own office phone. Leave it with me."

"Also, Lauren would like to help Amina with her basketball skills. Coop played university ball and could coach her on her shooting. I also think it would help Coop become more comfortable with the idea of adding Amina to our escape plan. I've started to lay that groundwork, but I think getting the two of them together often will help bring Coop onside. She really likes Amina."

"I will see what I can do to clear it with Demba. He has never had a very enlightened view of women, particularly young women, so he likely won't consider Lauren to be any kind of threat. After all, he just thinks she's a research assistant, googling things and taking notes. And Amina really likes Lauren, too. I think it would be good for her."

"It would be good for them both."

As we were about to re-enter the palace, Demba suddenly appeared.

"Could I see you in my office, Mr. Norval?"

"Sure, if you like," I replied.

Adama looked at Demba, a quizzical look on his face.

"I don't need to bother you with this, Mr. President. I'm just following up on an earlier conversation."

Adama nodded and headed to his office, as I followed Demba to his.

"Could I have your iPhone, please?" Demba said in a tone that severely undercut the question mark at the end of his sentence. "I will return it."

"Why do you need my iPhone?"

"Mr. Norval, turn your iPhone on and hand it to me."

I didn't feel as if I had a choice, so I did what he demanded.

"Which voice recording app do you use for your research conversations with the president?"

"Voice Memos," I replied.

He found and opened the app, then scanned the recordings I'd made in Adama's office while masquerading as a writer seeking insight on coups and their aftermath. I was willing to bet that Demba had already listened to our earlier conversations courtesy of the listening devices planted in the president's office.

"There is no audio file from the walk you just took with the president, yet it was obvious that you were recording him. Explain this. Now!"

Uh-oh. I smiled and then looked a little sheepish.

"I'll tell you if you promise not to tell Adama."

"I do not give promises. But I can and will give you grief and even pain if you do not explain yourself," he blustered.

My mind was racing.

"Well, the fact of the matter is I deleted the audio file from my phone as we approached the palace," I explained.

Demba's eyes narrowed as I continued.

"You see, the president was tired and, well, just between us, he didn't say anything on our walk of any value to me as a writer."

Demba seemed to relax and nodded.

"Yes, I know, he sometimes talks without saying much. He has since he was a young boy."

"Ah, I see," I replied. "Anyway, I have limited memory capacity on my phone, so I just deleted it to save space."

He nodded again.

"Please, Mr. Dembele, I like Adama very much, so I'd appreciate it if you didn't tell him about the deleted recordings."

"So, clearly you are wasting the president's time. You take him away from his duties for thirty-eight minutes exactly, and then delete the file. When are you leaving? The president must focus on the important challenges Mali is confronting."

"Well, to be more accurate—and please do not pass this along to the president, either—I would say that technically he wasted my time, not the reverse," I said. "Ooooh, that sounded harsher than I wanted it to. I mean, we had a good talk. It just wasn't helpful to my novel. You understand."

"Again, I ask, when are you leaving?"

"Oh, right. I don't expect we'll need any more than another week. Unless, of course, our trip to Kéniéba is . . ."

No longer smiling, Demba waved his hand in front of his face to get me to stop yammering. Then he tossed my iPhone across his desk to me and merely pointed to the door. I got up and left. Demba was a scary man.

CHAPTER 10

Mali: Day 3

THE NEXT morning, Coop was allowed to spend time playing basketball with Amina. As had been clear at our welcome dinner, they'd taken to one another hard and fast, as if both needed a friend—likely because they both did. I watched them shoot baskets and talk as I walked the grounds mapping out the step-by-step plan we were about to execute. Of course, my usual approach would be to write it all down, but obviously that wasn't an option. So instead, I walked and thought and walked some more to entrench our grand stratagem in my brain. In my inexperienced mind, it was a good plan, though not yet fully formed. I just hoped it lost no lustre in its execution. It certainly helped to have the president of Mali assisting with logistics.

He'd arranged for us to travel to Kéniéba the next afternoon to meet with Monique Tardif. For me, that was when our operation would feel real.

The hoops-with-Coop session ended when it was time for Amina to log in and start her online school day. Coop and I had to get cracking on our day anyway. We stood outside the palace's main entrance and waited until one of the black Escalades pulled up. Adama had kindly provided a car, along with a driver whose English was quite adequate for our needs.

"We're going to the Canadian embassy," Coop said after we'd settled into the spacious back seat. "It's on Avenue Al Quds."

"Yes, I know where it is," the driver replied. "It will take about twenty-five minutes, depending on how many other cars are on the road this morning."

We were going on the simple pretense that our embassy had asked that I check in there. My status as a novelist had prompted the invitation, or so we said, along with the need for some research on the region and a few interviews with the Canadian diplomatic team. The information and insight we expected our visit to yield would be important for my new novel, and, you know, getting the details right. Everybody seemed to buy our story. Of course, the truth was that we hoped to advance our plan by engaging our CSIS contact at the embassy.

The trip did take almost exactly twenty-five minutes by the time we arrived at the Canadian embassy, cleared the security barrier, and parked. Our driver stayed in the car. Coop and I walked into the embassy where a young woman waited for us in the reception area.

"I'm Kiran Hassan, and I'll be your principal liaison while you're here in Mali," she said.

We introduced ourselves, and Kiran led us to an elevator. When the door closed, she hit the B2 button and we descended.

"My embassy cover is as an officer of Export Development Canada, but I'm the lone CSIS operative here. Welcome to Bamako."

I kept my yap shut and let Coop take the lead, largely because, well, she was in fact in charge of our little CSIS mission.

"Have you been briefed on the operation?" she asked.

"Yes, but let's wait until we're in the sitroom," Kiran said.

"I thought that was a term only used in the White House and thriller novels," I said.

"Nope. You'll find it in both those places, but we use it, too. Maybe we stole it from one of your books, but we've been calling it the sitroom for as long as I've been here."

She led us down a corridor to a large, heavy door with no window. She inserted a card in a slot, then pressed her index finger on a circle of glass to scan her print. Only then did the door click open. Inside was a small boardroom with two large digital monitors arrayed at one end. A slim laptop rested on the boardroom table, its cord snaking down a hole in the middle to an outlet in the floor.

We sat down, and Kiran pulled the laptop towards her.

"Vivian Kent briefed me on the basics of the exfil op," she said. "But I'm hoping you can fill in some of the details. It seems a little sketchy right now."

"Well, there's a reason it seems sketchy," I offered.

Kiran had stopped talking, but it took me a few seconds to realize she was waiting for me to complete my thought.

"And?" she prompted. I guess I was too slow.

"Oh, sorry. Well, it seems sketchy because, um, it *is* sketchy," I replied.

"That's it?" she asked.

"What James means," Coop said, "is that we won't be able to fill in all the details until we meet with Monique Tardif in Kéniéba tomorrow and do some reconnaissance. We'll be confirming numbers, the crossing site, optimal timing, and routes, along with any obstacles that may be in our path."

"Right, yes. That's what I meant," I said, adding nothing to the conversation.

"Well, then let's move directly to the sat photos, and we can worry about the plan when we actually have a plan to worry about."

Kiran typed away on the keyboard as the two screens flickered to life.

"Here's the index of sat photos for Kéniéba and the Falémé River," Kiran explained. "The dates the photos were shot are in the far-right column."

"How recent are they?" I asked.

"The bird is in medium earth orbit, so we usually get two passes every twenty-four hours. These shots are from yesterday."

Kiran threw up photos on both monitors. She used a digital pen on the laptop screen to mark useful elements in the shots.

"The river crossing Vivian proposed is just west of Kofeba and north of Boulandissou," Kiran said. "The route from Kéniéba is along a highway known as the RN2 all the way to Kofeba. It's just under ten miles and should take about forty minutes from the Tardif mine site at the speed limit."

Kiran then zoomed in to show a dirt road on the outskirts of Kofeba that seemed to get narrower and rougher as it got closer to the Falémé River. There were trees and other vegetation on either side of the road, which would give us at least a little cover. Other than Boulandissou, there were no villages or towns in the area, so if the road was passable, we should be able to make it to the river without alerting hordes of people. The dirt road eventually devolved into two tracks with grass in between before it ended at the river's edge. That was where we'd wade across into Senegal.

"But there's a small issue that we hope doesn't grow into a bigger problem," Kiran said. "One of our embassy staff is a bit of a weather nerd, and he reports that the seasonal rains in Guinea have been much heavier the past few weeks."

"Well, we're not going to Guinea, we're headed for Senegal," I said, confused.

"Yes, I know, but the Falémé is fed by rivers in Guinea. So, the heavier the rainfall there, the higher the water levels in the Falémé."

I looked at the sat photos on the screen. The river was not high enough to reach either of its banks, so I assumed it was low and wadable.

"It still looks like the river is no higher than my ankle," I said, pointing to the screen.

"Yes, but the volumetric flow is now twice what it was ten days ago," Kiran said, putting up the earlier photo on the other screen. "See?"

She was right. The photo shot ten days earlier showed barely a trickle between the banks. We could probably have crossed into Senegal without getting our feet wet a week earlier.

"So, you're saying we have no time to waste?" Coop asked.

"You should be okay if you can make your move in the next week, but I wouldn't want to wait much longer. The river usually runs deep and fast by mid-September, and this year's rains have been heavier than expected."

"We're headed for Kéniéba tomorrow afternoon to talk with Monique Tardif and figure out how to get from her gold mine to the river crossing site undetected," Coop said. "Then we can lock down the plan and execute before the Falémé River is swollen and raging, and better suited for whitewater rafting."

"I'll be your liaison with the Senegal security and CSIS field teams, so keep me informed on operational timing," Kiran said. "We want to make sure they'll be ready on the other side in case you're coming in hot with pursuers on your tail."

"If we're being chased when we arrive at the river, something has gone terribly wrong," Coop said.

We spent another hour or so reviewing sat photos to familiarize ourselves with the Tardif mine site and the living compound a short drive away, as well as the surrounding terrain and our route to the river. By the time we shut down the monitors, Coop and I had a clear sense of the region's geography and topography, even though our more pressing concern was meteorology. Little rain was forecast for Mali, but in neighbouring Guinea, continuing heavy rain was predicted. (At about this time in a Hunter Chase movie, the ticking stopwatch would be heard.)

Coop and I had agreed not to mention the whole taking-Amina-with-us gambit—I need a better name for it, I know. It was true that Coop and Amina had clicked from the first time they'd met, but I was still surprised that Coop had moved so quickly from a hard no to at least a tentative yes on the idea—not that I was complaining.

Kiran gave us a secure phone number so we could reach her, day or night. She also gave us a clean burner phone for Monique Tardif to connect with her whenever necessary. Finally, she agreed to arrange for an inconspicuous car—read dusty, rusty, and beat-up—to be parked in the side street behind Restaurant Fanta Sow in Kéniéba by noon the following day. The restaurant was right on the RN24 and about a fifteen-minute walk from the Tardif compound.

"On another front," Coop said, "if we can persuade the president that he should tour the Tardif mine operations, would you work with Monique Tardif to make it happen?"

"Well, considering the new regime has essentially commandeered the company and all of its profits, we normally wouldn't bend over backwards to help them," she replied.

"True, but in this case, we're trying to get the Canadians out of there and thought you might, just in the interests of building a relationship with the new government, be open to helping arrange such an excursion."

Kiran was nodding.

"And that's exactly how I would justify it to the ambassador, along with mentioning that it would be assisting an important CSIS operation."

"Great. We'll keep you posted on that, but it could happen quite soon," Coop said.

"Finally," I said, "I think we're going to need some kind of knockout drug if we're going to pull this off."

"What are you talking about?" Coop asked.

"I'm just looking ahead," I explained. "I assume it'll be most efficient to drive our homesick Canadians to the river crossing in the bus that carries them to and from the mine every day. Ideally, we'd do this in the early evening, when the light is fading. I suspect there'll be a bus driver and at least one guard on board, so we'll need a way to put them out of commission so we can hijack the bus. If we can spike their water bottles after we leave the mine property, I figure no one will be the wiser for at least half an hour or so, and we should almost be at the river crossing by then. We'll wade across to Senegal while the driver and guard sleep it off on the bus. Just a thought."

"Were you planning on sharing it with me sometime?" Coop asked.

"It just occurred to me as we were looking at the sat photos," I said. "Who else would I tell but you?"

"Let me look into the narcotic," Kiran replied.

"Thanks," I said. "We'll either need a few doses of knockout compound or a baseball bat. I know which one I'd prefer."

They both looked at me and waited.

"What?" I asked. "I thought it was obvious. The knockout drug, of course. Hunter Chase might prefer the bat, but I was never very good at baseball."

We walked through our bare-bones plan and identified the holes that Monique Tardif would have to help fill. A chime sounded as our conversation started to wind down.

"Ah, right on time," Kiran said, reaching for the illuminated green button built into the table. "It's time for your lunch with the ambassador."

"Just before you open the door, does the ambassador know why we're really here?" Coop asked.

"She knows you're part of a CSIS operation, but she doesn't know what the mission is, and she won't ask."

"Understood. Thank you."

Kiran pressed the button, and I heard the door unlatch. Two young women entered the boardroom, dressed similarly in dark pantsuits, which seemed to be the standard-issue embassy wardrobe.

"This is Jorjah, who works on the ambassador's staff, and she'll take you to your lunch in our private dining room," Kiran said. "And this is her colleague, Selema, and I'm afraid I don't yet know what you do around here."

"Oh, I just started a week ago, so I'm still shadowing Jorjah for the time being, just getting up to speed."

"For a minute there, I thought we each got our own personal lunch escort," I said, for some unknown reason. I felt Coop's eye roll, though I didn't look for it.

We thanked Kiran for her time and help. Then Jorjah and Selema led Coop and me on a long, circuitous journey up to the ambassador's dining room on the embassy's second floor.

The ambassador was waiting for us seated at the dining table, which was set for three. She rose and smiled as we entered. Clearly, she eschewed the dark-pantsuit trend—today it was in favour of what I thought was a rather elegant cream-coloured dress.

"So delighted to welcome you to Bamako, Mr. Norval," she said, extending her hand to shake mine. "I'm a big fan of your novels."

"Thanks so much, Madame Ambassador," I said. "And, call me James, please. This is my colleague, Lauren Cooper."

With a quick glance, the ambassador acknowledged Coop's presence.

"Yes, of course, nice to meet you," she said over her shoulder while still clinging to my hand. "Now, I may not be your target demographic, but I have read and loved all of your novels."

"Well, thanks for reading them," I said.

After I had managed to extricate my hand, I held Coop's chair out for her, and then the ambassador's.

"It's lovely to have you in Mali," the ambassador said when we were all seated. "I know you're here for some intelligence matter for which I am not cleared. But please know that we will extend whatever support we can to make your visit a success, whatever 'success' may be."

And that was the last statement of any substance that emerged from the ambassador's mouth for the duration of the two-hour lunch—two hours we would never recover. Over the years, I've gained many important and helpful skills, including the ability to appear deeply engaged in a conversation while thinking about something else entirely. That was the kind of lunch it was. Don't get me wrong. I'm grateful for my readers and how supportive they are. Without them, where would I be? But my mind was not riveted to our ambassador's long-winded recitation of her so-called diplomatic journey, and I'm sure Coop's wasn't, either. We had other issues to worry about.

We bailed as early as common courtesy allowed and headed back to the palace.

CHAPTER 11

Mali: Day 4

ACCORDING TO Google Maps, driving from Bamako to Kéniéba would take eight and a half hours in the very best of traffic conditions. We didn't have that kind of time. So, early the next afternoon, I was relieved to hear the familiar *whomp-whomp-whomp* of a helicopter as it settled to the ground on a demarcated grassy space behind the palace. It would only take the whirlybird about two and a half hours to fly to the Tardif mine. A single guard from the PPPF would accompany us. This did not surprise us, but it could complicate matters.

I'd flown in several private helis in my writerly travels, particularly when on location shooting Hunter Chase films in remote corners of the globe. But the beast that was conveying us to Kéniéba, while quite fast, was by far the oldest and most rickety chopper in which I'd ever had the pleasure of flying—and by "pleasure," I do not mean pleasure. It was louder in the cabin than front-row seats at a Metallica concert, though perhaps slightly less troubling to my ear. No offence to metalheads the world over, but heavy metal is not my thing.

The flight was uneventful—long and loud, but uneventful. The terrain below was neither scenic nor interesting. It was scrubby, occasionally green and lush but mostly brown and barren. It was certainly not like flying over the Serengeti plains. Even though we were never particularly high above the ground, we saw no wildlife from the air. No herds of antelope or giraffes, no hippos, not even a lowly meerkat. No matter. We had more important things to worry about—and more of them than we'd like.

As we were descending to the Tardif site, the full scale of the open-pit surface mining operation became clear. It was one gigantic brown and dusty hole in the ground, with dozens of big trucks, heavy excavation equipment, and lots of workers going about the task of extracting *gold from them thar hills*—apologies to Mark Twain. There were several buildings on the site, including what I assumed was the mining operations office, centrally located on the property.

No one greeted us when we landed on the large square patch of asphalt off in a corner of the grounds. The guard stayed in the cockpit with the pilot but motioned to us that we were free to leave and commence our "research." I guess he felt that having us on a secure site meant that his job was essentially complete upon landing, at least until we travelled to the Tardif living compound for our two-night stay.

Shouldering our own bags and backpacks, Coop and I walked about two hundred yards to the single-storey building that served as the offices of Tardif Resources. Atop the flagpole out front flew the green, yellow, and red Malian flag, with a Canadian flag just below. We walked inside. There was a large bullpen of office cubicles, populated by many of the Canadian execs we were there to help escape—though none of them had any idea. Pressed into the far corner of the open space was a single office, with half-walls on the inside and glass running the rest of the way up to the ceiling. I didn't need to see the name on the door to know I was looking at Monique Tardif as she sat at her desk. I'd been active on Google and YouTube the evening before, refreshing my memory of her.

No one leapt up to greet us. They all seemed stressed, busy, and unhappy. I suppose that was to be expected, given their situation. So, we just walked to Monique's door and knocked.

"Come," she said without looking up from her desk.

She had brown but greying hair tied back from her face, which was quite lovely despite her stony expression. I knew she was fifty years old, but I thought she looked younger. She wore a grey work shirt with lots of pockets, the kind Marlin Perkins used to wear when hosting *Mutual of Omaha's Wild Kingdom*, one of my favourite nature shows as a kid. I assumed she was wearing pants of some kind, but her desk blocked her lower half from view.

We walked in, and I closed the door behind us.

"Ms. Tardif, I'm James Norval, and this is my research assistant, Lauren Cooper," I said. "I believe President Camara called you about meeting with us today."

"Was that stunt supposed to impress me?" she asked, still not looking up. Even though she was born and raised in Québec with French as her first language, she spoke English with almost no discernible accent. She finally put her pen down, took a deep breath, and lifted her eyes to her guests—or intruders, depending on her perspective.

"Look, you should know that if Camara hadn't called, you wouldn't be here," she said. "I'm trying not to aggravate the president, or worse, Dumbo, given that they now hold power over every aspect of our little lives. But I'm extremely busy. I do not have time to spend on helping a wealthy thriller writer I've never heard of and whose books I've never read write his next blockbuster."

"Wow, thank you for your warm welcome. I'm sorry we've intruded, and we'll certainly try not to take up too much of your time," I said, reeling a little from her harsh reception. If we'd been in court, I'd have asked the judge for permission to treat her as a hostile witness. But I don't write courtroom dramas.

She put her hands up in surrender and took another deep breath.

"I'm sorry, you didn't deserve that opening salvo of mine," Monique said. "It's just that it's been a very stressful month or so since the coup. Obviously, I must work on my temper. And I don't want to expose my team to any more hardship by being a hard-ass with the new regime."

"Of course not," I said. "But what kind of hardship?"

"The last time I was obstinate and argued about one of Dumbo's—sorry, Demba's—demands, our ten p.m. lights-out curfew was advanced to eight p.m. for an entire week. My team was not happy. And then, when I refused Demba's directive that our Malian workforce put in more hours than they safely should, he had the hot water turned off in our living quarters for a week. That did not go over well with my team, either."

"So, you agreed to see us because it was easy and you could be seen to be co-operating on a low-stakes issue," I suggested.

She smiled for the first time.

"Yes, I suppose that's as good an explanation as any."

"Um, I know our formal tour of the mine site is not until tomorrow morning, but would you mind terribly just quickly showing us around, if only so that we're better prepared for what we'll see then?" I asked.

"It's really not a good time," she said.

"Just a very quick spin around the grounds? No more than ten minutes?" I said, making meaningful eye contact with her.

She seemed to understand and sighed heavily.

"All right, all right, but try to keep up, and I can only give you ten minutes," she conceded. "Okay, let's go."

"Thank you, Ms. Tardif," Coop said.

"I don't know any Ms. Tardif. Call me Monique."

With that she was out the door, with Coop and me hustling to keep up with her. Just to close the wardrobe loop now that she was out from behind her desk, Monique was wearing work pants the same colour as her shirt, and workboots of some kind. Just your standard, garden-variety mining engineer dressed for her workday.

She led us around the periphery of the mine site. We didn't descend into the pit. That would happen tomorrow. She pointed out some of the different buildings and explained what they housed. She also detailed how the gold was literally torn from the earth's clutches. Coop slipped up beside Monique.

"Just keep pointing things out to us as we walk in case anyone is watching," Coop said. "We needed to move our meeting outside because we know there are listening devices, and probably cameras, too, in your office. Now, you should know that we're here to get you and your team out, and we have a plan to do just that."

"Who has a plan?" she asked without breaking stride.

"Well, technically, the Canadian government, but through CSIS," Coop explained. Then I weighed in.

"Monique, we believe that as soon as you've taught these thugs how to operate the mine, you and your team immediately become expendable, and we don't want to find out what that really means. So, we're getting you and your execs out."

Monique's facial expression never changed as we revealed who we were and what we were there to do.

"And why is a writer involved in a CSIS operation, anyway? Wait, are you really a writer, or is that just a cover story?"

"No, I actually am a thriller writer. And I'm here because, for better or worse, I seem to be President Camara's favourite writer. That got us into the country so we can now get you out."

"Well, I'm certainly happy to have you rescue the others. They are scared and didn't sign up for this. But I'll be staying," Monique said. "I've invested too much time, money, and energy in this mine and this community just to bail on them now. And besides, who would take care of Pierre? No, I'm not leaving."

"Pierre?"

"Our Malian rescue dog," she replied.

"You don't sound like a mining mogul," I said.

"My father was the mining mogul, and he's not in charge anymore. I am."

"But if you're imprisoned or your mine is shut down, the community you've worked so hard to improve will suffer even more," Coop said. "We're going to get you out so you can live to fight—or invest—another day."

"I want you to get the others out," she said. "I can manage ongoing operations here. But I will not abandon the mine or the broader Kéniéba community we've worked so hard to lift up. I won't do it, so you can stop asking."

"We can revisit this later, but we don't think we should tell the others about our real role here," Coop said. "The more who know, the more likely it is we'll be blown. So, let's stick with our cover story for now."

"Understood," Monique replied.

Adama had told us about Monique's generous investment program to bring much-needed social services and infrastructure to the surrounding community. Thanks to Monique, Kéniéba had come to symbolize how foreign companies ought to approach effective community investment in developing countries. I wondered how pleased the other mining companies were with Monique now that she'd single-handedly moved the community-investment goalposts for everyone else.

Just as we were returning to the office, Coop spoke up again.

"Just a reminder that we cannot speak of any of this inside the buildings, either here or at the living compound, and you probably know why."

"Understood," Monique replied. "I've never known for certain, but I've always suspected as much."

"Just before we go inside, with others likely listening in on your conversations, you may want to go with Demba rather than Dumbo," I suggested.

"Tabarnak," she whispered, shaking her head.

We spent the next hour in Monique's office acting out a writer's research interview with a subject-matter expert. My questions about the gold-mining process were not too detailed. My readers don't care about the particulars of gold's journey from the earth in Mali to a vault in Fort Knox. They're more interested in who has (or stole) the gold, what services (or weapons) are purchased with it, and whether the transactions will (almost certainly) upset the delicate geopolitical balance to the point where a guy like Hunter Chase has to get involved. So, we kept it high-level. I'd ask a few questions, then Coop would chime in with a supplementary or two for appearance's sake. I actually thought Monique's responses were thoughtful, informed, and insightful. For someone who claimed she only had ten minutes for us, she gave us much more.

At five o'clock, I could see through the glass wall of Monique's office that the other Canadians had started packing up their stuff. Monique followed suit. I turned and watched out the window as an old school bus pulled up in front of the office.

I figured within the week, it would probably end up being our getaway car, er, bus.

"Okay, people," Monique shouted out the door. "Let's go. We have guests for dinner, and they're staying a couple of nights with us, too. I'll introduce you on the bus."

Nobody responded, but I did see a young woman in the far corner indulge a deep sigh.

Everyone seemed eager to leave their workplace, and ten minutes later we were all seated on the bus, including our PPPF guard. I'd been right in that there was one other guard seated near the driver. Our escorts were grossly outnumbered, but the automatic rifle slung from the shoulder of the guard up front balanced out the odds somewhat. As soon as the doors closed, the bus rumbled along the gravel driveway to the security checkpoint on the edge of the property, where we slowed to a halt. Stopping wasn't a choice. An access barrier was blocking our path.

A guard boarded the bus with a clipboard and did a quick head count. He ignored Coop and me until the very end.

"Êtes-vous Norval et Cooper?" he asked, referring to his list.

"Oui," we said in unison.

Without another word, he stepped off the bus and raised the barrier. The bus pulled off the property and onto the road heading towards Kéniéba.

A few minutes later, Monique stood up at the front of the bus.

"Before we make it home, I wanted to introduce the famous thriller writer James Norval and his research assistant, whose name I seem to have forgotten."

"Lauren Cooper," I said.

"Right, Lauren Cooper," she repeated. "James is researching his next novel featuring his recurring character, whose name I also seem to have forgotten."

"Hunter Chase," I said.

"Oh, yes, Hunter Chase," she said. "Such a Hollywood name."

Several people laughed.

"I love those books," one of the guys said from the back of the bus. "I have four of them back at the compound."

"Anyway, I know we all have a lot to do, but if either James or Lauren has any questions about mine operations or your role in particular, please take a minute and speak with them. The sooner they conclude their research, the sooner they'll be gone, and we can get back to focusing on our jobs. Thank you."

Ouch. Monique then sank into her seat, one row in front of us. No one sat beside her, or even in the seats across the aisle from her. I had watched her team when she was speaking. As they often say about NHL coaches when rumours of their imminent dismissal are rampant, I could tell that Monique had lost the room, if she'd ever had it in the first place. In our Madrid briefings, all the intel we'd been given on Monique Tardif confirmed that, while she was a brilliant, workaholic mining engineer, she could be difficult, prickly, challenging, just not very nice. Having already spent some time with her, I agreed that "prickly" aptly summed her up. But I sensed we didn't yet have the full story. I was sure she had many admirable qualities. We just hadn't yet found ourselves in a situation where they could emerge.

Beyond Monique Tardif, Coop and I hadn't yet determined when we would tell the other fourteen Canadian expats that we were getting them out. Fourteen was a big number, and the possibility that the plan might inadvertently—or purposely, for that matter—find its way into the wrong hands made telling such a large group a significant risk. As well, we wanted them acting normally, as they would on any other day, when the bus left the mine site on E-Day—you know, Exfiltration Day. I favoured keeping them in the dark until we were literally driving their escape bus and could finally bring them into the light. Coop seemed to agree.

Twenty-five minutes later, we turned right off the badly paved two-lane road we'd been travelling on and onto what was obviously the Tardif living compound. It was completely encircled by an eight-foot-high chain-link fence topped by another two feet of razor wire. At the security station, once again a guard and his clipboard climbed onto the bus and repeated the head-count procedure, finishing up with Coop and me. He then lifted the barrier and granted us access to the compound. Apparently, Coop and I were on his guest list. The bus drove through and parked a short distance from a nice-looking two-storey brick structure. It wasn't groundbreaking architecture. It looked like those nondescript motels you'd see on a highway heading into, or out of, any Northern Ontario town. Still, I'd seen uglier buildings in downtown Toronto.

A happy-looking Golden Retriever—Pierre, I assumed—was sitting waiting for us in front, his tail pumping up and down. When Monique stepped off the bus, the dog rushed her and was rewarded with Monique's ardent ear scratching and belly rubbing.

Monique was talking to the dog and smiling throughout. She looked genuinely happy. Then she stood near the front door of the bus as her fourteen employees filed past her, with none of them even acknowledging her. No *See you at dinner* or *Have a nice evening*. Nothing. They gave her a very hostile version of the silent treatment. I looked at Coop and she shrugged.

"So she's not Boss of the Year. Not everyone can be a leading mining engineer and a brilliant, motivational human-resources savant at the same time," she whispered. "She's their boss, not their best friend."

The PPPF guard assigned to us was among the first off the bus. He walked with the driver and the other guard to a Quonset hut back near the security gate. Clearly, keeping tabs on us wasn't a high priority as long as we were inside the chain-link fence.

Coop and I were the last to step down from the bus. We had to trot to catch up with Monique as she headed for the building where the Tardif team lived—where they were forced to live.

CHAPTER 12

TWO LOCAL Malian cooks, working in a fully stocked kitchen, provided breakfast and dinner daily for the Canadian expats. In the dining area, there were three circular tables—two large and one smaller—at which the seventeen of us gathered for dinner. Coop and I joined Monique at the smaller table, which was set slightly apart, while the others divided themselves between the two remaining tables. Pierre curled at Monique's feet, his head resting on his paws. He seemed to be the only one of the Tardif crew prepared to spend time with her—then again, Golden Retrievers aren't known as the most discerning judges of character.

I was happy to learn that it was pizza night at the Tardif compound. The two cooks arrayed seven pizzas and several bottles of red wine on the long stainless-steel counter that bordered the kitchen. There were also pitchers of cold water, but I don't think

I saw a single person pour a glass of H_2O. Finally, there were two different salads—though I'm not sure why. Pizza is pizza. It's meant to be eaten on its own. No need for any green and nutritious accompaniment. What's the point?

We let the other two tables rush the pizzas first. By the time we filled our plates, there were only two bottles of wine left. Monique claimed them both for our table. The pizzas were not bad at all—quite good, in fact, though they tasted a little different from what I was used to. The dough and the herbs and spices gave my slices of pepperoni pizza an exotic flavour. Different, but still good. The wine was flowing freely at our table.

"Do you normally sit with the others?" I asked Monique.

"I guess I do, usually, but I imagine the rest of the team prefers this arrangement," she replied with a sigh.

"I'm sure that's not true," I said.

"I really don't think you're in a position to know that after two and a half hours on-site."

Of course, she was right. And the evidence we'd seen so far, from the team's body language and facial expressions to the unmistakable vibe in the place, told me Monique's claim held more truth than mine.

"Do they do good work? Are they a good team?" Coop asked.

There was no pause for contemplation before Monique responded.

"I've worked at many different mine sites in many different countries, and I think this is the best team I've ever seen."

"Are they well compensated?" I asked. "What about the benefits, perks, and vacation time?"

"All are above industry standard, as are their accommodations," she said. "You should see where other mining expats live. This is luxury."

"Sounds like they're doing pretty well here," Coop said.

"Oh, they are, but apparently I don't work and play well with others," Monique replied. "I'm not warm and friendly. I'm not a cheerleader. I'm not a shoulder to cry on. I'm trying to work this site as effectively and efficiently as I can. That's what mining engineers do. That's what grown-ups do. I don't have time for hand-holding."

"Well, everyone, you included, must be incredibly stressed out being confined to barracks, as it were, and having your freedoms curtailed. I'm not surprised some of your team may need a little extra care," I said.

She turned to look at me.

"Is that supposed to make me feel better?" she asked.

"Um, sorry, no, not really," I said. "I just have a gift for ill-timed, ill-conceived observations. Apologies."

"What about when your father was in charge?" Coop asked, giving me some cover.

"Ha! Everyone loved my father," she replied, "except me. No, that's not true. I loved him. I just didn't always like him. But he's a tough act to follow."

Partway through dinner, Coop and I approached the other two tables in turn and introduced ourselves to the fourteen Tardif team members. The situation—you know, interrupting their dinner—didn't exactly lend itself to meaningful exchanges, though a few commented favourably on my books. They all seemed nice enough but were clearly fearful given their predicament. Who could blame them? We worked each table quickly and then retreated to our own.

The more I thought about it, the less sense it made to tell them what was in their immediate future. It just seemed too risky to bring another fourteen people into our little circle of secrecy. They were in a vulnerable state and may not have had their best decision-making powers available just then.

When we made it back to our table, Monique was standing up.

"I need to take Pierre for a walk."

"I'll go with you," I said.

She gathered our dishes and carried them over to the counter, where the two cooks stood ready to receive them. Pierre shadowed her every step. I followed with the two empty wine bottles. I'd had a few glasses at dinner, as had Coop, but that still left a lot of wine for Monique.

"We'll see you when we're back," I said to Coop, to pre-empt any intention she had of joining us. I didn't want us to overwhelm Monique.

Coop just nodded.

The sun was still shining just above the western horizon, but the light had begun to fade. Despite the excruciating heat of the day, it was a beautiful evening, with even a slight breath of cool—or rather, less hot—breeze. Pierre escorted us around the perimeter of the property. It was not a particularly scenic stroll, but that was hardly the point of our walk. Pierre was one of the most well-behaved dogs I'd ever encountered. He seemed devoted to Monique and stuck by her side from start to finish. I got the sense that Pierre would happily lay down his life to save her should such a need ever arise.

"Are your rooms all right?" she asked.

"They're great," I replied. "I mean, they're not like living at the palace, but they're just fine for our purposes."

She smiled but didn't look my way as she continued walking.

Coop and I had been given our own rooms. They were just big enough for a single bed, a bedside table, a small dresser, and a set of bookshelves. We shared a communal bathroom with two other Tardif expats who lived across the corridor from us.

"Sorry, again, about my thoughtless comment at dinner," I said. "I was just trying to figure out the dynamics of this place. It's important as we try to pull off this little operation we're lining up."

"Don't fret. I've already forgotten about it," she said.

"Until I reminded you."

We walked without saying anything for a few minutes. Eventually, Monique spoke.

"You know, when my father started Tardif nearly forty-five years ago, he was only thirty years old."

"Did you always want to follow in his footsteps, or is that what *he* wanted?"

"I've been asking myself that very question for years," she said. "I go back and forth on the answer. Like most daughters who adore their fathers, I really wanted to please him. I guess that might have influenced my career choice. But when I got to McGill, I just loved the mining engineering program. It was perfect for me. I stopped thinking about pleasing Dad and immersed myself in the work to please myself."

"Did you always work with your father?"

She shook her head.

"I worked at Tardif in the summers while at McGill, but when I graduated, I took a job with another big gold-mining company."

"Really? The competition? How did Dad take it?"

"I think he was disappointed, but with my last name, I never wanted my first job to be at Tardif. I feared I'd never know for sure how good I was at my job. You know?"

"Of course. I get it," I said. "Being the founder's daughter would be very difficult. So, you charted your own course."

"I did, for a time. And as it turned out, I didn't return to Tardif until I was forty years old."

"So, you only worked with him for five years before he died," I said, doing the math in my head.

"Correct, but they weren't happy years for me. We fought a lot about company strategy, priorities, and direction, but he was always the final decision-maker. It was his company."

"You mean, you just weren't on the same page?"

"Well, at least not where the business was concerned," she admitted. "But I think I figured out why, years later. I was born an idealist. Or perhaps more accurately, I'm a born idealist. My father tempered that a little, but I kept a lot of it in me and it started coming between us," she said. "He thought the only mission of the company was to make money. Nothing else. And I thought it was all about making money so the company could contribute to something—the national interest, the local community, society, sustaining the environmental health of the planet. Something meaningful and lasting, bigger than the company or ourselves. I mean, Kéniéba is an impoverished community with almost no infrastructure and very few social services. Our investment in Mali should not just be about the extraction of gold, leaving the land ugly and scarred behind us. The company should pay a dividend to the community that offers up those precious minerals. The government benefits, the company benefits. Why shouldn't the community also benefit?"

That seemed a little Pollyanna to me, so I said nothing, and we just kept walking.

"Even hearing myself say that out loud sounds naive. That's certainly what my father thought. But that's the truth. That's how I felt back then, and it's how I still feel now."

"And yet, here you are, the CEO of Tardif."

"Dad had the succession plan all laid out, just waiting for me to come back to the company. When we clashed on basic questions about the future of the business, I'm sure he was tempted to look for someone else to succeed him. Someone who thought like he did. Someone prepared to sustain his vision. But he never did. The succession plan was etched in stone. But I'm sure it never occurred to him that a heart attack would trigger it so early. That was five years ago, and ever since, I've been running the company in a very different way, with a very different set of priorities."

"I'm sure he'd be proud of what you've achieved."

She smiled and looked at me.

"Again, I really don't think you're in a position to know that after, let's see," she said, consulting her watch, "after just three and a quarter hours on-site."

"Fair point, but by all accounts, the company is doing very well, no doubt because of you."

"We are doing well, but I honestly don't know how much of that can be attributed to my so-called leadership."

In the spirit of reciprocity, I talked a bit about my writing life. I even told her the whole sordid story of when I'd crashed into the final hurdle in my race to become a CSIS intelligence officer thirty years earlier. She made sympathetic noises.

"Failing, and not knowing why, has stayed with me all these years," I said. "Rightly or wrongly, it just seems to hang over me. It's always there, diluting the happiness and satisfaction my writing brings. It's hard to explain."

"I think it simply means that you really wanted that opportunity, that life. You invested your vision of the future and all of your self-worth in that career. So when you didn't get it, after coming so close, you were devastated, and it still hurts. Seems logical to me."

"Well, I was about to say, I really don't think you're in a position to know that after just three and a quarter hours, but as it sinks in, I think your analysis may have hit the bullseye."

She laughed. For the first time, she laughed. Based on the confused look on Pierre's face, I don't think it happened very often. He sort of tilted his head, and one ear perked up. Monique seemed to be more relaxed and, well, more human than when we'd first met her.

"You know, it's weird," I said. "I haven't told anyone about my CSIS crash-and-burn experience for nearly thirty years, yet I've now told both Coop and you in the space of a few days. Not sure what that means."

"Perhaps it means you're starting to get over it, maybe because you're now part of that life you always wanted, at least temporarily."

"If you ever get bored in the mining business, you might just have a future as a psychoanalyst."

Again, she laughed. And again, Pierre looked perplexed.

"I don't know about that," she said. "It could just be the wine."

We again walked for a time without talking, enjoying the clear, comfortable evening. Some people have difficulty enduring, let alone enjoying, silence with another person. It seemed not to be a problem for Monique. I didn't mind it, either. It felt like the silence drew us closer together, simply because neither of us felt the need to fill it. We were both comfortable, at ease, with it. As earlier in our walk, Monique spoke first.

"In case this may have some bearing on the plan to get the team out—though I don't know how—I thought you should know that we've recently discovered diamonds on our site. And unfortunately, that has meant frequent contact with Demba Dembele."

"Well, this is new information," I replied. "I know nothing about geology, but I didn't realize that gold and diamonds could be found in the same chunk of earth."

"Not to get too technical, but the Kéniéba region is one of the few places on the continent where diamonds and gold can be found in close proximity," Monique explained. "It was one of the reasons we wanted to explore this part of the country. We knew there was gold on our site, but we'd all but given up hope of finding diamonds. Then, five months ago, we hit a small but rich diamond deposit, and we've been working it ever since."

"What does that do to your operations when you're all set up for gold and then you suddenly find diamonds?"

"It hasn't changed that drastically. It's a different part of the site. We hand-selected and trained a special team of trusted workers to handle the extraction. And we also built a very thick-walled concrete bunker to process and securely store the stones. It's under guard twenty-four seven."

"Makes sense," I said, remembering the squat concrete bunker of a building I'd seen earlier on our brief tour.

"Prior to the coup, the government of Mali owned twenty per cent of this mine. So of course we reported the diamond find to Mali's Ministry of Mines, Energy, and Water, as usual. Post-coup, Mali allegedly now owns one hundred per cent of the mine, and that snake Demba has been here several times to 'review' the diamond holdings and 'supervise' secure transport back to Bamako," she said, using air quotes. "In fact, Mali is a signatory to the Kimberley Process to stop the distribution of conflict diamonds. Naturally, Demba is personally handling the Kimberley Process reporting. In other words, I'm sure he's not reporting the full extent of our diamond yield—if he's reporting any at all—and may well be pocketing the diamonds and selling them on the underground market. I suspect Demba is the only entity benefiting from our diamond deposit."

"You're kidding. That's terrible. That's outrageous!"

"And it's also the way of the world in a country with such a long history of corruption."

"And just when you thought you couldn't hate Demba any more than you already do, you should know that he is not only corrupt but also the power behind the government. He's in control and is forcing Camara to do his bidding by threatening to harm his daughter."

"What a dick!" she snapped, catching me a little off guard.

"I, um, couldn't have put it more eloquently myself," I replied. "And I'm supposed to be a writer."

I didn't yet know what to do with Monique's news about the diamonds and Demba. But it was more grist for the mill as we finalized what I had come to think of as our exit strategy, and that included, I quietly hoped, changing the balance of power at the palace.

By this time, we were almost back to the main building.

"Um, I have another favour to ask of you," I said. Monique was silent and kept walking.

"Part of our plan is to have President Camara and his daughter fly here for a tour of the mine and to see your important investments in local community services. A dinner would be catered at the mine site. The Canadian embassy would foot the bill. Then, early in the evening, after the dinner is over and the president and his daughter have taken off to fly home to Bamako, we would commandeer the school bus and drive your team, and I hope you as well, to a location on the Falémé River where we could wade across into Senegal."

"Just to be clear, I'm still not leaving, but I will do everything in my power to ensure that you succeed. Senegal is very close.

It seems like a sensible plan, except for the commandeering the bus part. There's an armed guard on board, you know."

"Well, we're still kicking around that part of the plan, but we think we've figured out a way to make it work safely," I said. "Oh, and one more important reminder. We still don't intend to tell your team about the operation until we're on the bus and heading for the Falémé. We just think it's too risky to tell them any sooner. One innocent slip of the tongue from any one of them and we'd all be done for."

She nodded as she thought it through.

"I see what you mean. I agree. I won't mention it to anyone."

I still said nothing about Amina joining the exodus. Monique didn't need to know at that stage, and the fewer who did know, the better.

Coop was waiting for us outside on the driveway when we returned.

"Now that I've had the grand tour, why don't I show you around?" I said to Coop.

"Sounds like a plan."

"I'll say good night, then," Monique said. "And thank you for the risks you're taking to get the team out."

"Okay, spill it," Coop said when we were alone. "You were out here for a good forty-five minutes. So come on, dish it."

It took me fifteen minutes or so to share everything I'd learned. I hoped I was not forgetting anything. After I'd finished, Coop took a minute to let it settle in her mind.

"Okay, so to summarize, Monique's relationship with her father is still messing her up a bit. Crashing out of CSIS is still messing you up a bit. But then she put you on the couch and it seems you're doing a little better lately. I'm almost done. We now have diamonds in the play. Demba is still a dick. And Monique agrees we will say nothing to the others until we're en route to the river crossing. Does that about capture it?"

"Nicely done, Coop. I think you've got it."

"Well, then I don't know why it took you three-quarters of an hour."

"Neither do I," I said. "But while we're on the topic of Demba, I have an idea percolating that could put him on ice. He's broken so many laws already and is basically stealing from the citizens of Mali. I know the priority of course is getting the Canadians out, and in the best of all worlds, Amina, too. But after that, if we could somehow actually give Adama the power Demba currently wields, that would be a very positive development."

"James, we're not exactly authorized for regime change—check that, we are definitely not authorized for regime change. CSIS is not in the business of overthrowing governments, whether they're legitimate or not," she said. "We have a narrowly defined mission to exfiltrate Canadian expats. That's where the operation begins and ends. And if adding Amina to our little group in any way threatens the success of the mission, we're going to have to leave her behind."

"Okay, okay, I get it. But I'm not talking about regime change. Adama Camara is currently the president, and he will continue to be president. I just want Demba out of the picture."

"Well, that's still meddling in the internal affairs of a sovereign nation. That is not our mission, nor is it part of the CSIS mandate."

"Look, to clarify, I'm not proposing that we personally derail Demba's corrupt reign. I'm just suggesting we pass along my idea to Adama and his supporters."

She didn't say no. But neither did she run in slow motion across a crowded room, accompanied by an orchestral soundtrack, to warmly embrace my clarification. But again, she didn't say no. So, I took that as a yes.

CHAPTER 13

Mali: Day 5

THE TOUR of the open pit the next morning was less interesting than I had hoped. As its name suggested, it was literally a large open pit, where local workers extracted gold, often by hand, from the earthen walls. Coop took notes, purely for appearances' sake, while Monique kept up a running commentary and I kept up a friendly interrogation. The tour was suddenly more interesting when Monique led us to a different part of the site and the concrete bunker of a building where the diamonds were processed and secured. The two guards outside the lone door immediately stood aside. And calling it a door hardly does it justice. It looked like the entrance to a bank vault or a nuclear waste storage facility.

After what can only be described as the multi-step process of opening that very secure door, Monique entered the bunker, and Coop and I filed in behind her. With my help, Monique swung the massive door closed behind us, then relocked it from the inside. There were counters along one wall of the bunker, and cupboards and shelves along another. A sink and a large safe were set into one of the concrete walls, and a central table with some scales and other instruments rounded out the furnishings.

Monique walked over to the wall safe and started yet another multi-step process to open it. It took a few minutes, but she got there eventually. She swung open the heavy door, pulled out a drawer, and showed us some of the rough diamonds that had been mined on the property. They were not lustrous and glittery, but rather dull, rough-edged, and irregularly shaped.

"These samples are actually extremely high-quality and, when cut, will be visually stunning and of extraordinary value," she explained.

On a hunch, I pulled out my mobile phone and was pleased to see that there was absolutely no cell signal registering within the diamond bunker.

"Can you both check the cell signal on your mobile phones?" I asked.

"Mine was confiscated," Monique said.

"Right."

Coop complied and turned her phone to show me that she had not even the slightest hint of a signal bar.

"Excellent. Thank you."

While my phone was in front of me, I noted the time.

"We should get going," I said to Coop.

After emerging from the bunker and thanking Monique for the tour, we walked to the security house where the guards were hanging out. I found our PPPF guard and told him we were walking into Kéniéba for lunch and to explore. He didn't look very happy and released a heavy sigh. He was still in the process of raising himself to his feet when Coop and I walked underneath the raised security barrier and started along the road towards Kéniéba. A few minutes later, I looked behind me and saw our guard dragging his feet quite a distance back, but still in sight of us. It was a hot day, but walking was part of our plan.

We strolled along the right-hand shoulder of the RN24 into town. It took us about twenty minutes. Perhaps predictably, Kéniéba, much more than Bamako, reflected Mali's reality as a developing nation, a country still struggling to find herself. A few long-in-the-tooth low-rise buildings in less than great shape. Slums not far off the main road. An old man herding goats through the streets. Dust in the air. Dilapidated market stalls with sparse offerings. Old, beat-up cars—some running, many not. And again, the dust. It was just how Kéniéba had been described in our initial briefings, so I ought to have expected it. But an antiseptic location briefing in Madrid was just not the same as being right there on the streets.

We reached our destination and walked through the front door of Restaurant Fanta Sow. Without slowing down we moved right past the dining area, into the kitchen—where we nodded to the staff—and then out the back door into an alley. And exactly where Kiran said it would be, just a little ways down the alley, we found a banged-up black Toyota Corolla. Discreetly, Coop reached up under the rear bumper, pulled out the keys, and opened the door. No more than ten seconds later, we were driving away from the restaurant, with Coop at the wheel. Our guard was nowhere to be seen—just as we'd planned.

"So, you're finally commuting in a Toyota Corolla," Coop said.

That made me laugh.

We drove south for a time before taking a right turn to head west and connect with the RN2, the highway to Kofeba. There were lots of other cars on the road that looked like the Toyota we were driving. We kept a vigilant eye out for tails, but none appeared.

Forty minutes later, we reached Kofeba. There wasn't much to the small village, which was just fine with us. We drove through the western outskirts and managed to find the dirt track we had previously only seen in satellite photos. To be sure, I also used my phone's GPS and followed the moving arrow on my screen directly to the Falémé River and our crossing point. It was slow going, but we eventually made it to the end of the road, the river beckoning just beyond. There was not a soul around that we could see. We were in the middle of nowhere. It wasn't just rural—it was untouched scrubby outback.

We got out of the car and walked to the river's edge.

"It's running deeper and faster than I expected," I said.

"Yes, but it's still manageable on foot, at least right now."

The water was only about a foot deep in the middle and still did not stretch from bank to bank. But there was definitely more water than in the original satellite shots that Vivian had shared in Madrid, and maybe even more than in those Kiran had shown us the day before.

Looking at our surroundings, we agreed that the bus could make it along the dirt track, though it would be a rough ride, and that there was room on the flat riverbank to park close to the water before we started wading across to Senegal. So far, so good.

I admit, it felt strange looking at the far riverbank, knowing that it was in fact the sovereign territory of Senegal. It was right there in front of us. Crossing seemed simple enough. We could have easily trotted across right then if we'd wanted to. The harder part of the operation would be getting all seventeen of us to the river safely and, ideally, undetected.

We gathered as much info as we could and then drove back to Kéniéba, parking the car just where we'd picked it up. To complete the charade, we walked through the Restaurant Fanta Sow, this time from back to front, as if we owned the place, and started strolling back to the compound. We didn't see our guard, though we certainly weren't making a show of looking around for him. The town was hopping so we blended in, and we made it back to the Tardif mine site in good time. We presented ourselves at the security gatehouse and found our PPPF guard lounging inside with the other security staff. He scowled at us but said nothing. We had gambled—and won—that he'd never report up the line that he'd lost us. It would not reflect well on him, and if Demba's reputation was well-earned, there would likely have been unpleasant repercussions. At any rate, it seemed we were expected, and we were admitted.

I was quite tired by the time we made it back to the Tardif site office. I was hoping to head back to the compound and lie down for a bit before dinner. But Monique had other plans.

"Glad you're back," she said when we appeared outside her office. "Let's go."

She stood up and walked past us to the front door. We followed. What else could we do? A Ford Explorer with the Tardif logo on the door was parked outside. Two guards were in the front seat, so the three of us climbed into the back.

I hoped she was taking us back to the compound for my aforementioned nap. But no such luck.

"I want to show you what we've done in the community. It's a big part of our story," she said. "You've seen the mine, but we've also invested heavily in Kéniéba. You should see that, too."

"Lead on," I said.

I'm not sure what I was expecting, but what Monique had achieved in the community was really impressive. It took an hour, but we toured a family planning and health clinic, a secondary school, a fully stocked pharmacy, a small library—including several computers with internet connections—and a career counselling service, all conceived, built, and funded by Tardif Resources. You might expect that there would be large and colourful Tardif logos plastered on every flat surface, but you had to look carefully to see any corporate identity at all. When I asked where all the Tardif branding was, Monique shook her head.

"That's not how we work," she said. "It's not about the Tardif brand, it's about the delivery of much-needed services to an underserved population that has never had access to the basic social infrastructure and community supports that much of the world takes for granted."

"This is definitely not your father's company anymore," I said. "Congratulations."

"It's very impressive, Monique. Really great," Coop said. "I think President Camara needs to see this, too."

The guards dropped us off at the Tardif compound before they drove back to the mine site. The three of us walked the dog again so we could speak freely.

"Okay, we made it to the site of our river crossing today without any issues," I said. "And there were no real surprises. It still seems like the right plan."

"But we have to move as quickly as possible," Coop cut in. "The water levels in the river are rising, and it could be impassable in another week or so."

"So, what can I do?" Monique asked.

"Well, you can respond quickly and favourably to the request for a presidential visit to the mine and a tour of the community."

"So that's going to happen, is it?"

"I figure I'll be writing the official request as soon as we get back to Bamako," I replied. "But to respect diplomatic protocols, it will have to go to the Canadian embassy first. Then they will reach out to you. The sooner you say yes, the sooner we can get it all arranged and nail down the date. But we're talking a matter of days, not weeks. We're in a race with the river."

"Got it."

Coop looked around and then reached into her pocket. She pulled out the cheap phone that Kiran had provided and handed it to Monique.

"This is a burner phone with no ties to you or to us. It's totally clean," she said. "You can use it to reach us, and we may need to call you on it, so keep it close, but hidden. We don't want to draw attention to the fact that you all of a sudden have a mobile phone. I've put the ringer on vibrate. Do not call anyone else on it but us."

"Understood," Monique said, as she pocketed the burner. "I'll keep it safe and close."

CHAPTER 14

Mali: Day 6

ON THE way back to the mine site early the next morning, once again the guard sat up with the driver of the school bus. I positioned myself in the second row so I could surreptitiously watch the driver, just to familiarize myself with the business end of driving the bus. After all, I'd be the laughingstock of the intelligence world if we succeeded in putting the driver and guard out of commission on E-Day but were then stymied because I couldn't figure out how to put the bus into gear. But it all looked quite straightforward. I noted that both the driver and the guard were drinking from plastic throwaway water bottles. Good to know.

As we turned onto the mine site, we heard and saw our ride back to the palace. The presidential helicopter was cruising in to land, right on schedule. Monique walked us over to the helipad as it touched down.

"If the second part of our plan—the very unofficial, never-to-be-admitted part of the plan—is to even have a shot at success, Demba has to be here the morning after we cross that river," I said.

"Yes, but he'll have plenty of incentive to be here when he finds out the entire Tardif team—minus Monique, of course—and the two of us have turned up in Senegal," Coop replied.

"Yes, but just to be sure, I think I have an idea that will almost guarantee Demba will be here that morning, whether or not we've made it to Senegal."

"Well?" Coop prodded. "Go on, then."

"Right. Okay. Well, what if Monique were to call Demba sometime during the presidential tour and suggest he come up ASAP because of a particularly bountiful diamond harvest, including the biggest diamonds yet extracted? Let's capitalize on Demba's greatest weakness—his greed."

No one said anything for a few beats as we approached the chopper.

"I like it," Monique said. "Believe me, his greed knows no bounds. He'll make the trip. You can count on it."

"Of course, when you call him, don't use your . . ." Coop started.

"I know, I know, don't use my burner phone," Monique interjected. "I'll call him from my office land line as I usually do."

"Good," Coop replied. "Just making sure."

By that time, we'd reached the helipad.

"Thank you for having us up here, and for agreeing to help us get your team out. There's no way we could do this without your support," I said. "You know, you can still change your mind at the very last second and come with us."

"I know I can, but I also know I won't," Monique replied. "But I'm grateful for everything you're risking in getting my people out. The team has been through a lot. They deserve to be safe."

"So do you," Coop said.

"I'll be just fine," Monique replied, "and so will the mine, and the community, too."

What happened next surprised me. Monique hugged us both before turning and heading back to her office. She didn't strike me as the hugging type. By the surprised look on Coop's face, she hadn't expected Monique's embrace, either. Maybe we hadn't quite figured out Monique as well as we thought we had. The hug felt good, and it occurred to me that the ever-evolving Monique was growing on me. Perhaps I was beginning to see what Pierre saw in her.

I felt a little sorry that we hadn't told her about Amina, but it was too risky.

We were seated in the presidential compartment for the chopper's return trip to the palace, while our PPPF guard was up front in the cockpit with the pilot. As with our flight to the Tardif site, there wasn't much to see on our return journey, so my eyes were wandering around Adama's luxury cabin. Yes, it was a rickety flying machine, but the president's compartment was done up right. There were curtains on the windows, extra soundproofing, three comfortable chairs—the kind you see on private jets—and a single bed made up and ready, positioned against the aft bulkhead. Painted in red letters across the bulkhead were the words *Emergency Escape Hatch*. Hmmmm.

The idea came rushing in, fully formed, filling my mind as if it were a vacuum—and believe me, sometimes it is. I let it sit, steeping in my brainpan for a time as the scrubby terrain rolled by below us. Each time I reviewed the idea, it was still in one piece at the end. Somehow, it held together. Then I waited a little longer—I thought about something else for a time. I wondered if I should grow a moustache. I wondered why I still wasn't able to touch my toes with my legs straight. I even wondered where Amelia Earhart might be. And then I came back to the idea once more. And still it held.

With all the rotor noise in the cabin, Coop and I could speak freely, but still I leaned in close to her ear and explained my idea, step by step.

"Run it by me again," was all Coop said in response.

I did as I was told. Partway through my second recitation, she started nodding, and kept it up until I finished.

"That's not bad, writer man. Not bad at all," she said. "I can't think of a better way to pull this off, despite all the inherent risks. But if Adama does his job well, it could just work—it should work—and then maybe, just maybe, Demba goes down, too."

"That's my favourite part," I said.

"Since you came to the palace, has Amina ever been off the property?" I asked the president that afternoon, not long after we landed.

Coop, Adama, and I were once again doing what we always did when we needed to speak freely. We were walking outside, through the palace grounds, passing the lovely flora growing along the path. By this stage, I'd had my fill of the presidential gardens, but it remained the only option we had for conferring with one another free from prying ears.

"Twice so far, that I can think of," Adama replied. "Her online teacher has taken her to our national museum and to the art gallery. For security purposes, both institutions were closed to the public so Amina and her teacher could tour them on their own. Demba permitted it but he required four guards and me to accompany them."

"Good, there's precedent," I said. "If this is going to work, we have to get Demba to agree to let Amina accompany you on the mine visit."

He nodded.

"Could you instruct Amina to ask her teacher if she could do a special project on mining?" Coop asked. "Then it would make more sense for her to go with you on the Tardif visit."

"Hmmm, I see. Very clever," Adama said. "Yes, I think Demba would permit it as a school project. There would already be guards accompanying me anyway, so that might just work."

"Good. So that gets Amina to the Tardif mine," I continued. "We haven't yet finalized precisely how to get her on the bus with the Canadian expats, but we're close. We do know it will require some theatrics on your part, particularly when you land back in Bamako after the trip to Kéniéba."

Adama nodded, a determined glint in his eyes.

"'All the world's a stage, and all the men and women merely players; they have their exits and their entrances, and one man in his time plays many parts.' For my daughter's future, I can play any part."

I stifled a smile and the early inklings of a giggle when I realized he wasn't goofing around. I actually thought his response was a little corny. And maybe more than a little. But then again, I'm not a father, so what do I know? I decided not to spoil the moment. He had a lot riding on this plan. For one, his daughter's freedom. So, I cut him some slack on the Shakespearean soliloquy. Even Hunter Chase would never reach for Shakespeare, and believe me, I've put some cheesy lines in his mouth over the years.

"There's one more thing, Mr. President," Coop said. "To make sure Amina understands what's happening and why we need her to be ready to play her role in all of this, you may want to tell her the truth about Demba and why she is living in what you described as a gilded cage. It's obvious she is intelligent beyond her years—she's the smartest ten-year-old I've ever met. She can handle the truth. And it may give her the resolve and the motivation she's going to need when the big moment comes."

He nodded, thinking it through. "Yes, I see. I agree. I think she deserves the truth. We will have a walk together tonight and I will tell her everything then. You're right, it may be what brings her through what lies ahead."

By then, we had walked Adama through the plan as it stood. There were still some refinements to be made, but the key elements were in place. Earlier, I'd used our satphone to reach out to Monique on her burner. We had a couple of long and rambling conversations as I walked the palace grounds. I barely noticed the time passing. It was nice. Happily, Monique was a supporter of any effort that would clip Demba's corrupt wings. And luckily, she liked my idea, contributed some enhancements, and was prepared to do her part. Otherwise, my little bringing-down-Demba idea would have been stillborn. In fact, its success turned on Monique's participation.

I thought the plan was a winner, but Coop's natural reserve prevented her from being too enthusiastic about it. She'd seen great plans blown up through bad execution, bad timing, bad weather, bad luck, perhaps even bad karma. But in my blissful innocence, or perhaps ignorance, I continued to feel good about our strategy.

Beyond extracting the Canadians from Mali, I also really wanted to see Demba escorted off the playing field and stripped of his power. Then Adama could, with different and trusted advisors around him, start to wield the power his office gave him, rather than simply follow Demba's orders. I understood Coop's concerns that CSIS was not in the business of toppling governments, even corrupt governments. But putting an end to Demba's reign wasn't regime change in the strict definition of the term. Adama would still be president. From the outside, the regime would be the same. Status quo. Plus, in the idea I'd been working on, Demba's downfall would be an internal Malian initiative and would actually unfold after the fourteen Canadian expats, Amina, Coop, and I were already safely out of the country. Didn't sound like regime change to me.

Coop headed over to the basketball court to shoot a few hoops with Amina. That worked out well, as it meant I could speak freely with Adama about Demba.

"We've been working on a second little initiative that we hope might result in what I've been calling Demba's Downfall," I said. "CSIS would not officially be involved, and it would happen after we've left the country. But with your blessing, and if it goes well, Demba would be out of the picture and facing corruption charges. Then you could start to govern according to your own democratic principles and beliefs, free of Demba's control."

He said nothing for a time but was clearly deep in thought.

"What would be involved?" he asked.

"Well, you'd need help. But Monique Tardif is on our side and will do her part. I think she'd like to see Demba brought to justice as much as you would."

"I am not excited about Demba being tried for corruption. He was my friend for so many years," Adama said, almost in a whisper.

"Adama, he's also the guy who's been threatening harm to Amina to keep you under his thumb," I said. "So, why would you have any sympathy for him at all?"

He paused for a moment before responding.

"I want to believe the Demba I once knew is still buried there inside him somewhere," he said, before shaking his head. "But he no longer serves the people of Mali. He only serves himself, and that cannot stand."

"All right. Good. Can you quietly reach out to your friend, the Minister of Defence, without Demba knowing?" I asked.

"Yes, as a matter of fact, we have a Cabinet meeting here tomorrow and Oumar Sissoko will attend," Adama explained. "We often walk together after our meetings to catch up. Demba knows we've been friends for many years. He also knows Oumar's wife is very ill, so he won't be surprised if I'm seen with him, offering comfort at this difficult time. Demba has known Oumar as long as I have, but they don't much like one another."

"Okay, if you're convinced the defence minister will step up and do the right thing in the interests of Mali, here's what we propose."

I walked Adama through Operation Demba's Downfall, twice, just to be sure.

"Simple but effective," Adama said. "I like it, and I think Oumar will, too. But it means Demba has to be in Kéniéba for the plan to work."

"True, but he'll have plenty of incentive to get up there. As soon as you arrive back here, he'll know that Amina is missing. She's the key to his power. We're convinced he'll want to fly up to Tardif and lead the search personally. He must protect his principal asset. But just to be sure, we're also counting on his avarice, his greed. Monique will have called him to share the news that they've just extracted their largest and most valuable diamonds yet. And that's another multi-carat reason we think he'll be eager to get to Kéniéba, and fast."

Adama nodded.

A few minutes later, we found ourselves at the door to the palace. Adama went back inside to his office to prep for the Cabinet meeting. I had one more call to make, so I turned around and headed back out on the garden path.

I called Kiran Hassan on her secure line.

"Just wanted to give you a heads-up that an official presidential request for a tour of the Tardif mine site will be arriving within the hour," I said. "And a timely response is important given the rising water levels in the Falémé."

"I'll be watching for it," she replied. "I can reach out to Monique Tardif by phone to save time and then get back to you fast with a formal invitation from the embassy."

"Perfect, but I hope we won't be slowed down getting the ambassador's approval," I said. "We're very short on time."

"No worries. I don't need her to approve this. I'll tell her about it later without giving her the full story. All will be good."

"Great. Thank you, Kiran."

By 2:00 p.m., Amina's special project on mining in Mali had been officially sanctioned by her lovely but unwitting teacher. That was the first domino toppled in our little scheme.

We decided that Adama would not mention Amina's mining assignment and the Kéniéba trip to Demba. We were leaning on the old "beg forgiveness rather than ask for permission" strategy that had worked so well for so many for so long.

By 2:30 p.m., I had drafted on presidential letterhead, for Adama's signature, a formal request to the Canadian ambassador for a visit to the Tardif Resources mine site in Kéniéba. It took me about seven minutes. We printed it out. Adama signed it. And by 3:15 it had been hand delivered to the Canadian embassy. But to keep the wheels turning while waiting for the hard copy to reach Kiran, I also emailed it to her, and to Monique. As in comedy and boiling eggs, timing is everything. While it may have looked like a request, when the president asks to visit a gold mine in the country he governs, rest assured, it will happen at the time of his choosing. Ready or not, here we come.

By 3:45 p.m., a formal invitation from the ambassador had arrived via email—the second domino—confirming that Tardif Resources would welcome a day-long visit from the president, his daughter, and others from his staff, to tour their operations. They would also be serenaded by a community choir, have lunch on-site, and visit the social services facilities in Kéniéba funded by Tardif Resources. The date had been set for two days hence, the earliest possible time given the Cabinet meeting at the palace the next day.

By 4:05 p.m., Demba had already heard of the visit from the president's scheduler, as we had planned. At the same time, Coop and I were meeting with Adama in his office, also as planned, for another interview about my upcoming novel. We could hear Demba lumbering down the corridor, right on cue.

"What's this trip to Tardif all about and why is Amina invited?" Demba said, before he had fully entered the office.

"Oh, I thought you knew all about it," Adama said, looking puzzled. "Amina was recently assigned a school project on mining in Mali, and at the same time, Monique Tardif invited me to visit the gold mine in Kéniéba. So we are, as they say, killing two birds with one stone."

"No. You're not going," Demba said, making a horizontal karate chop motion with his right hand in case his words were not clear enough. "There'll be too much work coming out of Cabinet tomorrow. We've wasted enough time already."

"Please, Demba. Amina has not been off the palace grounds for a very long time, and her teacher is so pleased that she can visit a real mine and see the future of Mali's economic prosperity. Please, Demba, it's one day. We leave in the morning, and we'll be back by nightfall. Please. Think of Amina. She's ten years old, locked up here, and she has no friends. She has a fine mind. She's curious. She needs this field trip. It's an important project for her. Please . . ."

Demba sighed and looked at the ceiling, exasperated. Then he shook his head and held his hands up like the victim of a holdup.

"All right, all right, enough whining, Adama. Make the trip, but please clear these unplanned excursions with me in the future, and do not schedule them for the day after Cabinet."

"I won't. It was just because Amina's deadline was quickly approaching," Adama said. "Thank you. Thank you."

Demba paused in the doorway and turned back to Adama. He seemed to notice Coop and me for the first time.

"Mr. President, forgive my tone. I only have your best interests, and Mali's, in mind."

Adama nodded.

Demba then wheeled out of the room without another word. Given the cameras in the office, we were careful not to show any outward signs that we were celebrating. But internally, I, for one, was doing handsprings. Outwardly, we just looked at one another and shrugged.

Well played, Adama, I thought to myself. That was an important moment. Our third domino had fallen. Getting Demba's "yes" for the Tardif visit was probably our most important achievement thus far on the road—or, more accurately, the river—to Senegal. Without it, our chances of success would have plummeted.

"I guess we're going to Kéniéba," was all I said.

CHAPTER 15

Mali: Day 7

WHILE THE Cabinet was meeting the next day at the palace, Coop and I again visited the Canadian embassy, ostensibly for a briefing on industrial development in West African countries. I had already made it clear that I hadn't yet chosen the nation where my next novel would be set, hence the need for such a briefing. Details matter. Of course, as soon as we arrived, the briefing was miraculously "cancelled," thus freeing up our time to work on other pressing matters, like the imminent and risky exfiltration of fourteen Canadian mining executives and a certain ten-year-old Malian girl.

Kiran, Coop, and I met in the same briefing room where we'd first gathered. I found it hard to remember when we'd actually landed in Bamako. It felt like a very long time ago, yet it was only a matter of days—a week, to be precise.

"Okay," Kiran said, calling us to order and handing a small vial to Coop. "This is a specially engineered benzodiazepine solution, whose effects are limited to deep and nearly instant sleep."

I was so relieved to hear this. It had been one of the remaining question marks in our plan. Without it, wresting control of the bus from the driver and the armed guard would have been much more terrifying.

"Add only one capful of this potion to a standard single-serve water bottle," Kiran continued. "If the target takes two mouthfuls, that will be enough to knock him out for about an hour. If he drinks the full bottle, he'll be down for five hours but will recover quickly with no after-effects. It's actually quite safe."

"When this is all over, I just may try it myself, recreationally," I said.

They both just looked at me. Inside my head, I counted down: *three, two, one*. Coop rolled her eyes before I hit two.

We talked about the mechanics of safely drugging first the guard and then the driver, ensuring our ability to bring the bus to a safe stop before I took over at the wheel. I'd be monitoring the driver's reaction closely, while Coop would loiter next to the guard. My plan was to literally—perhaps physically is the better word—lift the driver's right foot off the gas pedal when he started to lose consciousness, then put both my hands on the wheel, guiding us slowly over onto the shoulder of the road. In the worst case, I had easy access to the emergency brake located on the floor on the right-hand side of the seat. I didn't think it would be easy, but when I played out the various scenarios, I had a course of action to manage each one.

We spent the next two hours talking with Monique on a secure speakerphone while she moved, seemingly purposefully, around the mine site. Her burner phone was in her pocket, while her earbuds were situated where earbuds seem to work best. To anyone watching, she was just making her rounds to important locations, singing along to the music in her ears from her old iPod, making sure everything was operating as it should be.

We walked through the plan several times, step by incremental step. Kiran guided our discussion.

"Monique, you'll need to disable the bus's air conditioning. We need the driver and guard to be really thirsty when that bus rolls out."

"Well, how do I do that?" Monique asked.

"There are two ways to do it, but one is much better than the other," Kiran explained, as she consulted the appropriate school bus manual. "Beneath the dashboard, just to the left of the steering column, is a fuse box about three inches wide and six inches long, with a black plastic cover. You can't miss it. Pry off the cover just using your hands and you'll see two columns of fuses. They're about an inch long and look like little glass cylinders with metal ends. The fourth fuse from the top in the right-hand column is for the AC. Use a knife or a flat screwdriver to pop out just the fourth fuse. If you happen to remove the fifth fuse, the bus likely won't even start. So, make sure."

"I assume I need to do this without being seen," Monique said, her voice flat and calm as it always was. "Any suggestions?"

Coop piped up.

"We suggest taking Pierre for a late-night walk when the compound is asleep. The bus doors are unlocked and can be swung open from the outside. Bring a knife, a small flashlight, and whatever book you're reading. If the bus is parked where it usually is, the doors cannot be seen from the security station or your living quarters. They're on the other side of the bus. So, open the doors, bring Pierre onto the bus, and settle him on a seat with something he likes to eat. Don't forget to close the doors again. Get down on the floor beneath the steering wheel with your flashlight and knife and get to work. Remember to keep the beam of the flashlight tight on the fuse box beneath the dash. We don't want stray light leaking out of the bus. The whole procedure should only take you a minute or so. Then check your surroundings before you leave the bus, and you'll be back in bed in no time."

"All right. That sounds quite straightforward, except for one thing," Monique said. "Why should I bring my book with me?"

"This was James's idea," Coop said, giving me the floor.

"That's so if anyone sees you, or hears a noise on the bus, and comes to investigate, you can just tell them you were walking Pierre and remembered you'd left your book on the seat next to you. Then you wave the book around a bit and casually head back to bed."

"Okay, got it. Now, what's the second way to take out the AC?"

"Oh, well, it's not really viable, as it requires you to open the hood and cut through an insulated hose to drain the coolant. It would be hard to do that discreetly. I shouldn't even have mentioned it," Kiran conceded.

"I see," Monique replied. "Okay then, let's go with popping the fuse."

"Monique, while we have you on the line, is the security team at your living compound notified when to expect the bus after a workday on the mine site?" I asked.

"Only if we don't leave the mine at the regular time. Then the guard on board calls to let them know when to expect us. Or I've let them know on a few occasions," Monique said. "Since I'm not joining you on the bus, my plan was to work late at the mine site and sleep in my office. I've done that several times and it's never been an issue, as long as I tell security."

"Smart," I said. "We're also trying to buy us some time to get to the river crossing before anyone raises the alarm. We're hoping you'll call the guardhouse at the compound around the time we leave on the bus to let them know that the president's visit has delayed our departure for at least an hour. By the time anyone starts to wonder about the bus, we should be in Senegal."

"I can do that," she said. "I don't have a phone, of course, but I can use the radio in my office to reach them. I've done it before so it shouldn't register as unusual. I'll also tell the guard on the bus that I'll take care of it so that he doesn't have to. He's lazy so I'm sure it will work."

"Good," Coop said. "Thank you for doing that. It could very well make the difference."

"Monique, it's Kiran. Are you sure you won't reconsider and get out with your team? I'm a little worried about your safety if you stay behind and it becomes clear you aided and abetted their escape."

"As I keep saying, my mind is made up," Monique replied. "But if we think it through, I actually believe I'll be safer afterwards. I will then be the only person in the country who knows how to manage the mine's operations. Besides, Demba is most interested in the diamond side of the business and I'm the lead on that. Really, no one else on our team knows much about the precious stone operation. So, he won't let anything happen to me as long as he's profiting from our diamond production. I'm staying. No need to ask again, please."

"Well, I tried." Kiran sighed.

With Kiran in the room and who knows what CSIS listening devices, we didn't want to talk to Monique about the follow-up stratagem that we hoped would spell the end of Demba's foray into power and corruption. I'd have to bring her up to speed when we arrived in Kéniéba the next day. I'd already briefed Adama, and he had his marching orders with respect to his friend the Minister of Defence. The pieces were falling into place. Then again, this was my first clandestine operation. So, who could be sure? But by the time we left the embassy late that afternoon, Coop and I felt we were in as strong a position as we could be to pull this off.

Adama was hosting a dinner for his Cabinet to round out a busy day for the fledgling government of Mali. I saw him briefly on his way to dinner. He shook my hand, smiled, and pulled me into a collegial embrace. While in close, he whispered, "Amina knows all, and is ready. Green light."

He then broke away and headed for his dinner. Coop and I ate with Amina, then squeezed in a walk outside to make sure she was all set for her role in the next day's events.

"So how are you feeling about all of this?" I asked Amina as we strolled the gardens. "It's okay to be a little nervous. But we'll be watching over you the whole time."

"Now that I know what is really happening here, I'm not nervous about the plan and what I have to do," she said. "I know you'll both be there. But I am worried about Papa. I wish he was coming with us. Why can't he come, too? It's dangerous to stay."

Coop reached out and held Amina's hand as we walked.

"Your father's first priority is your safety, and as confusing as it may sound, protecting you means he needs to stay here to, um, fix a few problems, before you'll be able to come home. He's really doing all of this for you—for your future—and for Mali's. Your father knows what he's doing, and we believe he will be safe."

"I know, I know. That's just what Papa told me," she said. "But it's still scary. I just want it all to be over."

"Actually, after tomorrow, it *will* be nearly over," I said. "We have a plan. It's a good plan. And tomorrow we make it happen. The three of us are going to make it happen."

"I'm ready," Amina said, leaning against Coop as we walked. "I just want my father back."

She was nervous but determined. We took that as a good sign. We'd had a long day, so we retired early. We had a very early start the next day and needed our sleep.

CHAPTER 16

Mali: Day 8 (E-Day)

THE NEXT morning broke clear and cloudless. It was not yet excruciatingly hot, but the heat would surely come.

"So, this is it," Coop said as we sauntered around the grounds before breakfast. "Are you okay? Are you ready? We really need to be on our game today. There's a lot riding on us both."

"Is this your idea of a pre-game pep talk?" I asked.

"Maybe it is, but this is not a game," she replied.

"Fair point. I actually feel good about it all—or at least I did—but now you've ramped up my anxiety."

"Good, that was my intention. I always find that I'm sharper when my stomach is a little tight," Coop said.

"Well, I don't mind when my stomach is tight, but I'm not sure it's helpful if it leads to projectile vomiting. You know, everything in moderation, including pre-mission jitters."

Coop put her hand on my arm as we walked.

"We're going to be fine," she said, almost in a whisper. "I'm ready. You're ready. Amina the wunderkind is ready. We've gone through the entire operation step by step countless times. And that repetition to ingrain the plan is important. It frees up mental bandwidth so we can deal with anything unexpected that comes up. And you know something unexpected will come up. It always does. But we'll deal with it."

"Thanks, Coop. You've managed to loosen the knot in my stomach a little."

"You know, I really did not want to involve a civilian in this operation, let alone a famous writer."

"Yes, I seem to recall you made that very clear, very early on, right to my face."

"I wasn't finished," she said, smiling. "But even considering you blew our cover an hour after we landed, this has all worked out much better than I expected. At least after you understood we wouldn't be detonating explosives, calling in air strikes, and firing curare-tipped blow darts."

"Nice, Coop, very nice," I chided. "I didn't even bring my blowgun."

"Anyway, whatever happens today, I'm now officially glad you came along for the ride."

"Me, too. Let's make sure that the ride takes us all the way to Senegal."

—

About half an hour later, Coop, Amina, Adama, and I boarded the chopper and occupied the president's cabin. The four PPPF guards assigned to us sat in the forward compartment. We lifted off the palace grounds at seven thirty sharp. Amina, her father having shared with her the truth about their situation, looked as stoic and determined as a ten-year-old could. Adama also looked a little different that morning. He knew what he had to do to get his daughter out of the country and to give himself a shot at governing without the corrupt control of Demba Dembele. But knowing what you have to do is not the same as doing it. Coop looked as calm and cool as ever. She had told me that she usually felt anxious leading up to an operation, but that when it started, all of sudden she was at peace. She certainly looked tranquil as we began our descent to Tardif Resources only a couple of hours later, aided by a tailwind. I wouldn't say that "tranquil" accurately described how I was feeling, but I felt ready. Anxious, but ready.

As we settled onto the helipad, I could see the children's choir from the community school Tardif had founded, lined up in neat rows on risers in front of the main building. The choristers were dressed in navy-blue shorts or skirts, and white shirts. To accompany the choir, the school's band was set up to the left of the risers, ready to play. I have no idea how Monique managed to get them there on such short notice. I flashed back to our arrival in Bamako and the military band that sounded like each performer had swapped instruments with the player in front of them. I was praying for a better performance from the school band.

As the engine died away and the main rotor wound down to a stop, I had to force myself to act normally. My heart rate was elevated. This was the start of a long day. And if our preparation paid off, and everything unfolded as we'd drawn it up, we'd all wake up the next morning in Senegal. But if our plan blew a tire along the way, I had no idea where I'd be spending the night.

Monique was waiting for us outside the chopper. She had dressed up a bit—well, as much as a working mining engineer in West Africa could. She was still wearing khaki cargo pants and a work shirt, but they were clean and pressed. And she'd added a scarf in Mali's national colours. A nice touch. We waited in the presidential compartment until the four PPPF guards had disembarked and lined up next to Monique. When all was ready, I opened the sliding door and folded down the stairs. President Camara, holding hands with Amina, stepped down onto the helipad's asphalt and approached Monique. Given that his government had seized ownership of her mine and detained her entire executive, she could have been forgiven for unloading on the president with a piece of her mind. But she knew the score and that this visit was critical to getting her team safely out of Mali. So, she was cordial and respectful, without fawning all over him. Actually, I can't imagine Monique fawning over anyone or anything. But she shook his hand and then bent down to greet Amina, who smiled in response and shook hands like a veteran diplomat.

Coop and I hung back. This welcome ceremony was not about us. Then the band started playing the Malian national anthem and the choir started singing. I think everyone in earshot would have preferred it if the choir had been much louder. They were good, but the band drowned them out, and not in a good way. As I'd hoped, they weren't as bad as the airport military band, but that still left a lot of room to be bad. And they were.

After the choir and the band had finished and the applause had petered out, the president and his daughter moved closer to the young performers, applauding and beaming at the children. While that was happening, Monique came over to greet Coop and me. When we shook hands, she left something in mine. I pocketed it discreetly without yet knowing what it was. Monique then approached Adama and Amina, interrupting their little love-in with the children's choir and band. She led her visitors towards the mine and the start of their tour. When it was safe, I checked my pocket and discovered the AC fuse from the bus. Well done, Monique, and her accomplice Pierre, too.

The rest of the morning was consumed by the grand tour. Several of Monique's team supported her in giving their special guests not just a thorough exploration of the pit and the gold that it surrendered, but also of the processing journey the precious metal took thereafter. Everyone on the tour—including the four PPPF guards—had donned hard hats, steel-toed boots, and ear protection. Amina looked like a cartoon character with her over-sized protective gear, but she managed just fine. Ever ready, she clutched her notebook full of the questions she planned to ask her hosts. Having gotten to know her a little, I had no doubt it would be the best mining project Amina would never hand in.

There wasn't much for Coop and me to do while Monique was showing Adama and Amina around. All the pieces were in place. We were ready. I just wanted to turn the clock forward and get us to the moment we'd been anticipating. Coop felt the same way but had an easier time dealing with it. I spent part of the morning singing the chorus of an old Tom Petty song, anchored by the line *The waiting is the hardest part*. Yes, I know, I'm quite literal.

An hour after the tour had started, I happened to be watching from the air-conditioned comfort of the office as Monique and her small tour group emerged from the big pit and walked over to visit the diamond bunker. I wondered if Adama knew the full extent of Demba's corruption when it came to the Tardif diamond yield.

As Coop and I surveyed the scene, it was clear that Monique had aced the tasks we had assigned her. Most important was the placement of the bus. Because of the hastily erected risers for the choir, the bus could not occupy its traditional parking spot—just as we had intended. Instead, it was now parked much closer to the helipad and, more to the point, the chopper. The bus was oriented so that its door faced away from the helicopter and was essentially out of sight from any curious eyes in the immediate vicinity. Perfect.

When we saw Monique, Adama, Amina, and the four bored-looking PPPF guards walking towards the main building at eleven forty-five, Coop and I headed into the dining room. It had been transformed. On short notice, a local restaurant had stepped up to cater the lunch, and they had provided tablecloths, polished silverware, glassware, and flower arrangements, too. A black baby grand piano sat in one corner, with a young, well-dressed woman seated on the bench, at the ready. These additions alone transformed the room. Who knew there was a black baby grand piano in Kéniéba?

Those on the tour cleaned up in the washroom off the dining room before taking their seats. As soon as Adama settled into his chair, a team of four waiters emerged from the kitchen carrying trays, and the pianist started playing. I was anxious and not particularly hungry. I picked at my lunch without eating much. Hard to eat when my stomach was tighter than a snare drum. Adama, Amina, and Monique kept up their conversation, with Amina periodically putting down her fork so she could take notes. I was relieved when the wait staff started clearing the tables.

After lunch, when Adama and Amina were touring the sprawling equipment garage next door, Monique and I stepped away and slipped into her office. She activated the speakerphone on her desk and dialled, while I pulled a mining text off a bookshelf and busied myself flipping pages and taking notes in case there were cameras as well as listening devices in the room.

"Mr. Dembele, it's Monique Tardif calling."

"Yes, Ms. Tardif, what do you want?"

"I just wanted to assure you that the president's visit is going very well. Both he and Amina are learning a lot about gold mining."

"I don't really care, but fine. Anything else?" he asked, with undisguised impatience.

"Yes, the real point of my call is to tell you that yesterday and this morning, the yield from the diamond vein included the seven largest stones we've ever found. They are enormous. Not quite the Hope Diamond, but in that category."

"Seven?" he asked. "Are you certain?"

"I'm quite good with numbers, Mr. Dembele, even though I needed the fingers on both hands to confirm the count. Yes, seven.

And there are signs of more to come. They're still in their raw state, but initial assessments suggest they are of excellent quality."

There was silence on Demba's end of the line for about ten seconds. His heavy breathing filled the room, along with what I thought just might be the subtle sound of his synapses firing.

"I'll be there first thing in the morning. At first light."

"Fine. I'll already be here," Monique said. "This presidential visit has cost me a precious workday, so after he leaves, I'll be in my office late and staying on-site for the night. I'll see you in the morning."

He hung up without saying goodbye.

Monique and I said nothing as we left her office to catch up with the tour. But I was enjoying a few more internal handsprings.

At three o'clock, a makeshift presidential motorcade arrived, featuring one aging Lincoln Continental and two military jeeps. Adama, Amina, and Monique rode in the Lincoln, with one PPPF guard joining the driver in the front seat. The other guards travelled in the jeeps. Monique took her guests on an extended version of the community tour she had given Coop and me a couple of days earlier—though it felt like at least a week ago.

Once again, Coop and I skipped the tour, twiddling our thumbs and counting the minutes. We passed the time by walking the grounds and reviewing, over and over, each little step in what would follow. I also loaded several cases of bottled water that Monique had secured into the large fridge in the kitchen. The colder they were, the better—we were counting on a very hot bus later in the day.

The presidential visit had been a great success. Amina had learned a lot about mining in Mali for her fictitious school project. Adama had been impressed with everything he'd seen, particularly Monique Tardif's commitment to community development. He already knew that Tardif had done more on this front than any other foreign-owned company in all of Mali. But he was pleased to have seen first-hand what it had done for the people of Kéniéba. I hoped that what remained of the day, and the evening that followed, would be just as successful. It was nearly time.

During the dinner, I noticed a big flatbed truck making its way up the driveway towards the main building. I couldn't tell what was loaded on the truck because it was concealed beneath a dark-green tarpaulin. After the driver parked in front, one of the crew pulled off the tarp to reveal a gigantic lion made out of what seemed to be scrap wood, and lots of it. I estimated it was about twenty feet long and eight feet high. In the cracks between the pieces of wood I could see what looked like straw. The flatbed then lifted upwards at one end to become a ramp. Four workers proceeded to drag the lion down the incline and onto the gravel. Next, the crew erected a makeshift wooden barrier that completely surrounded the lion, presumably to keep people a safe distance away. I still didn't understand . . . until I did.

We really needed a distraction to coincide with the departure of the presidential chopper. At that moment, we desperately needed everybody's eyes fixed on something, on anything, other than the helicopter. Our success depended on it. Monique came over when she saw what I'd been watching. She leaned down behind my chair, put her hands on my shoulders, and whispered in my ear.

"Voila, your distraction."

Monique was a miracle worker.

Despite being immersed in a high-stakes escape plan with many moving parts, it still somehow occurred to me that Monique's hands resting on my shoulders felt warm, and good. As with Coop, her initially icy demeanour seemed to be thawing.

It was after seven o'clock when the dinner ended, and it was time for Adama and his entourage to depart. The light had started to fade but it wouldn't be fully dark for nearly two hours. And that was partly why we needed a distraction.

At the end of the dinner, Adama rose, and everyone fell silent. I hoped he was not just going to the washroom. That might have been awkward. But no, he had something to say. He spoke in English and repeated his message in French.

"I would like to thank Monique Tardif and her team for such a wonderful day, not just for me, but for my daughter, Amina, who so seldom has the chance to travel with me. Though you tired her out. She's been nodding off at dinner and I'm sure will sleep on the flight back to Bamako," Adama said. "I'm grateful for the chance to spend time with you, and I wish you well as you strive to realize the full potential of this gold- and diamond-mining enterprise. I know that some of you may not appreciate the changes my government has made in some industries, including mining. I understand, and I can tell you that we are still learning. And it is days like today that help advance my own understanding of the situation here on the ground—or in this case, *in* the ground—and that can lead to better policies in the future. I look forward to coming back here.

"I also commend Tardif Resources for your enlightened approach to community investment. I was just as impressed with how you've transformed Kéniéba and the lives of its citizens as I was with your mining success. Thank you all again for your efforts, not just today, but tomorrow when the work begins again."

"Thank you, Mr. President," Monique said, as she rose to respond. "We would be pleased to have you and Amina back for a visit anytime. Thank you for coming. And now I invite everyone out onto the front driveway, where we'll witness a made-in-Mali spectacle created by Pyrotechnic Arts, a company based right here in Kéniéba. Please join us around the great wooden lion that now sits in front of the building. Of course, it is symbolic of the Mali lion. See you out there."

Amina had been sitting next to Coop. In fact, she'd been leaning heavily against her. She appeared to be very tired. But she roused herself now as we all moved towards the main door.

I was still back on the Mali lion. Mali lion? I'd never heard of such a thing. I was enlightened by a quick Google search on my phone. Yes, there is a Mali lion. Had I known, I might have been a bit more careful wandering around outside. Then I read a little more, only to learn that the Mali lion is found mainly in one region: yep, the Falémé River basin! I tried to put that out of my addled mind and focus on the job at hand.

When we stepped outside into the stifling heat of the early evening, I was happily surprised to see that a crowd of community members had shown up for the spectacle. Many of the volunteers and staff from the Tardif-funded community agencies were there, as well as dozens of the local mine workers and their families. The more people crowding the site, the better.

Adama and Amina waved to the assembled throng before turning and joining Coop and me for the long walk to the chopper, the four ever-present PPPF guards walking behind us. We had carefully mapped out the split-second timing of this part of the operation. The start of the chopper's engines and the turning of the main rotor were the triggering events. The pilot was already ensconced in the cockpit, ready to go. Three of the guards climbed aboard the helicopter and took their seats in the forward compartment. We said goodbye to Adama and Amina. Then they boarded, while the fourth guard waited outside the president's cabin. Coop slipped away and I stood back a dozen paces or so to watch.

While I was not on board the president's helicopter at that moment, I knew exactly what was unfolding within. I could picture Adama tucking Amina into the small bed—really, it was more of a camp cot—inside the president's private cabin. I counted off the timing as I stood there. In my mind's eye, I could see him reaching down and unlatching the emergency exit hatch, before hugging Amina and whispering words to give her strength for what was to come. Then, I watched Adama step back out of the chopper, as the fourth guard closed the main door behind him. Adama and the guard joined the others in the forward compartment and secured the front door.

I knew what Adama would do next. He would bang twice on the cockpit wall behind him to signal they were ready for takeoff.

I think I actually heard the wall-banging from where I stood. Or perhaps I just imagined it.

Right on cue, the engines started to turn over and rev up to speed. I looked over my shoulder to make sure that Monique, who was running the great wooden Mali lion distraction show, had heard the chopper starting up. She had. Immediately, she turned to two guys hovering near the lion and exchanged a few words. They both nodded and pulled something from their pockets.

Not yet. Not yet. Not yet.

Finally, the main rotor started to turn slowly. Showtime.

When I looked back again, the lion was already smoking. A few seconds later it was fully engulfed in flames. The crowd gasped, their eyes glued to the lion. I turned back to the chopper just in time to catch a glimpse of Coop huddled underneath the bird and swinging open the emergency exit hatch. A second later, Amina had slipped through and was crouching on the ground while Coop closed the hatch. They both stayed low and scrambled towards the rear of the helicopter, before darting to the right behind the school bus conveniently parked there. It was hard enough for me to see them, and I'd been standing close and watching for them. So, again, given my vast experience in covert intelligence missions, I was confident we'd pulled it off. We'd know soon enough. And if you're wondering whether opening the emergency escape hatch might have triggered a warning light on the chopper's instrument panel, well, wonder no more. Coop and I had already downloaded and read the manual for the helicopter and there was no such sophisticated warning-light system. After all, the helicopter was thirty-one years old.

I smiled at the pilot and waved. He nodded. With my left hand I gave him a thumbs-up, though it really wasn't for him; it was the all-safe sign for Adama, whose face I could see peering out a side window. The chopper lifted into the air. I watched it climb and turn towards Bamako, then walked back to watch the burning lion. As far as I could tell, not a soul was watching the chopper as soon as they torched the big cat.

CHAPTER 17

NOW THAT I was among the crowd near the incendiary sculpture, it really was quite the spectacle. The fire and the glowing wood gave the lion an eerie, swirling, orange outline. I didn't know how they had done it, but the lion held its form. I figured out their secret when the flames eventually died away. I had thought it was the wood that formed the shape of the Mali lion, but in fact, the wood was attached to a sculpted metal-pipe frame. The illuminated shape of the lion was formed by the metal piping heating up and glowing orange. Anyway, it had been an extraordinarily effective distraction. Even I'd been distracted.

I felt Coop sidle up beside me as the festivities died down.

"All good?" I asked, looking straight ahead.

"All good."

"Man, it is hot."

"Yes, it is. Though I'm not sure standing so close to a giant flaming bonfire of a lion helps much."

Within twenty minutes, most of the community guests had left for home. With the president no longer on-site, and the lion fully combusted, there was little to keep them there. The pipe frame of the lion had cooled and been reloaded onto the truck so it could be covered with wood and straw and ignited all over again at some future event.

Then the bus driver pulled his vehicle around and stopped as close to the building as he could without rumbling over the risers the choir had sung from earlier. It was time to go. I fetched the chilled bottled water from the fridge and loaded it onto the front seat of the bus, across the aisle from where the guard typically sat. At Monique's urging, her team piled on board, ready for some downtime back at the compound. I counted fourteen expat Canadians as they filed past me and down the aisle like it was just another end-of-shift bus ride. And as far as they were concerned, that was exactly what it was. Then the armed guard boarded and took his regular seat just behind the driver.

"It's stinking hot in here," someone shouted from the back.

The bus driver yelled from the front as he fiddled with the AC controls.

"La climatisation est en panne!"

A collective groan rolled up to the front.

Monique stepped briefly onto the bus to tell the guard in French that she'd radio the compound and let them know we were on our way. The guard just nodded. One thing off his list.

Coop and I casually waved to Monique through the window as the driver closed the door and we started down the driveway. She waved back, Pierre at her side. Then she reached for the radio she'd brought from her office. I could see her talking into it to buy us some much-needed time.

I waited until we'd left the mine site and were driving on a relatively quiet two-lane road before I broke out the cold water. The guard across the aisle from me reached for a bottle.

"Allow me," I said. I pulled out two bottles and opened them. I first handed one to the guard, who wasted no time in draining it completely. I waited another minute before handing the second bottle to the driver. He too guzzled the full bottle. The two plastic caps I still cradled in my hand each had a little black dot on them. Coop asked one of the guys on the Tardif team to distribute the rest of the water to the others on the bus. Then she grabbed one of the bottles and casually walked to the back of the bus, where, for some reason, she opened the last overhead luggage compartment, rooted around a little, and then closed it again. I noticed she was no longer carrying the water bottle when she returned to her seat across from the guard.

As planned, the guard exhibited the telltale signs first, right on schedule. His eyelids fell to half-mast. Then his head fell forward, before he snapped it back and opened his eyes with a look of alarm. He glanced around as he realized something was not right. The second time his eyes closed and his head fell forward, his body followed, as if he were performing a vaudeville pratfall. Coop caught him and gently reclined him on his seat before disarming him. He was out cold and would be for quite some time.

While Coop had been dealing with the guard, I'd been focused on the driver. I wondered if we'd overplayed our hand drugging the driver of a moving bus, or, more to the point, *our* moving bus. I stood up beside him, close. He was starting to drift across the road's white centre line as his eyelids drooped.

"Hey, watch the road!" I shouted.

He woke up and brought the bus back into the right lane, but he was losing it fast. Two or three seconds later, he fell forward onto the steering wheel, unconscious. I was ready, but really, how ready can you ever be to take control of a moving bus when the driver has just passed out? I'd practised it in my mind and in my darkened room many, many times. But this was no rehearsal.

I grabbed the wheel with my right hand and kept the bus going semi-straight. With my left hand, I pulled on the driver's pant leg to lift his foot from the accelerator, and, as you might expect, the bus slowed down. Then, as planned, Coop grabbed him around his torso and managed to drag him from behind the wheel. Somehow, she muscled him onto the two seats across the aisle from the guard, who, of course, was still out cold. By this time, I'd slid into the driver's seat and accelerated back to the speed of traffic before the cars around us suspected anything was amiss. I assumed that was going to be the most hair-raising moment of our escape. Yeah, right.

While Coop was securing the ankles and wrists of both the guard and driver with heavy-duty zip-ties, the fourteen Tardif mining execs had fallen silent. Earlier that morning, before they'd driven to the mine site, Monique had told them in small groups that whatever happened that day, they were to do exactly what Coop and I told them to do, that we were there to help them. She refused to give them any more than that.

With everything secured up front, Coop rushed to the back of the bus, reached up, and opened the last overhead compartment. Amina stretched out her arms and Coop gently lifted her down to the seat below, as several freezer packs and empty water bottles tumbled down in her wake. But Amina wasn't quite ready to let go of Coop. The hug carried on for another few seconds. I was still driving but had caught the scene in my rear-view mirror. As soon as Amina emerged from the overhead compartment, the Tardif team freaked out a bit. It caused a bit of a ruckus.

"Calm down, everyone!" I shouted. "All will be made clear shortly. Just give us a moment, please."

Soon thereafter, Coop and Amina, still holding hands, moved up to a row of seats near the front of the bus. Amina sat down and finally let go of Coop's hand, but I don't think she wanted to. Coop handed her two more bottles of cold water and a towel to deal with the perspiration running down her cheeks. I can only imagine how hot it was up there in the overhead compartment.

"Okay, listen up, Team Tardif," Coop started as she faced fourteen confused faces. "Just to get this out in the open right from the start, I'm Lauren Cooper, but I'm not really a research assistant to a famous thriller writer. As to my true occupation, I'll let you draw your own conclusions, but let's just say I'm employed by the Government of Canada."

There were some rumblings from the expats, but I suppose that was to be expected.

"However," Coop continued, "this really is James Norval, who is in fact a famous thriller writer. We came here to get you out of Mali and back to your families. We'll soon be crossing the Falémé River on foot into Senegal, where a Canadian field team is expecting us. You're going home."

That's when the spell was broken, and the Tardif Fourteen broke into applause.

"What about Monique?" someone asked. "Is she meeting us there?"

"We really wanted Monique to come with us and we tried hard to convince her, but she declined. She wants to continue her work at the mine and, just as importantly, her work with the community. She's a very compassionate person, even if that's not always obvious," Coop said. "We think she'll be safe because she's the only one left who can effectively lead the mining operations."

"If I'd known this was happening," a young woman said, "I would have brought my guitar and my passport."

"Yes, well, that's exactly why we didn't tell you," Coop replied. "That may well have tipped our hand. It was safest to leave all your possessions back at the compound, as if it were just another normal day at the office."

Just then, we came upon a section of the road with a wider shoulder. I took advantage to pull over and turn off the ignition. Then I slipped down onto the floor by the steering column. Other than a memorable moment in a particularly demanding game of Twister that I'll say nothing more about, it may have been the most uncomfortably contorted position my body had ever assumed. Yet it only took me about ten seconds to reinstall the air conditioning fuse that Monique had slipped me. I replaced the black plastic cover on the fuse box and managed to return to my normal upright position, and we were back on the road inside of four minutes with the AC blasting. A few minutes later, another round of applause from the expats confirmed the cool air was moving again.

"I nearly forgot," Coop said. "There's something I need to do."

I watched in the rear-view mirror as she grabbed the mobile phones of the guard and driver, removed their SIM cards, and threw all of it out the window into the bush along the road. I remembered that Kiran had told us that mobile phones could be tracked as a crude but effective way of monitoring the bus's progress. Done.

"Okay, but there's more," Coop continued, addressing the Tardif Fourteen. "Yes, your eyes are not deceiving you. We have the president's daughter on board, and she'll be getting out with all of us."

"What, you've kidnapped her?" someone asked.

"No, of course not. We're bringing her with us at the president's request. I'm not at liberty to explain why, but rest assured, we are the good guys in this situation and are acting with the president's support. That's really all I can say, and all you need to know, right now. You'll all be debriefed in Ottawa."

I heard some low-level murmuring from the expats, but all in all, they took the news well. So Coop carried on.

"We'll be at the Falémé River and the site of our crossing soon. We're going to try to get this all done with some light left in the sky. So, try to relax and gather yourselves. I am in charge.

You need to do what I say, when I say. That's our best chance of getting everybody out and home safely."

"But if we don't arrive at the compound in about fifteen minutes," a woman observed, "they'll know something is wrong."

"Not true," Coop replied. "You can thank Monique again, because she radioed the security station at the compound just as we were leaving and told them that we'd been delayed because the president's visit ran long. So, Monique gave us enough breathing room to get you all across the river before anyone knows we're gone. You can thank Monique for a great deal. Without her and what she's done, we would have had no chance of pulling this off."

By then, we were on the RN2, just heading into Kofeba. As we had a few days earlier, I managed to find my way through the outskirts of the town, then turned right onto the dirt track that ran straight to the river. We were on schedule. As before, there seemed not to be a living soul around. Armed with recently acquired information, and the knowledge we were about to traverse the Falémé River, I was no longer concerned about encountering people, be they friend or foe. No, I was worried about the possibility of coming face to face with a Mali lion.

With only about twenty-five minutes to go before reaching the river, I suddenly realized that I felt different, more alive, buzzing. We'd been in Mali for a number of days by then, yet up until that moment, when I could almost see the river ahead, I hadn't really felt like I was engaged in a potentially dangerous clandestine operation to exfiltrate fourteen Canadians and a presidential daughter from an unstable nation. I'd been staying at a palace, collaborating with the new president, touring a gold mine, inspecting raw diamonds, and getting my steps in walking an awful lot through the palace's lush gardens. I had never once felt in danger or threatened, not even when Demba's suspicions occasionally flared. So far, my time in Mali had not even approached the peril of my situation in that Tajik interrogation cell a week before. But now that we'd knocked out the driver and guard and were approaching our crossing from one country to another, from detention to freedom, I was finally feeling the pressure of the moment. That pressure manifested as excitement, and a curious lightheadedness.

It took me back more than thirty years, to when I'd had my heart and my head set on making intelligence work my career. Well, as you know, for reasons I still didn't understand, it never happened. And you also know that it had haunted me ever since. I certainly could not complain about my Plan B. I had enjoyed writing novels and all the rewards that came with it. But deep down, that failure three decades previous had left a hole inside me that even my unexpected international success as a writer could never quite fill. Yet in that moment, just minutes away from the Falémé River, I sensed that liberating fourteen Canadians unjustly detained in a distant nation, might just be a start.

I felt Coop standing beside me.

"How much farther?" she asked.

I just pointed towards the windshield. She looked up and in the fading light we both saw the banks of the Falémé—and, just beyond, Senegal.

I pulled to within about fifty yards of the river and turned off the ignition. The sound of the engine died away and was replaced by the unwelcome roar of rushing water.

"Uh-oh. That's not good," I said, as I slid out of the driver's seat. I pulled the lever to open the doors and stepped out.

"Please, everyone, stay on the bus while we check out the crossing," Coop said, before following me down the steps and out the door.

We trotted down to the riverbank. The closer we got, the bigger our problem became. Those unexpectedly heavy rains in Guinea had done a number on our escape route. When we reached the water's edge, we could barely hear one another. Just a few days earlier when we'd been there reconnoitering, we could easily have waded across. It would have been a walk in the park with wet feet. But now, less than a week later, it sounded like we were standing next to Niagara Falls. The water looked thigh-deep at either bank, and at least up to my waist in the middle. But the depth was not really the issue. It was the volume and speed of the water. And man, it was rushing fast. I'd never actually tried one of those touristy whitewater rafting experiences, but this set of rapids looked too treacherous for even the most relaxed liability insurance company to sanction.

Holding on to Coop, I took a step into the water, then another. The pressure on my legs was strong, and the heavy current created little whirlpools on the downstream sides of my thighs. It was a violent maelstrom. There'd be no wading across this river.

Coop hauled me out. While the sun was on its way down, it was still bright enough to see the far side of the bank. That was when we saw the flash of light from the shoreline directly across from us. I'd been so consumed with the problem of the raging river that I'd nearly forgotten about our CSIS field team across the churn in Senegal. We watched as the expected pattern of light flashes repeated. In response, Coop pulled the flashlight from her pocket and returned fire, as it were, with our designated response.

With our respective identities confirmed, we watched as a figure stepped out of the trees and waved. We were already out in the open, and Coop waved back.

"That's Steve. A positive ID. He's CSIS," Coop said, smiling as she waved. "We're good to go."

"Well, I'm not sure we're good to go anywhere except perhaps the stockade in Bamako, because we're not making it across this river."

"You didn't think it was all going to be smooth sailing, did you?" she asked. "Every op I've ever done has gone off the rails at some point. Welcome to our derailment."

We watched as Steve scrambled down to the shore, where he tried to throw us what looked like a big white plastic bottle on a long rope. He swung the bottle around his head faster and faster—not unlike the technique used in the Olympic hammer throw event—before releasing it to soar up into the air and out over the raging river. You could tell that the bottle was weighted with something, probably stones or sand or both. He tried it four or five times. It always landed a good twenty-five feet short of us and was washed downriver until Steve hauled it back in to shore.

He took a few tentative steps further into the river, struggling against the whitewater, and hurled the bottle yet again without it landing close enough for us to retrieve it. Finally, with Coop holding onto my outstretched arm, I waded out as far as I could, and Steve tried one more time, confirming what I already knew. I was twenty feet or so away from where the weighted plastic bottle landed. I was nowhere near close enough. Without the rope, we simply could not cross. Frankly, I wasn't convinced we could make it even with the rope.

"Well, what now?" I asked.

"Well, the by-the-book response would be to abort," Coop replied.

"Abort? And just load up the bus again and drive them all back to the compound? Apologize for drugging the driver and guard and promise not to do it again? We'd be checking out of the palace and into a Bamako prison for a very long, and not so luxurious, stay."

"Now who's minoring in sarcasm?" Coop asked. "Why don't we follow the river for a bit, in either direction, and hope we find another crossing point?"

"Coop, you remember the sat photos and why we chose this precise location in the first place. This is the narrowest point on the Falémé for ten miles."

"I know, okay! I know," she snapped.

"Maybe we get back on the bus and try to run one of the border crossings. If the security barrier is not too hefty, a speeding school bus should make short work of it," I suggested.

"Except they'd shoot out the tires, or, worse, strafe the bus before we'd make it to the other side. The bus is heavy, but its walls are thin and flimsy. There'd be body bags. So, no."

I looked at our heavy school bus and then at the rushing river, then back at the bus again.

Coop started to say something to me, but I had stopped listening. I had an idea. I walked along the bank about thirty feet to our right, where the river's edge was a pebbly beach. Again, I looked back at the bus. Where we stood, the river was only ninety feet wide. Yes, I had an idea. I know I should have discussed it with Coop—that's what a colleague would normally do—but I also knew my idea would work. I just knew, and we were running out of light and time. We couldn't spare a moment to debate it. It was our only option. I hurried back to the bus and climbed aboard.

"Okay, everyone, please step off the bus and gather next to the tree right over there," I said, pointing. "Just stay there, keep your voices down, and don't move. We're trying to reduce our visibility. Okay, let's go. Oh, and take our two sleeping friends with you."

Two of the bigger guys dragged the driver and guard off the bus and gently laid them on the ground beneath the tree, while I slipped into the driver's seat. I waited until the Tardif Fourteen and Amina were gathered in front of the tree. Coop arrived and stuck her head in the door.

"What the hell, James!" she said. "What's going on?"

"Please, Coop, just trust me," I pleaded, and pointed towards the river, dead ahead. "It's our only option, and I think it might even work."

She looked out the windshield to the raging Falémé as understanding dawned. She nodded slowly, coming to grips with what I was about to do.

"Amina looks like she needs you. Make sure she's okay. I'll be fine. We both know this is our only way across. Go. Go!"

I feared she might refuse. Why would she leave me at the wheel of a school bus on the shores of a rushing river? But then she did. For some reason she did. Without another word, she stepped off the bus and walked over to stand with Amina. Coop knew what I had planned. She had to. I mean, it wasn't rocket science. Or perhaps she was just so impressed with how I'd conducted myself since arriving in Mali that she fully trusted my judgment in such matters. Okay, that seems like a stretch. Let's just go with the former.

I started the bus, shifted into Drive, inched forward so I could straighten the wheels, and then dropped the hammer. I stepped on the gas and accelerated directly towards the pebbly beach and the whitewater beyond. And I didn't stop. I was probably only up to twenty-five miles per hour or so when I hit the beach, but a school bus is a heavy beast, and the momentum it mustered was impressive. I plowed into the water, sending spray high into the air, but kept my foot heavy on the pedal.

CHAPTER 18

I GAUGED my stopping distance pretty well and lifted from the accelerator only when I felt the rear wheels hit the water. By the time I was on the brakes and had brought the big orange bus to a stop, I figured I'd positioned us in just about the perfect spot—you know, in the middle of a rushing river. I threw the gearshift into Park, yanked on the emergency brake, and leapt from my seat.

Sure, the bus was heavy, but it was now parked broadside to the current and taking a pounding from the full force of the whitewater. The whole bus was shaking, but it wasn't going anywhere—at least not yet. I grabbed the shorter of the two coils of rope we'd stashed in the first overhead compartment and dashed to the rear of the bus. I threw open the emergency exit door at the very back and found Coop standing at the water's edge, gesturing for me to speed up.

"Come on with the rope! Let's go!" she shouted above the torrent's roar.

She understood.

The back door of the bus was only about fifteen feet from the shore.

I tied one end of the rope to the solid grab bar on the final row of seats. Then I gathered the rest of the coil and threw it to Coop. She caught it on the third attempt, largely because I missed her completely with my first two tries. I had to shout so that she could hear me over the rushing water.

"Okay, Coop, secure your end tightly around that first big tree, there. Tie it at about waist height, but it has to be as taut as you can make it."

She hustled over to the tree and tied off the cord. Following my kamikaze school bus gambit, the others had moved down to the shore and gathered around Coop. The guard and driver were still out cold and hadn't moved since being dragged off the bus.

So, we now had a tight and taut line running from a big tree on the shore right into the school bus. I stood at the open back door and shouted out the instructions.

"All right, we need as much weight on the bus as possible to keep it from being swept down the river. And we need that weight now. So, one at a time, heaviest people first, hold on to the rope and wade out to the bus. Coop will help you. I'll haul you up when you get here. When you make it on board, go directly to the front of the bus, where the force of the water is greatest and where we really need the weight. Okay, go!"

Coop took two steps into the river and anchored her feet as

best she could. Then, one by one, the Tardif Fourteen waded through the rushing water, holding on tightly to the rope, and clambered into the bus with my help. No one lost their footing. They filled up the front of the bus, and I could feel us become more stable as the additional weight pushed us into the sand of the riverbed. Coop then put Amina on her back and headed my way. A few seconds later, I pulled them both into the bus. Phase one was complete.

I was still figuring out phase two as I moved to the front of the bus. I needed to get out onto the front hood, but I couldn't open the front doors because of the water pressure holding them closed. And also because if I did somehow pry them open, the entire bus might well fill up with water. As you might imagine, filling up the bus with water just didn't seem like the outcome we wanted at that particular moment. I knew the water would eventually find its way inside—a school bus is not built to be watertight—but I hoped we still had some time.

So, I seized the only option left to me. I crawled out the driver's-side window and managed to clamber onto the hood. CSIS Steve, as I took to calling him, on the Senegal side of the river seemed to understand my idea. He immediately resumed his attempts to hurl the heavy plastic bottle out to the bus. On his first try, the bottle bounced off the hood and into the river. I just wasn't quite close enough to reach it, so I moved further forward onto the hood, where I clung to one of the side mirrors mounted on the front fenders. I caught his second throw. Well, "caught" is a slight embellishment. The plastic bottle kind of landed on my chest—knocking the wind out of me—but I somehow managed to grab it before it bounced into the water. That hurt, and I couldn't breathe for a few seconds.

With the bus parked halfway across the river, we had plenty of rope to spare. I untied the bottle and looped the rope through the side-mirror mounting struts on both front fenders, to more evenly distribute the tension that would soon be borne by the rope. Finally, I tied it in a big granny knot to the left front side-mirror mounting strut. By this stage, Coop was hanging out the driver's window shouting encouragement. I assumed she'd also grasped the idea by then.

The newly secured fixed line was tight, but it would still be hard to hold on to and make it across, hand over hand, to the Senegal side of the river some fifty feet away through rushing water. But it was the only way, our only hope.

"Okay, Coop," I shouted. "Send up the strongest guy and let's get him across."

"Wait," she replied, eyeing the weighted plastic bottle I'd set down beside me on the hood. "We need some help." Then she disappeared into the bus.

I know she wasn't gone long, but when you're standing on the front of a bus as it vibrates beneath your feet with the force of rushing water slamming into it, time passes very slowly. When I looked up again, Coop was crawling out the driver's window to join me, shouldering that second coil of rope from the front overhead compartment.

"You know how the royal family never flies together on the same plane?" I said.

"Yeah," she grunted as I helped her to her feet. We were now both standing on the hood of the shimmying school bus.

"Well, I'm not sure it's a good idea for both of us to be in this less-than-secure location together."

"Save it," she said, cutting me off. "I have an idea. The water is running fast, and I think it's getting faster. It's going to be really hard for some of these people to make it across safely. We need some pulling power from the other side."

She reached into her pocket and pulled out a robust-looking carabiner that I'd earlier seen attached to the bus driver's backpack. It's funny what you think of in such high-stress moments. The first thought that popped into my head was that we were stealing his carabiner. I got over it, fast. Clearly, I'd forgotten the more serious sin of drugging him into dreamland.

"This is a really long rope, at least twice as long as the distance to shore," Coop said. "Why don't we throw this line over to Steve, tie the carabiner to it right here in the middle of the length of rope, and then clip it to our fixed line? Then we'll also clip the carabiner to the person crossing. That way, Steve and his team can pull from their end while we pay out the rope at our end. When they make it across, we'll just haul the carabiner back along the fixed line and do it all over again with the next person."

It took me a minute to follow what she was saying, but then it landed.

"Brilliant, Coop. That's just what we needed," I said. "I never believed what everyone said about you. You're okay."

For something completely different, she rolled her eyes, yet again, big time.

I was glad I hadn't tossed the weighted plastic bottle into the river when it seemed we wouldn't need it again. I grabbed it from where it still sat, in that space where the windshield met the hood, and tied it to the end of the long rope. Coop started waving to get Steve's attention and finally called over to him. He came down to the river's edge and I started swinging the bottle around my head as if trying to helicopter myself off the bus. Then I let go. The bottle sailed an impressive distance—easily long enough to make it across—but unfortunately, I'd hurled it straight downstream and nowhere near the opposite shore, let alone to where Steve stood waiting. I also stumbled in the effort and nearly rolled off the hood into the Falémé. Luckily, Coop grabbed me just as I was headed out over the front bumper.

"Thanks," I croaked, hiding how frightening my near-fall into the river had been. "Clearly I need to work on my release point."

"Well, working on your release point is a good start."

Nice.

My next two throws showed steady improvement, stabilized as I was by a crouching Coop, who held on to my belt from behind. My fourth throw landed close enough for Steve to wade into the river a few steps and snare it. He held his end while we tied on the carabiner at the right spot and clipped it onto the fixed line already connecting the bus to the Senegalese shore. And we still had plenty of rope coiled at our feet.

"Okay, *now* let's get our strongest guy up here and get him across," I said.

And off we went. Two minutes later Coop was back with a tall and muscular mining engineer named Lucien. Coop had briefed him, and he was keen to blaze the trail for us. We cut a short length of rope from our end—we had plenty to spare—and used it to fashion a harness of sorts, which we looped around Lucien's arms and legs. Then we clipped the carabiner—already linked to our fixed line—to Lucien's rope harness.

"Ready?" I asked.

Lucien just nodded and sat down on the front right fender of the bus. Coop and I grabbed him under his arms and slowly eased him into the maelstrom. Water splashed up onto us as his shoes disappeared under the roiling water. A few seconds later, his feet hit terra firma. The water was up to his mid-thigh and pressing him against the bus. He grasped the fixed line with both hands and started to move his feet, shuffling across the river. Coop signalled to Steve, who started pulling on the rope. Lucien slowly, hand over hand, step by step, made his way across, aided by Steve, who pulled from the Senegalese shore. At the river's deepest point, the water pushed Lucien's feet out from under him and his kicking legs rose to the surface. But he maintained his grip on the fixed line and kept hand-over-handing it, as Steve, hauling on the line, kept the big mining engineer moving in the right direction. Lucien's feet eventually found the riverbed again, and Steve was soon able to grab him and pull him ashore.

Coop and I high-fived, but gently so that neither of us tumbled into the river. I confess, the feeling of elation at that moment was simply indescribable—so, um, I guess I'll not try to describe it. One down, sixteen to go. The others had been watching Lucien's technique and progress out the side windows of the bus, and they clapped long and loud when he collapsed on the opposite shore—in Senegal, not to put too fine a point on it.

I hauled back the carabiner and makeshift rope harness, and we were ready for the second transit. There was a little light still lingering in the sky, but we had to move quickly if we hoped to get the rest of the team across while we had some visibility. Coop was helping them out the window and up onto the hood one by one. The next four—two men and two women—made it across with much the same experience as Lucien's.

I worried when the first woman to go lost her footing a little earlier than Lucien had. But being harnessed to the carabiner and to the fixed line worked well. It took all of her weight, and Steve just kept pulling her across until her feet again touched solid earth. We shouted encouragement and instructions all the way across and that seemed to help.

As more and more of the Tardif Fourteen left our front-hood departure gate on schedule for their crossing to Senegal, the bus, relieved of their weight, became less and less stable. It was rocking more violently, and the much lighter back end was starting to slip downstream in small but growing increments. We were not just running out of light; we were running out of time.

We continued sending team members one by one, as quickly as we could, until two very lean and light women, numbers thirteen and fourteen, stood with us on the hood. Suddenly, the tail of the bus lurched downstream a good five feet, nearly throwing us all into the river. We hung on to each other and to any other handholds we could find, and somehow managed to stay on the front of the bus. Fortunately, the weight of the engine and the people standing on the hood kept the front end from moving. But we were on borrowed time. So, we decided to send the two young women together, in one go, to enhance our efficiency. Combined, they still weighed less than Lucien, so we figured it would work. Harnessed together, they clung to each other and gamely worked their hands and feet. With Lucien joining Steve on pulling duty, the two women were soon safely on the opposite shore.

"You're taking Amina next," I said to Coop, as I again pulled on the rope to bring the carabiner back to us. "No arguments."

She nodded and helped Amina out onto the hood. I worked the harness around them both and clipped them to the fixed line. Amina was facing Coop with her arms and legs wrapped around her, hanging on with everything she had. Coop alone would be gripping the fixed line. They slid slowly off the fender and into the churning water. Amina kept her eyes closed and Coop kept up a running, comforting commentary as she moved hand over hand along the line. Even when the roar of the water drowned her out, I could still see Coop's lips moving and Amina nodding.

Lucien and Steve did their part. I watched as Amina's eyes and mouth opened wide when they reached the deeper section of the river and Coop's feet lost touch with the riverbed. But soon, just like everyone else, she recovered her footing, Amina regained her stoic composure, and strong-like-ox Lucien pulled them both onto dry land.

As I pulled the carabiner back along the fixed line for the last time, even the front end of the bus was now shifting downstream, straining the line and putting pressure on the steel side-mirror mounting struts. Uh-oh. The right front metal strut started to bend under the strain. That was not good. I rushed to slip into the makeshift rope harness and pulled it tight. Then I clipped onto the carabiner. That's when the bus suddenly jerked downstream another foot, putting even more tension on the fixed line. Too much tension. With a crack that sounded like a gunshot, the right-hand mirror and mounting strut broke free from the fender and shot across the hood at terrifying speed. Luckily, their progress was slowed by—well, by my left wrist. The dull thud of metal on skin, muscle, and bone was a little unnerving.

After the strut hit me, it carried on, dragged by the rope, to jam against its matching counterpart still fixed on the left-hand front fender. That's when I noticed that the lines of my left forearm were no longer exactly straight. There was a small kink in the middle. That's also when I noticed the excruciating pain. It wasn't really the new angle of my wrist that told me it was broken. It was the pain. Oh, the pain. On the positive side of the ledger—and believe me, I was checking that column often—I was amazed to find myself still on the hood, though sprawled on my back. It was a miracle the blow hadn't snapped the fixed line and taken me clear into the water. But back to the negative column: the bus was on the move again.

Everything slowed down then. I know that's almost a cliché, but it's truly what happened. The weight of an entire school bus, along with the force of tens of thousands of gallons of whitewater pushing against it, was then borne only by our fixed line and the one remaining side-mirror metal mounting strut. And that lone strut was failing, slowly . . . and then not so slowly. I could see it folding in on itself. I knew it would let go soon, and that simplified matters for me in a way. It meant I would not be walking through the rushing water, holding on to the fixed line, and then be pulled ashore by Lucien and Steve, like those who had gone before me. We had run out of time. More to the point, I had run out of time.

Through the last of the light, I could just barely see Coop standing on the shore, with both hands covering her mouth. I motioned to her with my good arm—pointing to me and then down into the river—to indicate what I was planning. She shook her head and mouthed *no*. But there really was no other option. She eventually saw the inevitability of it and nodded. I just hoped they knew what to do when it all went down—and when I went down.

As tightly as I could, I grabbed onto the taut fixed line with my right hand. Then I put my left foot on the remaining metal strut to stabilize myself so I could kick it with my right foot with every ounce of strength I had left—and by that stage, I really only had ounces left. I was pretty well spent. It took five kicks before the side mirror finally gave way and ripped off the fender. Therefore, I, too, was ripped off the fender, and slingshotted into the river. I wondered if my mind was playing tricks on me, but I could have sworn that I heard gunshots over the river's din, just before I disappeared beneath the surface.

I'd somehow managed to keep both my feet pressed against the newly liberated metal mirror strut, helping to support my weight so I wasn't just holding on with one good hand. I never would have made it otherwise. As I sank down into the water, I could only hope that Coop and those on the Senegal side did their job. And eventually they did. By then, I was under the water, the torrent tossing me around. A few seconds later I suddenly felt more tension, not just in the taut line I was holding but in the second rope to which I was harnessed. Yes, yes, I could feel it. They were hauling me in to shore against the raging river. The only question was, could I hold my breath long enough to make it back to the surface, let alone to land?

When my lungs felt like they were just about ready to give out, my feet brushed the ground beneath me. Then my butt made contact. A second or two later, I felt hands grip my right arm as they hauled me up to break the surface. I sucked in two lungs' worth of air in one desperate and needy inhalation. Then some other helpful soul grabbed my left arm and yanked. So I expelled that fresh air in one anguished yelp, surely heard over the water's roar by any living being within a quarter-mile radius. He or she meant well, and I assume had no idea my left wrist was broken. I never did find out who it was. Probably for the best.

Less than a minute later, I was still hyperventilating, writhing in pain, but safely concealed in the brush up the bank and away from the river. And then I knew my mind was not deceiving me. There were definitely gunshots coming from the Mali side of the river. Every time a shot rang out, I heard shrieks from a few terrified Tardif escapees. I heard soothing but authoritative voices calming them down and keeping everybody flat on the ground. We were assured that, given the near darkness and our cover in the trees, we weren't in any danger. Still, for some reason, bullets whizzing over your head can be somewhat disconcerting. Who knew? Our Senegal field team gamely returned fire, just to ensure our pursuers stayed on Mali's side of the water. Whoever they were, they gave up after about five minutes and the shooting ceased. Oh, and I was told later that the school bus tumbled a further two hundred yards down the Falémé, where it finally stopped, jammed upside-down against some boulders in the middle of the river.

In the midst of it all, someone gave me four or five painkillers, which I gratefully swallowed. Whatever they were, they actually helped, and in short order I was feeling quite relaxed—not exactly high, but heading towards giddy. I made a mental note to ask for more of those.

I was still resting in the bush when Coop and Amina approached and sat down beside me. Amina gave me a gentle hug, mindful of my broken arm. I knew she was worried about her father, but she was brave. Coop knelt down next to where I lay on my back, still holding my wrist. She confirmed that all of us were safe, present, and accounted for. The Tardif Fourteen, plus the three of us, had made it. My left wrist seemed to be the only casualty.

"Well, Norval, you put on quite a show in the last hour or so," Coop said, as she laid her hand on my shoulder and gave it a little squeeze.

"Well, sorry I went all Hunter Chase on you, but I just couldn't see any other way across," I said.

"There was no other way. As Hollywood as it was, it was our only option," she conceded. "Nice job."

"But the plan would never have worked without your carabiner innovation. That's what really got Team Tardif to Senegal."

"All right, enough with congratulating each other," she said. "Save it for the debrief."

We fell silent for a short time. Then Coop looked at my arm.

"Oh, and sorry about your wrist," she said, changing the subject. "At least you're not left-handed. You can still write."

"I'll survive," I said. "So, who was shooting at us?"

"Who knows? Maybe they tried to call the guard on the bus and couldn't reach him. Then perhaps they tried the bus driver's phone and couldn't reach him, either. That might be when they raised the alarm."

"Right, that makes sense. But how did they know to look for us right here at this particular spot?" I asked.

"They could have been tracking the guards' phones for the first part of our journey, before I chucked them out the window."

"Well, that would only lead them to the location where you popped out the SIM cards, and that was miles from here. I don't get it."

"We may never find out, but the point is we made it across. We made it. But we need to focus on more pressing matters," Coop said, holding up a mobile phone. "You have some content to post. Remember?"

"Right! Whose phone is that?" I asked.

"Steve's, and before you ask, yes, it's secure and his Current Location function is always switched off. Secret activities wouldn't be secret for long if it were turned on. So, you're clear to post."

Coop held the phone for me so I could use my one good hand to navigate to my website. I grabbed the image I needed, then signed into my Facebook account. I then posted the cover art for my novel *Safe*, noting that it had been published exactly ten years earlier. It was the sort of innocuous anniversary post I regularly sent out to my three and a half million followers, to give them what my publicist called "semi-personal contact with their favourite writer." I'd been told it also helped sustain a high social profile, which in turn helped sell books. Always a good thing. But this post in particular meant a lot more to Monique Tardif, who had been quietly monitoring my Facebook feed for the last hour or so. Adama wouldn't find out until shortly before he landed back in Bamako and just before his Oscar-worthy performance started. I knew they'd be relieved, but both of them still had an important day ahead of them, and critical roles to play if Operation Demba's Downfall was to succeed.

"Before you return that phone, can you dial Monique on her burner?" I asked. "It's time we told her about Amina."

Coop said nothing but started dialling. I guess she agreed. Then she handed me the phone.

"You should tell her," she said, smiling. "It was your idea that got her out."

The phone rang several times before Monique finally answered.

"Sorry, I was in my office, but now I'm outside," she said. "So, you made it out! You did it! I just saw your Facebook post on my laptop."

"Well, it had its moments, but yes, I'm calling from the banks of the Falémé, thankfully on the Senegal side. Yes, we made it. Everyone is safe. The plan worked, with a few minor adjustments we made on the fly. And your team was fantastic. They really stepped up."

"I'm not surprised."

"But I need to tell you something we couldn't mention to you before. You see, um, we brought Amina with us, at Adama's request. She's safe now and out of Demba's reach."

I didn't give her time to react, but quickly walked her through what would happen as soon as the presidential chopper landed back at the palace and it was discovered that Amina was not on board. I told her about the search likely to start the following morning and that we were still full steam ahead on the Demba part of the plan. She listened carefully.

"Brilliant. You've taken Demba's power away. Just brilliant."

"That was the idea," I replied. "Your office phone may ring quite soon with the news from Bamako that Amina is missing. So, Demba may instruct the on-site security team to look for her at the mine site even before the reinforcements arrive in the morning for a more systematic search."

"Understood."

"So be sure to act surprised if Demba calls about it in the next little while," I said. "And please be careful tomorrow. We'll be thinking of you the whole time. It's no exaggeration to say that it could be a new beginning for Mali if you can pull it off."

CHAPTER 19

WHEN WHOEVER had been taking shots at us from the Malian side of the river had packed up and gone home, we walked about half a mile along a trail until we hit a dusty gravel road. Someone had fashioned a makeshift sling to support my broken wrist. It certainly made walking easier and less painful. And when I say "less painful," I mean it still really hurt. A bus was parked on the side of the road between two—yes, you guessed it—Cadillac Escalades. An ambulance idled just a little farther up the road. I was impressed CSIS Steve had thought to bring an ambulance and pleased that he'd only brought one. He apparently had liked our plan and hadn't seen the need for any more.

The Tardif Fourteen boarded the bus, while Coop, Amina, and I climbed into the ambulance.

"You don't need to come in the ambulance," I said. "I'll be fine. Get on the bus. It'll be more comfortable."

"No thanks," Coop replied. "We started this thing together, and yadda yadda yadda. You know the rest."

I looked at Amina.

"I don't know what 'yadda yadda' means, but if she is going in the ambulance," she said, pointing to Coop, "I am going in the ambulance."

The drive was only long enough for the Senegalese paramedic to give my wrist a quick examination.

"You have broken your wrist," she said.

"Um, yes, I know," I replied. The medication I'd been given did reduce my pain somewhat, but its real strength was in making me prone to giggling. That should have been on the warning label: *Liable to induce sudden laughter at inappropriate moments.* I barely managed to contain myself.

"How did you break it?" she asked, as she continued to palpate my less-than-functional forearm.

"I was struck by a side-view mirror and its metal mounting frame that had broken loose from the front fender of a school bus."

"I see. That is very specific."

"Well, that is specifically what happened," I said, stifling another laugh.

"Yes, wrists are not meant to withstand such trauma," she said solemnly. "Please try not to put yourself in such a situation again."

That's when I burst out laughing. Coop gave me a stern look.

"Sorry, sorry," I backpedalled. "I don't know why I laughed—except for the drugs, I mean. But of course, you're right. I will do my best in the future to avoid metal objects flying towards my wrist at high speed."

"I'm going to splint it to immobilize the ulna and radius until a doctor can reset it," the paramedic explained. "I will apply the splinting material from the proximal palmar crease, wrapping around the elbow and extending to the dorsal metacarpophalangeal joint."

"Excellent, I was hoping that's how you would do it," I replied before cracking up again. I quickly reined myself back in. "Sorry, again. I know there's nothing funny about a broken wrist."

"Now, this may hurt a little."

She then proceeded to splint my wrist using the technique she'd so clearly and comprehensively described.

"Yeeeeooowwwwww!" I yelled. "Yes, I can confirm that I certainly felt that. In fact, I'd suggest changing your warning from 'this may hurt a little' to 'this will definitely hurt a lot.'"

Then I laughed again for some reason, as the waves of pain began to subside.

Soon thereafter, we pulled off the road and into a clearing of sorts next to a large gravel pad. Three choppers sat there, all sporting the gold, blue, and green crest of the Senegalese Air Force. Two were regular troop carriers, which the Tardif Fourteen boarded in two groups of seven. The third was a medevac helicopter. For obvious reasons, the ambulance pulled up in front of it.

My splinted arm, by then supported in a proper sling, was still painful, but I'd been given another dose of the laugh-inducing opiate and was back to my giggly self in no time. As Coop, Amina, and I stepped down from the ambulance, the other two choppers lifted off. I was helped into the medevac heli, where a doctor and a nurse sat me down and helped me secure my seat belt. Coop and Amina sat across from me. We could just as easily have flown with the others. Even though we were in for a long flight, I had a broken wrist, not a descending aortic aneurysm. (I'd researched that often-fatal cardiac event for one of my novels.) The doctor looked over my splint and gave it her seal of approval. That was the extent of her medical ministrations.

Coop and Amina played cards. So, I reclined my seat as far back as it would go and tried to sleep. The near-deafening noise of the engine and main rotor should have made it difficult, but Coop told me later that I was out like a light in less than five minutes.

I woke up as we were landing near Dakar, Senegal's capital. I would have liked to have seen the city, but we were nowhere near downtown. We landed at the air base at Ouakam, on Dakar's outskirts. Sitting on the tarmac at the far end of the base sat two Challenger jets with Royal Canadian Air Force markings. I brilliantly deduced that these were the aircraft that would take us home. They were a very welcome sight.

After we touched down, Coop and Amina joined the Tardif Fourteen in a reception room attached to one of the hangars, while I was escorted to the medical centre on the base. An RCAF physician was waiting for me.

"Mr. Norval, I'm Dr. Helen Redway with the RCAF, based in Ottawa," she greeted me, shaking my hand. "I don't know what you've been through, and I've been told not to ask, but I understand that congratulations are in order."

"Thank you, but I'm still not exactly sure what I've been through, either."

"Understood. But my job right now is to reduce your obvious wrist fracture so you can get back home."

"Thanks, Doctor," I replied. "And does that involve yanking my broken wrist in various directions until the bones are aligned properly? And if so, that sounds like it might be a tad unpleasant."

"Well, yes, after checking out the X-ray I'm about to take, I will likely need to manipulate the arm a little, but you shouldn't feel a thing. We'll be using local anaesthetic to numb the entire area."

And that's just what happened in the end. The X-ray revealed that the two major bones in my wrist were clearly and cleanly broken, but not wildly out of alignment. Dr. Redway administered the local anaesthetic, and we waited a bit until the numbness took hold of my arm. Then, I looked the other way while I felt her tugging and turning my wrist. But there was no pain. Within forty minutes, I walked out of the medical centre with a spiffy new navy-blue fibreglass cast on my left forearm. It actually felt quite comfortable, and I liked the secure, solid feeling it gave my wrist.

Two hours later, the Tardif Fourteen, along with Coop and Amina, had all received medical clearance to fly home. We split up into two groups—the Challengers only seated a maximum of twelve passengers—and boarded the two RCAF jets for the flight back to Ottawa. From there, various domestic flights and trains would deliver each of the Tardif Fourteen to their homes and families, but only after they'd been debriefed and told not to discuss how they got out of Mali. It was just past three in the morning when we finally took off from the air base at Ouakam. Seems an odd time, I know, but there was really no point in delaying our departure till later.

Coop, Amina, and I kind of kept to ourselves on the plane. It was standard operating procedure in CSIS, and in most intelligence agencies, for operatives to distance themselves from civilians in the field, particularly when an operation was over. So, Coop sat us at the back of the Challenger. But the four Tardif staff on our flight apparently were unaware of what I call the CSIS "post-mission aloof protocol." Over the course of the long flight, they all ventured back to where the three of us sat, to express their thanks. The exchanges were a little awkward, though well-meaning. They knew not to ask any questions, but made it clear they were grateful for our help in getting them out of Mali and home again. While some suspected, none of them knew for certain that this had been a CSIS operation. Of course, Monique knew, but we'd agreed not to share that with anyone else. As far as the fourteen were concerned—and, for that matter, Amina, too—we were friends who could be trusted.

Coop and Amina sat across the aisle from me and spent the first forty minutes of the flight talking and laughing until, eventually, Amina crashed. It had been a very long day, and it had all finally caught up with her. I sat on my own, head back, eyes closed, and tried to get used to having a cast on my arm. My wrist still hurt—as it was supposed to, only eight or so hours after a flying metal mounting bracket snapped it—but whatever pain relievers I'd been given were still doing their job reasonably well.

“So how was it?” Coop asked, knowing—eyes closed or not—that I was not asleep.

“How was what?”

“You know exactly what I mean, Mr. Norval. How was it?”

I sighed, opened my eyes, and turned to look at her.

“I guess I do know exactly what you mean,” I said. “It was . . . well, incredible, extraordinary, mind-blowing. And not mind-blowing because of what we did, what we made happen. Mind-blowing because of how it made me feel.”

She said nothing but nodded with the beginnings of a smile that I took to be of recognition, of understanding, of familiarity. (Yes, I really did get all of that from her nascent smile.)

“At the risk of sounding like a greeting-card sloganeer, it all just makes me feel so good, so fulfilled, so alive, so proud,” I continued. “Don’t get me wrong, writing a novel that hits number one feels great, too, but it’s not even in the same universe as the endorphins still coursing through me right now. Those people sitting up there are safe and going home because of something we did.”

“I know,” was all she said.

“It feels like the most important thing I’ve ever done, and probably will ever do. And strangely, it feels just as I thought it would when, nearly thirty years ago, I imagined one day being a part of a covert operation. But, you know, it also makes me sad, and I guess a little angry, that I couldn’t have been doing this kind of work for the last three decades. That I was denied my shot, without ever knowing why. I feel . . . robbed.”

"Yeah, but if you'd made it through back then, the world would have been deprived of Hunter Chase and his over-the-top, special-effects-heavy, take-no-prisoners, save-the-world adventures."

I must have been primed for catharsis, because her jibe just struck me as the funniest line I had ever heard. Obviously, and being generous, it was only moderately humorous. But I was in a vulnerable state and under the influence. I busted out a laughing conniption that had our fellow escapees up front turning around to see if I required additional medical attention. The tears were streaming down my cheeks, in a good way. Fortunately, it only lasted about fifteen minutes. I had clearly needed that.

Coop waited until I returned to a semblance of my former, normal self before she spoke again.

"I do know exactly what you're feeling," Coop finally said. "Do you play golf?"

"No, why?" I replied, perplexed at her non sequitur.

"I don't play, either, but someone once told me it's among the most frustrating of sports. You can string together over a hundred bad shots in a row, and you wonder why you ever took up this asinine game. Then, on the eighteenth hole, you somehow hit a miraculous shot, one of the best you've ever made. And all you want to do is come back the day after and play again."

I didn't respond but just looked at her, staring intently at a tiny piece of dirt lodged near her eyebrow. Oh, and I guess I was also waiting for her to complete her thought.

"My point is, we just took a fantastic shot across the Falémé River, and now all you want is another chance to get back in the game."

Okay, she'd nailed it. She was dead right. I was reminded once again just how smart and perceptive she was. Our relationship had stumbled out of the gate, but sitting on that plane, still thousands of miles away from home, I realized I was going to miss Coop and the roller coaster we'd just ridden together.

Eight and a half hours after takeoff, our wheels touched down at the Ottawa Macdonald–Cartier International Airport. We were home.

PART 3

CHAPTER 20

WHEN WE arrived back in Ottawa, it was hot. Perhaps not quite as stifling as in Mali, but not far off, either. And humid, too—so humid I felt like I needed an umbrella when I stepped off the Challenger. Non-Canadians seem to have a hard time accepting that in summer, temperatures in Ottawa, among the world's coldest capitals, can stay in the sizzling thirties for days on end. But there you go. It was a Friday morning in August. I can't tell you the actual date because I had lost track of my days. But I was home—well, at least, in Canada. I didn't make it back to Toronto right away, but I would soon.

Landing on a scorching summer Friday proved to be excellent—if fortuitous—timing on our part. Nobody wanted a long meeting on a steamy Friday afternoon. Vivian did not insist on an immediate debrief, I assume due to the success of our operation.

Not to mention that we were all exhausted—physically, mentally, emotionally, and, I don't know, perhaps geographically, musically, gastronomically, and maybe even astrologically, too—and needed some downtime. Plus, I had a broken wrist. Even after snoozing on the long flight, I still felt pretty well wiped out when we arrived. So, Vivian gave us the weekend off. The pilot conveyed this good news shortly before we started our descent into Ottawa. The two Challengers landed within minutes of one another and taxied into an empty hangar on the perimeter of the airport, far away from the busy commercial terminal.

Of course, none of the Tardif Fourteen nor the three of us had passports when we landed on Canadian soil. But apparently Vivian and Angus had arranged for a streamlined entry process that did not require our passports or any other government-issued ID. Each of us simply signed an affidavit attesting to our identity and country of citizenship. Officials would match each one up with a passport at some date in the future. Besides, none of us had anything to declare beyond the clothes on our backs—including, in my case, one fresh fibreglass cast—and collective, unbridled relief.

Much to my surprise, Coop told me she had promised Adama that Amina would stay with her in Ottawa. She said that neither she nor he trusted the diplomats at the Malian embassy in Ottawa. They'd been appointed by the previous corrupt regime, not by Demba's corrupt regime. I didn't recall reading in the CSIS Intelligence Operations Handbook that operatives were encouraged to take personal custody of ten-year-old foreign nationals—let alone the daughter of a president. But I was glad. I thought

Coop had mellowed a little since meeting Amina a week earlier. They seemed to bring out the best in each other. When Coop was with Amina, I barely recognized my hard-nosed, rule-following, badass partner in all things clandestine.

"So, does Vivian know you'll have a roommate for the next few days?" I asked Coop, as the three of us sat in the back of a government car driving in to Ottawa.

"She does."

"And she had no concerns?"

"Oh, she had a few, but none could match the case I made," Coop replied with a Cheshire grin. "In fact, I'm taking Amina to meet Aunt Vivian tomorrow."

"We are going to hang in," Amina helpfully added in her ever-improving English.

Coop whispered in her ear.

"I mean, we are going to hang *out*."

"Well, that will be a blast," I said. "You'll like Aunt Vivian. She's really nice, and lots of fun, too. And she's a boss."

Amina looked puzzled.

"I mean, she's, um, smart and powerful and kind."

Amina nodded, no doubt stowing away the new word for future use.

We soon pulled up to the front entrance of a modest low-rise condo building in downtown Ottawa, not too far from the canal. The driver opened the trunk and pulled out two duffel bags. One tag said *Cooper*, the other AC.

"I was told to give you these," the driver said, handing Coop both bags.

"That Vivian thinks of everything," she said, then turned to me. "I'll see you Monday morning for the official debrief. I've already given Vivian the thumbnail sketch, and all seems to be well. Though you never know. But I think we're all good to go with the whole truth and nothing but the truth."

Coop then put down the bags and hugged me.

"Not bad for your first op, Norval. Not bad at all."

Amina hugged me, too.

"Yes, not bad, Mr. Norval," she said.

I figured I'd been on the receiving end of more hugs in the last week than I had in the previous year. That was not a complaint.

I asked the driver to wait until I'd seen Coop and Amina breeze past the concierge. They both waved and disappeared into an elevator.

Amina seemed to be holding up well. I thought back to shortly after we'd landed in Ottawa. By the time we'd disembarked and gathered in the hangar, it was already early afternoon in Mali. While we waited for our driver, Coop had called Monique on the burner phone for an update on the secondary operation, the oft-cited Demba's Downfall. We'd pushed our heads together around the phone so we could both hear. Monique wasn't in a position to speak freely, but she was able to confirm that everything had gone exactly according to plan. Or as she put it:

"Let's just say your name for the operation was completely fulfilled."

The others around us had seemed a little alarmed as Coop and I, and eventually Amina, too, performed an impromptu celebratory interpretive dance on the hangar floor. It likely meant that it would be safe for Amina to go home soon and that Adama was now in charge—not just superficially, cosmetically, but substantially, truly. We'd have to wait for the details, but it sounded an awful lot like unqualified good news to me. Still, we weren't quite ready to cut the cake just yet.

After we dropped off Coop and Amina, it was only another five-minute drive before the car pulled up in front of the venerable Château Laurier hotel, right next door to the Parliament buildings. Vivian had kindly put me up there for as long as it would take to complete the debrief and our final operation report. I wasn't sure how long that would be, but staying at the Château meant that I didn't really care.

The driver popped the trunk again and reached in. He checked the tag on the last duffel bag and then handed it to me.

"Norval," he said. "Not a common name. Like the thriller writer."

"Right, I guess so," I replied. "I'd forgotten about that writer."

I thanked the driver and he pulled away. My mystery duffel bag and I managed to navigate the revolving door without banging my left arm, and I was soon deposited in the beautiful lobby of the Château Laurier. The Château was, and still is, a world-class hotel. A young woman was waiting for me just across the threshold. I could tell at a glance she was not on the hotel's staff.

"Welcome home, Mr. Norval," she said, reaching out to take the bag from my right hand. "I'll take that, if you please."

"Oh, hello," I replied. "Nice to have a welcoming committee."

"Well, a committee of one," she said. "I'm Charlotte. I'm with CSIS, and part of my job is liaising with the minister's office. So, I have the pleasure of working with Vivian Kent whenever the MO is involved in operations. Hence my presence here today."

"Very nice to meet you, Charlotte."

"We're circumventing the typical hotel check-in procedures. Here is your key. I'm quite sure you'll enjoy the suite. Ms. Kent felt it was the least we could do after the week you've had."

"Well, that's very kind of her, and the people of Canada," I replied. "Thank you so much."

"You must be exhausted," she said, leading me to the elevators. "I'll see you up."

The elevator opened on the fifth floor, and we walked down a carpeted corridor until we reached a corner of the building. The sign on the door said *Presidential Suite*.

"Wow," I said, as I entered the expansive and expensive suite.

There were several different rooms stretched out across what must have been two thousand or so square feet. It was actually bigger than my Yorkville condo in Toronto, and more lavishly appointed

"I guess this expense does not fall within the scrutiny of the Standing Committee on Public Accounts or the Auditor General," I said.

"I think, given the nature of our work at CSIS, our financial accountability operates a little differently," Charlotte replied. "I'll leave you to rest now. You're expected at CSIS on Ogilvie Road, Monday morning at nine o'clock, where you and Ms. Cooper will be debriefed. A driver will pick you up here at eight fifteen.

Lauren Cooper will meet you in the CSIS lobby. Oh, and I've been asked to remind you that this operation is completely off the books and so you're not to speak to anyone about it, except for Ms. Kent, the minister, and Ms. Cooper, of course. But I think you already know that."

"I'm glad to be reminded. Thank you," I said. "Is there still an Apple Store in the Rideau Centre?"

"Yes, there is. Have a restful weekend, and thank you for whatever you've been up to in the last week or so. By Vivian's demeanour, I assume it was important and successful."

In the duffel bag, I found two or three changes of clothes, a pair of casual but dressy-enough-for-the-office shoes, boring but presentable pyjamas, and a well-stocked toiletries bag. I spent twenty minutes in the bathroom showering and shaving. With a fibreglass cast, showers were fine, but washing my hair one-handed took a little concentration. Then I tried on the most comfortable-looking pairing of the new pants and shirts I had spread out on the bed. As usual, everything fit perfectly. CSIS obviously shared my view on the importance of getting the details right.

I headed down to the lobby and back out through the revolving doors towards Wellington Street. I waved off the bellhop—I didn't need a taxi—and strolled down to the corner of Colonel By Drive and Rideau Street. I crossed at the lights, walked into the Rideau Centre, and headed straight to the Apple Store—and by "straight," I mean I wandered aimlessly around the multi-floor mall until I eventually stumbled upon my destination, utterly by fluke, after about twenty-five minutes.

No need to bore you with a run-of-the-mill retail transaction, but half an hour later I returned to my room—sorry, suite—in the Château Laurier and, using the cloud, set up my new MacBook Air laptop. I'd left my older model in Kéniéba and wasn't sure when or if I'd be seeing it again. Fortunately, I always stored my files in the cloud, so there was nothing of any value on the hard drive. I'd let Monique know that my retired computer could be donated to the Tardif community-service operation of her choice.

It took me about an hour before I was happy with my one-armed laptop set-up. Then, I started scouring the Web for any news from Mali. If Demba's Downfall had indeed unfolded according to plan, it should have been over by then, and some news of it may have seeped out. But there was nothing. That concerned me. On the other hand, maybe it had all worked out, and Adama was sitting on the news for a bit as he strategized how best to proceed with any public announcement. Smart.

Then I opened my email. I had given Adama an obscure email address that I sometimes used when connecting with the intelligence sources I occasionally tapped for, yes, operational details to make my novels more real and believable. And I had helped Adama create an innocent-looking Gmail account with no apparent connection to Mali's head of state. I really hadn't expected to hear from him so soon, but there it was, topping my inbox. The subject line simply said, *Success!*

Given the size of the presidential suite, I don't imagine the neighbours heard my celebratory shout. I restrained myself and limited my histrionics to several enthusiastic but silent fist pumps.

My dear friend, JN,

Thank you for your earlier and welcome message about the anniversary of your novel Safe. I cannot adequately convey how it made me feel.

Today's schedule of events was successfully completed with the best possible outcome. MT was very brave. I'll tell you the whole story when I see you, which I hope will be soon. In the meantime, I will send official transport soon to make it easy for you to send my precious package back to me.

I am in your debt in so many ways. I am grateful beyond words.

AC

I had never experienced the sense of satisfaction and happiness that washed over me in that moment. I actually felt a little emotional about the news, as confirmed by the lump in my throat.

I waited for a few minutes and then called Coop's home number. She picked up on the first ring.

"It worked! The plan worked!" I shouted into the phone.

"Who is this?" she said.

"You know who this is," I replied.

"Yes, I guess I do. I was just messing with you," Coop said. "I was about to call you. I just heard from Adama. And he had a nice long talk with Amina."

"I can't believe our idea worked. Adama is now free to govern," I said. "And Amina is free to go to school and be a kid again."

"Exactly. And by the way, it was *your* idea. And yes, it looks like it worked, thanks in large measure to Monique."

"There's something about Monique. I'm still figuring her out. Ice queen at the outset, but then she warmed up and turned into a brave and willing co-conspirator in the end. She sure has spine. We could not have done it without her," I said.

"Well, obviously she just had to get to know us a little first," Coop replied. "After all, we are amazing. I knew she'd come around."

"So, I guess you won't have your new roommate for very long."

"No, likely just for a couple of days. He's sending a jet for her soon."

"Way to go, Coop. We did it."

"Yes, we did, Norval. You done good. See you Monday morning."

"Wait, did Adama give you any details? I want to hear how it all went down at the mine. I need the blow-by-blow account."

"Nope, I told him not to share the nitty-gritty over the phone. I have a feeling we'll get the whole story from the horse's mouth sometime soon."

I spent the weekend not calling my agent. Angela had been leaving me increasingly irate and frantic messages for the last week, after I'd failed to check in with her as I usually did, every few days or so. I hadn't told her I was going to Tajikistan, let alone pulling a covert op in Mali. I wasn't ready to share any of that yet. In fact, I'd never be spilling the Mali story to anyone. That was the deal.

So, I'd have to embroider the Tajik visit a bit. And neither was I ready to return to my writing life, even though I had dozens of items piling up on my to-do list. None of them seemed nearly as important to me after Mali as they had before. I just needed some time to recover and ease myself back into my old life. I needed a reset.

So, I coasted through the weekend. I bought a couple of books to read. I went to a movie by myself. I don't even recall what it was, but I remember that I liked it. I felt safe and secure sitting in the nearly empty, darkened theatre for a matinee. I walked up and down the canal in the sunshine. I ate breakfast at a diner. I spent Sunday afternoon touring the National Gallery, just a short walk from the Château Laurier. I even read back what I'd last written on my novel in progress, though my heart really wasn't in it. It would be at some point, but just not quite yet.

Angela racked up a few more calls but I let them all go straight to voicemail. I was still a little scared of Angela Prochilo, the only agent I'd ever had, even after all our success together. "Feisty" is far too sedate and tranquil a term to describe her. One of the reasons my advances were so large was that my publisher never wanted to go toe-to-toe with Angela. I admit it was an intimidating prospect. So, they just gave me what Angela asked for to avoid the battle. All good for me—and good for her, of course—but it also meant that I, too, was intimidated by her. I knew I was going to have to pay, and sometime soon, for not returning Angela's calls—but again, just not quite yet.

CHAPTER 21

MONDAY MORNING at the appointed time, I climbed into the back seat of the dark late-model Buick idling in front of the hotel.

"Good morning," I said.

The driver looked in his rear-view mirror, then checked his phone before replying.

"Good morning, but you don't look like Cassandra Stevens," he replied.

Just then someone knocked on my window. A young woman in yet another CSIS standard-issue dark pantsuit pointed to her car, parked a few spots behind.

"So sorry, my mistake," I said, employing my oft-used sheepish tone.

I made my way to the right car, also a dark late-model Buick.

"Apologies," I said, as I settled into the back seat.

"No worries," my chauffeur replied as she shifted into gear and pulled out. "It often happens when I pick up someone at the Château."

Coop and Amina were waiting for me in the lobby of the large triangular building CSIS called home. Amina was beaming and ran over to greet me.

"Did you hear that, um . . . you know, everything worked out at home?" she asked.

"It's great news, Amina. I'm very happy for you and for your father."

Coop was smiling, too. I sat down between them on a couch in the lobby's waiting area.

"Amina, I have to speak with James for a few minutes. Why don't you read your new book until we have to go up to the meeting?"

Amina nodded and pulled the book from her backpack. By its cover, it looked like a young adult novel in French, largely because that's exactly what it turned out to be.

Coop and I stood up and moved a few steps away.

"Okay, James, this is the official debrief. And that means that I take the lead in the meeting. That's what Vivian is expecting of me," she said. "It doesn't mean you won't be speaking, but I'm still the lead."

"Of course, Coop," I replied. "I wouldn't have it any other way. You let me know when I should chime in."

"The good news is, we can tell the truth from start to finish," she said.

"How do we handle adding Amina to our exfiltration manifest?"

"It was the only way we could secure Adama's assistance, and without it, the operation would have failed," she said. "We balanced the risks and benefits, and determined that it was worth bringing her out to ensure that we could get the fourteen Canadians home. So, we took her with us. End of story."

"Okay. And what about our explanation for leaving Monique behind?"

"We didn't leave Monique behind. She insisted on staying to continue her work. She made that call of her own free will. Besides, she played a crucial role in getting her team out and should be decorated for what she did."

"Finally, what about Operation Demba's Downfall? How do we explain that?"

"Well, first off, we must never call it Operation Demba's Downfall again," Coop said. "We were merely a sounding board for Adama as he considered his future. We neither encouraged nor dissuaded him. We just answered a few rudimentary operational questions as he thought through his options. We were not involved in anything that happened after we crossed over into Senegal. In fact, we still don't really know what happened."

"Wow, you are good," I said. "I think you're ready."

"Good, because here we go," Coop replied, eyeing the young woman walking towards us.

"Good morning, Ms. Cooper and Mr. Norval."

"Nice to see you again, Charlotte," I replied.

"As per Mr. Norval's greeting, I am Charlotte, and I'm Vivian Kent's CSIS liaison. I'll take you up now."

"Thanks, Charlotte. Vivian speaks very highly of you," Coop said. "And I appreciate you keeping an eye on Amina while we're in the debrief."

"Not a problem. We'll be in the outer office, just next door to the debriefing room."

As we made our way up an elevator and down several corridors, Charlotte spoke to Amina in a mixture of French and English. Amina warmed to her immediately and was happily in deep conversation with her when we reached our destination. I don't think she even noticed when Coop and I walked into one room while Charlotte led her into the next.

We were greeted by a beaming Vivian Kent. With some effort and perhaps pain, she lifted herself from her wheelchair to embrace Coop, her young charge, and then even gave me a hug.

"I'm sorry that you're flying on one wing, James," she said, eyeing my cast and sling. "I hope you're not in too much discomfort."

"I'll be fine, thank you."

We all sat down. Vivian had a thick file in front of her. The stamp on the cover was upside-down from where I sat, but I was still able to decipher the words *Top Secret* and *CSIS: Senegal*. It looked as if Steve had been a busy boy and worked the weekend to give Vivian a preliminary sense of at least the final stage in our little Mali escapade.

Holding up her hand, Vivian asked us to wait as she reopened the file folder and perused the final few pages, then closed it all up again.

"Right, then. Glad to have you both back safe and sound. But I confess, I'm having a hard time processing what I've learned of your exploits, and the creative and daring path you pursued all the way to the safety of a Senegalese riverbank," she opened. "I don't know whether to heap congratulations and gratitude at your feet for effectively dealing with unexpected complications, or to chastise you for broadening the operation from simply bringing fourteen fellow citizens home to rescuing the president's daughter and helping to install a more stable and responsible government in Mali."

Now, that was a mouthful. It seemed she already knew.

"Well, if we're voting, I support your door number one," I said, jumping in. "And, just to clarify, there was no regime change. Adama Camara was president when we arrived and he's still the president right now, as far as we know."

"Semantics, Mr. Norval," she replied, still smiling. "A writer's last refuge."

In one fleeting look of pure, unadulterated irritation, Coop very clearly reminded me that she was to lead, and I was to listen—you know, as we had agreed no more than three minutes earlier. I gave her the floor with an elaborate sweep of my one good arm and the hand attached to it.

"Well, sometimes the situation on the ground is not the same as it might appear from Madrid or Ottawa, or as it appears in an operational report from a colleague who was only in on the final play," Coop said, gamely entering the fray. "Our sole operational objective was to get the Canadians out, which we did. Anything else of consequence or benefit was merely an unintended by-product or completely disconnected from our operation."

I tagged in even though Coop had not yet invited me into the ring.

"Our suspicions that Adama Camara might not be the one actually running the country were confirmed early on. The president himself told us that Demba Dembele was in fact in charge and using the life of Adama's daughter as leverage. That realization necessitated changes in our approach. And in fact, without President Camara's assistance, it's unlikely we'd ever have succeeded in getting the Canadians safely out of the country."

Vivian nodded before speaking.

"Now then, let's not get ahead of ourselves. Like with all good stories, let's start from the beginning, when you touched down in Bamako," she said. "Take me through it, chapter and verse, and don't leave anything out."

And after I surrendered the floor again, that's exactly what Coop did. It took two days to tell Vivian the complete story, from the incompetent, tone-deaf band that greeted us on the tarmac all the way to having my wrist set in a medevac chopper near Dakar.

Even though Vivian was technically not with CSIS, but rather served on Angus's ministerial staff as his intelligence advisor, she never had any other CSIS personnel in the room with us. I assumed this was out of respect for her previous role as head of the agency. And it certainly made the long and gruelling session a little easier on us.

We started day two a little late, as Coop and I had to drive Amina to the airport. An older but serviceable Malian government jet was waiting there to whisk her back to Bamako, where she would no longer be in danger.

I pulled up to the security booth on a special airport access road. The commissionaire inside was clearly expecting us because he immediately lifted the gate and waved us onto the tarmac. I parked the car near the Malian jet, which sat just outside of a government hangar. Amina's teacher had been recruited to escort her back to Bamako. That was a welcome surprise, and the two embraced. When it was time, Amina came first to me.

"Other than Lauren, you are my favourite Canadian, and you were very brave," she said. Then she hugged me tight and whispered in my ear. "Thank you for helping my father find himself again. We've spoken on the telephone, and he sounds like he used to. He sounds like my father. Thank you."

"Now he needs you at his side to help him," I said. "He has a big and important job to do. You will remind him why he's doing it."

"I know," she said, nodding and smiling. "I know."

Then she reached over, grabbed Coop's hand, and walked her towards the metal staircase that ascended to the open door of the plane. Amina's teacher had already boarded and was waiting just inside the door.

The two stopped at the foot of the stairs. Coop lowered one knee to the tarmac and placed her hands on the young girl's shoulders. Amina looked at Coop, her bottom lip quivering just a little. Coop spoke to her for a minute or so, as Amina nodded periodically. Then they came together in a long hug. I could see Amina speaking in Coop's ear.

They were both laughing when Amina backed away, waving to us both. Then she climbed the stairs and disappeared inside.

We waited until the plane was taxiing towards the runway before we drove back to resume our debrief.

"So, what were you two laughing about just before she boarded?" I asked.

"Oh, nothing," Coop replied. "Just stuff."

"She told you that I was her second-favourite Canadian, didn't she?"

"I'll never tell. Okay, yes, she did," she said, dissolving in laughter.

Vivian had asked no questions on day one and instead just let Coop talk. On day two, Vivian stopped us a few times to seek clarifications. She was particularly interested in Monique Tardif and her unshakable decision not to accompany her team to freedom. We did our best to explain how different Monique's approach to mining in Africa was from that of her mercurial father's when he had been running the show. In the end, I think Vivian accepted that Monique was simply never going to abandon her post as the lead mining engineer at Tardif Resources and the de facto lead community investment officer in Kéniéba. Both, in equal measure, compelled her to stay to protect what she had built. And she was not to be moved. If we had forced the issue, it is likely that none of the Tardif Fourteen would have made it home to their families.

If Vivian hadn't held that view at the beginning of the debrief, I believe she got there by the end, courtesy of Coop's persuasive presentation.

But it took a bit more convincing to persuade Vivian that we'd made the right call in bringing Amina with us. Coop and I both understood that this point represented the shakiest ground in the operational terrain we'd chosen to navigate.

"To be clear," Coop said as our debrief was drawing to a close, "we didn't bring Amina with us because she was a child in danger, or because it simply wasn't right that she be played as a pawn in a power struggle she might not even survive. Of course, we were both outraged that Demba would use her—a child—in this way. But that's not why she crossed that river, clinging to me. Rescuing Amina wasn't our mission."

"And so . . ." Vivian prompted.

"We brought her with us because we didn't believe we could get the Tardif Fourteen out without Adama Camara's help. He got us up to Kéniéba in the presidential chopper. He got us onto the Tardif mine site. He ran interference for us time and time again. He took risks so that we could exfiltrate our Canadian expats. Sure, his love for James Norval's books alone would have guaranteed his hospitality, but it would not have been enough to gain his confidence, and thus his willingness to help fourteen Canadians escape his nation's custody. We brought fourteen Canadians home, but only because we agreed to do what Adama insisted we do—bring Amina, too. In the end, we thought the success of the operation was worth it."

Vivian didn't say anything for a while. Then she closed up her file with an air of finality and sighed.

"I would have made the same call, and perhaps even earlier than you did," she said. "And thank you for placing your decision to exfiltrate Amina in the broader context of the operation's success. That will make it easier to sell up the line, though I'm quite sure the minister will have no difficulty with it at all."

"Thank you, Vivian," Coop said. "It may not have been exactly what we planned, but it was what the situation demanded. And it worked."

"I've decided not to ask you any questions about what happened to Demba Dembele, and how or if that changes the government of Adama Camara. Since whatever happened on that front occurred after you made it to Senegal, let's just not go there, shall we?"

"That works for us," Coop said, as I bobbed my head in complete approval.

"In your final report, don't belabour your decisions to leave without Monique and bring Amina out with you," Vivian advised. "Don't make it sound too much like you're worried about justifying those calls. No need to be defensive. Couch it, as you have in this room, within the framework of the operation's success, and move on."

"Got it," Coop said, as I kept up my nodding. I was a veritable bobblehead.

We never saw Angus over the course of our time with Vivian. He was apparently overseas attending an annual gathering of the signatories to the Five Eyes intelligence alliance: the U.S., the U.K., Australia, Canada, and New Zealand. But he did send me a lovely handwritten note, filled with cryptic allusions to our operation that would mean nothing to anyone if the note fell into the wrong hands. But I knew what he was saying, and I appreciated it.

I probably should have burned his note after reading it. But that seemed a little dramatic, not to mention overdone. Besides, I wanted to keep it. So, I did.

My dear James,

I've been kept informed of your exploits and I gather congratulations are in order. I could not be more chuffed at the outcome. Upon meeting you some time ago, my gut clearly told me we had the right lad for the role. And after putting well more than sixty solar circuits on my curriculum vitae, I've learned to trust my gut, despite its incrementally increasing circumference.

I'm proud of you, lad, and of your, shall we say, supervisor, for the creativity, commitment, bravery, and unconstrained chutzpah you brought to an endeavour that was never going to be easy or straightforward. But we obviously had the right team on the job.

One day, this whole affair may well be bathed in public light. But even if your contribution remains shrouded in the shadows, know that we, on behalf of so many others, are forever grateful and in your debt.

Aye, lad, I'll say it again. We're so very proud.

AM

After our debriefing with Vivian, we tackled the final operation report. Coop bore the brunt of this effort, but I did help her wordsmith the more narrative sections, particularly when we needed to tread delicately. I like to think I know a thing or two about stringing words, phrases, sentences, and paragraphs together in a way that is clear and pleasing to the reader. I had to force myself to tone down my language, remembering that my words would not be sold in airport bookstores, but rather would reside, largely unread, in a secure CSIS database holding our most sensitive, top secret intelligence documents. Still, it was an interesting, even satisfying, experience.

My final night in Ottawa, after an early dinner with Coop, I was packing up what little I had into my new CSIS-issued duffel bag when the hotel phone rang.

"Hello?"

"Nice to hear your voice, James, as I agreed to call you," opened the Honourable Angus McLintock, his thick Scottish brogue front and centre, as always. "I assume my voice betrays who I am, so there's no need for you to say aloud my humble moniker or tiresome honorific."

"Yes, I certainly know who you are. Very nice to speak with you, um, sir," I replied. "And thank you for the kind note you sent my way. It meant a lot."

"I'm sorry I've not been in contact earlier, but my infernal schedule is not my own," he said. "Some days I know not where I've been, where I'm going, or ofttimes even where I am. But our mutual friend has kept me abreast of your escapades, and I must say, we're both mightily impressed. Your young colleague in the field also speaks well of your conduct in planning, and in that crucial time of execution that must follow. I'm proud of you, lad, and you, too, ought to be proud."

"Thank you, sir," I replied, touched by his words. "I found the whole thing not just exciting, but deeply rewarding. And it's given me new insight that I suspect will make its way into more conventional projects of mine in the future."

"Well, speaking of the future, I very much look forward to hoisting an ale with you soon and hearing about your travels and accomplishments. We will be having a private gathering in the coming weeks not far from where you stand right now, so expect a call with details in the days ahead."

"I'd like that and look forward to it."

We spoke for a few more minutes, but the minister's next obligation on his "infernal schedule" encroached and marked the end of our conversation.

I thought back to what I'd said to him and realized I hadn't been spinning him on how I felt about my first covert mission. Sure, it had been exciting, and seldom had my fear compromised my ability to act—at least, I didn't think it had—but when it was all over, I had been left with a strong but foreign feeling of deep personal satisfaction. When I thought of my time in Mali, I felt not just happy but fulfilled by the experience. Arguably a subtle distinction, but a distinction nevertheless. Yes, I felt fulfilled.

It made me feel better about my initial decision thirty years ago to apply to CSIS. And it made me a little melancholy that it hadn't worked out back then. A mélange of emotions.

—

After five days spent debriefing with Vivian and writing up our final report, Coop drove me to the airport.

"So, here we are. You're abandoning me and running back to Hunter Chase," she said, as we approached the terminal.

"Well, Hunter Chase doesn't argue with me as much, or really at all," I replied. "But he does require my attention, particularly as I've left him in a dangerous, spine-tingling predicament from which I must now extricate him."

"Perhaps navigating a dangerous and spine-tingling predicament of our own, as we just have, may give you greater insight when writing Hunter's next narrow escape."

"I'm counting on it," I said, as she pulled up to the curb and stopped. "Hey, um, thanks for not shutting me down over there when you were well within your authority to do just that. I quickly learned that I don't know nearly as much about the clandestine world as I thought I did. And I have you to thank or curse for that."

She laughed.

"Right back at you. Thank you for showing this 'by-the-book' intelligence officer that the manual doesn't always have the answers we need in the field. I have actually come around to conceding that by working together we achieved so much more than either of us could have on our own. We complement each other super well. What's the cliché? We were more than the sum of our parts. That's what you taught me."

"Well, as a writer, I've been taught to eschew clichés, but in this case you're right—or perhaps 'the shoe fits' would be more appropriate, since we're discussing clichés."

"Actually, you're the only one talking about clichés. I stopped listening quite a while ago."

Then she leaned over and gave me a hug.

"See you around, Norval."

"Later, Coop," I said, as I stepped from the car and headed inside to my gate.

I wasn't exactly feeling misty-eyed at how far we'd progressed after knocking heads when we first met, but had our farewell lasted any longer, I might have got there.

CHAPTER 22

WHILE IT felt good to be back home in Toronto, I also felt like something was missing. After having travelled halfway across the world, lived in a palace, hijacked a school bus after drugging the driver, and been dragged through a raging, rushing river with a broken wrist while being shot at, it was odd now to be back in the relative tranquility of my condo in Yorkville. My still-throbbing wrist was memory enough. It was not a bad break, but because it had been a blow from a flying, speeding metal side-mirror bracket, the resulting contusion peeking out from the edges of my cast, in all its colourful kaleidoscopic glory, was more painful than the actual wrist fracture. At least I could still type on my new MacBook Air without too much discomfort.

The novel about a West African dictator that I had completely made up to get me inside Mali's presidential palace was actually starting to take shape in my mind. Obviously, I'd need to change up the story from the one I'd just lived through, but my first-hand experience kept me coming back to it. Having spent time in West Africa also meant that much of my research was already done. Yes, I know, I pride myself on my research and on getting even the small things right, but it was a time-consuming—and sometimes life-threatening—exercise that I could avoid on this novel given my baptism by fire in Mali. Of course, I'd have to break the news to Angela that I was working on a different new novel and not the one she'd previously sold to my publisher. She would be a little perplexed at my sudden interest in West African politics and the dictatorships that drove them, but I'd figure out a way to explain it. I was quite good at making things up.

It did feel different being in Toronto. I noticed how much more vivid, sharp, and colourful the streets of my city seemed. It wasn't just the cleanliness of the urban landscape, or its plentiful parks and mature trees. No, I eventually realized that there was no dust in the air to mute the colours around me. After a little more than a week in Mali, I'd gotten used to the constant haze hanging over, well, everything. I hadn't noticed it as much in Bamako, but in Kéniéba I was reminded that Mali was a desert nation, with the Sahara beckoning in the northeast part of the country. When I woke up that first morning back in Toronto, when viewing my city, I felt like I'd upgraded my TV from a black-and-white to a colour LED 4K with Crystal Vision. Everything was so sharp. It was a little overwhelming. A sensory assault that took a while to ease and become the norm.

The morning after I returned home, my cast and I took a long, long shower. Then I read through, and responded to, some emails—so many emails. Finally, when I felt I could avoid it no longer, I called Angela in New York. She'd been my agent for more than twenty-five years. She didn't like to be out of the loop, and she'd definitely been out of the loop ever since I'd left for Tajikistan a lifetime ago. Now, somebody had to pay. I had to pay.

"I'm sorry," the irritated voice on the phone said, "I see the name James Norval on my call display, but I don't seem to remember anyone by that name. Wait, wait, it's slowly coming back to me. Perhaps I've just forgotten you because, despite leaving about two dozen increasingly desperate voicemails and twice as many emails, you never returned my calls or sent me even the briefest of emails. Not once. So, do remind me who you are again and how I might know you?"

"I'm sorry, Angela. I really am. I was, um, out of the country and really not able to communicate. There was next to no cell service where I was."

"You mean in Tajikistan?" she asked. "Yes, because I'm extraordinarily talented, I managed to find out you were in Tajikistan, of all places. Don't ask me how, but I do have a third cousin who's been crushing on me for decades and who just might happen to work at Langley—yes, that Langley, in Virginia. Anyway, your Tajik visa said you were supposed to be out of that godforsaken land two weeks ago. You see, you can't escape me. You can't ghost me. I will hunt you down. I will find you."

"Yes, right, Tajikistan," I backpedalled. "You see, I was detained, or rather, delayed, in getting out. It took a while to get the research done, but I now have everything I need. Oh, and good news, I may have an idea for my next novel."

"And that's supposed to take you off my nasty list for letting me stew these last few weeks about whether you'd been kidnapped or arrested or imprisoned or tortured, or worse?"

This phone call actually seemed worse than any of those fates, but I'd brought this on myself.

"Angela, I'm sorry about that. I was so wrapped up in my research. Oh, but speaking of torture, I did manage to break my wrist."

"Is it your writing arm?"

"Come on, Angela, would I ever allow the wrist of my writing arm to be imperilled? Of course I wouldn't. It's my left wrist," I replied. "And by the way, because I know you were just about to ask, I'm feeling much better, thank you very much, and I can still type almost normally."

"You mean slowly."

"Yes, for me, slowly is normally," I replied. "But the important thing is, I'm okay."

"Actually, I'm no longer certain that is the important thing."

It took me another forty minutes to coax her back in off the ledge and ease my way back into her good graces, or maybe just her indifferent graces. We had foreign rights agreements to sign that she had negotiated weeks ago, and several postponed meetings in L.A. on three upcoming feature film adaptations that we had to schedule. Finally, we had to approve new reprint covers for six novels on my backlist. It suddenly felt like I had returned to my old life. It almost felt good to be back, but I also realized I'd never felt more alive and renewed than I had in Mali. Too bad I could never share the real story with Angela, or anyone else.

By the time I'd been back home for two days, I'd already finished a quick freelance writing project. I was pleased with it and emailed it off. The next morning, I received a brief reply—*Perfect! Thank you!*—along with a URL. Two hours later, I clicked on the link and waited until the image of the now-familiar presidential palace in Bamako resolved on my screen, with the message *The president's address will begin shortly* superimposed in English. Soon my screen was filled with the same view of the president's office that I'd seen in his inaugural address, with his desk in the foreground and his bookcase behind. My novels were still arrayed on the presidential bookshelves, but this time, the display was in perfect chronological order.

I watched as Adama entered the room alone and took his seat behind the presidential desk. He was smiling and looking calm, almost at peace. He had told me that he would pre-record both the French and English versions of his remarks and they would be aired simultaneously. Then he began to speak.

"My fellow citizens of Mali, I am honoured but also sad to speak to you this evening about an important and positive development that sets our beloved country on a course for greater social stability, economic prosperity, and democratic integrity. I regret to inform you that a short time ago, my principal advisor and, yes, long-time friend, Demba Dembele, was arrested on multiple charges of corruption and crimes against Mali. I apologize to all of you for my error in judgment in appointing him to the very position of great power and influence that allowed him to profit at the expense of us all. I will not make that mistake again. In the wake of the infuriating discovery of Demba Dembele's corruption, I am moving quickly to secure Mali's future, our collective future."

Adama went on to announce a return to more measured and fair foreign-investment rules, those governing mining in particular. These reforms, he explained, were intended to strengthen the natural-resource sector and create a more resilient economy, while sharing revenue with the companies bringing their expertise to Mali and employing thousands of her citizens. He also committed to holding free and fair democratic elections within eighteen months, though he did not disclose whether or not he would be a candidate. Finally, he thanked, without naming, a few close friends of Mali who had helped him see the error of his ways in appointing Demba Dembele and then act on that knowledge for the sake of Mali's future.

It was an extraordinary performance. He spoke fervently and eloquently. He looked so much more comfortable and confident than he had in his inaugural address. But that was a different time, and he was a different leader then. My now good friend Kiran, from the Canadian embassy in Bamako, later reported to Vivian that there was a new calm in the capital, and that the people seemed to have embraced Adama after his confessional and inspirational address to the nation. Throngs of supporters had gathered outside the presidential palace as chants of *Camara! Camara! Camara!* rose from the crowd.

So, yes, if it weren't already obvious, I wrote Adama's address. He had asked me if I would, and I'd told him it would be a great privilege. And it was. He invited me to invoice him whatever I wished. I told him I would only do it pro bono. There was no invoice.

Now, not a high percentage of Malians had TVs in their homes—many had no homes at all—but the mainstream media, social media platforms, and word of mouth helped to carry the message across the country and, to a certain extent, around the world. I confess, I had watched with some pride. Not pride in the words I'd written for him but pride in how Adama had conducted himself, and in his commitment to doing the right thing in a nation where so often leaders had not. I had come to know Adama Camara and to believe that he was an honest leader who cared about his country, its citizens, and its future. That was the pride I felt.

But what about Demba Dembele, you ask? What was his fate? I had it on the highest authority that Demba would soon be tried in Mali for his crimes. It would take time, but Adama was confident that justice would be served, almost certainly sending his old childhood friend to prison to serve a long sentence. As for his decision to blow the whistle on Demba and have him arrested, Adama was sad, but certain.

The next morning, I sat before my laptop again and, with the help of the CSIS secure-comms network, clicked a link to start an encrypted video call. He was already on my screen waiting when the connection was made. He smiled and nodded when he saw me.

"Mr. James, my friend, I am glad to see you alive and well."

"Zafar, you look great, and I'm happy we could connect," I said. "I've wanted to do this ever since we parted ways on that road outside of that Russian base. But please believe me when I say that, for reasons I cannot reveal, this really is the first opportunity I have had to call you."

"I am just happy that you look healthy. And I was so surprised and so pleased with your unexpected gift. I picked it up yesterday. It looks beautiful. It drives so much better than my old car. It's like riding a flying carpet. So smooth. And thank you for not giving me a flashy car. It would just have been stolen around here."

"I wanted to give you a brand-new Mercedes, but in your line of work, I know you still need to blend in and not make a spectacle of yourself."

"Mr. James, it is perfect, and you really did not have to do that. You did pay me in advance for more days than I actually worked."

"Zafar, you may have saved my sorry life when you took the time and made the effort to contact my embassy in Astana. You didn't need to do that, and you went ahead and did it anyway. Thank you, thank you."

We talked for a few more minutes before a CSIS operator broke in to say the satellite window was closing. Zafar really had saved my bacon. Without his initiative—above and beyond the call in his trade—I might still have been locked up in Tajikistan's Correctional Colony No. 7, enjoying Yuri's company, and perhaps that of a certain Tajik periodontist. And I doubt I'd still be in as good working condition as I was when that irritable Canadian diplomat sprung me, saved me, and drove me to the airport. All that happened because Zafar acted when he didn't need to. He deserved more than a beat-up, but smooth-running, late-model Nissan Altima.

I had hoped to shed my fibreglass cast before returning to Ottawa for that mysterious event Angus had promised. But because I had broken both my ulna and my radius, the cast would stay for six weeks at least. So, I was still living with a sling and persistent low-level discomfort when I boarded a lunch-hour flight from Toronto's Island Airport bound for Ottawa. Having flown recently in Canadian government and private jets, I didn't find flying commercial much fun. On the other hand, I wasn't heading into an unstable country to undertake a secret operation with life and limb on the line. I was just going to Ottawa for a covert, but still unspecified, event.

"Can I ask, do we yet know who was shooting at us across the river and how they discovered our escape point? I mean, we had no cellphones on the bus to track. I thought we were free and clear."

I was sitting in a small boardroom in Minister McLintock's office on the second floor of Centre Block on Parliament Hill. Angus and Vivian sat on one side of the table, and I sat across from them. I was wearing a nice suit, as Angus had suggested. He was similarly attired, though my suit fit quite well. Vivian sat in her wheelchair wearing a red dress. She looked great.

"Excellent question," Vivian replied.

"Well, I don't like loose ends in my novels, and as it turns out, I guess I don't like them in real life, either."

"Kiran Hassan, our contact in the Bamako embassy, was able to find out that the bus itself had been equipped with a tracking chip," Vivian said. "But because of Monique Tardif's call back to the compound security team saying the bus would be delayed, no one in Kéniéba thought to check on the bus until it was too late. So, it took them a while to sound the alarm, track the bus, and deploy the border police. Then by the time they actually found the bus parked in the middle of the raging river—nice work, by the way, we heard that was your idea—you were literally being dragged through the rapids over to the far shore. So, they took a few blind potshots, but you were soon safe in Senegal's arms."

"So, I guess throwing those phones out the bus window was pointless," I said.

"Perhaps, in the end, but it was a wise decision at the time."

I asked a few more questions, but by that stage, I knew pretty well as much as anyone could know about what had happened that evening on the Falémé River. I'd been there, after all. In a brief pause in the conversation, I watched as Vivian pulled a file from her briefcase and placed it on the table in front of Angus.

"Ah, yes. Thank you, Vivian," Angus said. "Now, James, we're aware that you apparently fell just short of joining CSIS nearly three decades ago. We also understand that you received no explanation for their decision to take a pass on your offer of public service, despite your repeated requests. Finally, we have the sense that this has been a sore point for you ever since, and has prevented you from gaining what we now seem to call closure. Am I in the right neighbourhood, James?"

I wasn't sure what was happening, but his question was simple enough.

"Well, Minister—or rather, Angus, as I promised to address you, at least in private," I said, "I'm not clear on where this is headed, but you're not just in the right neighbourhood, you're standing on my front porch."

"Excellent. Now, this is a wee bit unorthodox, but we both believe that you deserve to know why you didn't make that grade, particularly when you seemed to be sailing through in the top of your cohort."

He opened the file in front of him.

"You'll be pleased to know that your test scores at the various stages in the recruitment process were exemplary, always in the uppermost quartile. And here's where it turns fascinating. There is a space provided for explanatory comments next to the rejection box, which in your case was unfortunately checked. Let me read the simple and clear explanatory comments from your file to illuminate what, for you, and for nearly thirty years, has been obscured in the shadows. And I quote: 'Too witty, too sarcastic, too quick, too thoughtful, too independent, too eloquent, too confident, and too opinionated. Ultimately, James Norval is simply too "memorable" for covert operations. For clandestine ops we need competent but dull and forgettable. Conclusion: Unsuited for field work.'

"And that, James, was the end of your CSIS ride," Angus concluded.

Nobody spoke for a time so that what Angus had revealed could find its way to me.

"We wanted you to know that, paradoxically, you washed out because you seemed too good in almost every respect. And being so good can draw unwanted attention. So, you failed for the very best of reasons," Vivian said. "And it was insensitive, even unkind, for them not to have provided you with these reasons at the time they made their decision. As a former head of CSIS, I apologize and have already taken steps—belatedly, I know—to ensure that other recruits who don't make the cut are not treated in the same fashion."

I exhaled slowly, nodding, relieved in many ways.

"Well, that could have been a lot worse," I said. "I'm touched that you would do this for me. I've wondered for, well, for a very, very long time, and now I know. Now I can finally close that book and move forward. Thank you for telling me."

"Aye, but this seems paltry recompense for what you've done for us, for your country, and, as I understand it, also for Mali," Angus said. "Under the circumstances, it seemed the least we could do."

"I'm glad and relieved after all these years to know what they really thought. But I don't understand how you've come to share this with me?"

"Despite our prowess at keeping secrets around here," Vivian said, "Lauren asked if we could find out what happened. She said that it was something you've wanted to know, needed to know, for a long time now. It was her request, and she pushed us hard to bend the rules. But we figured you earned it."

"Aye, we truly did," Angus agreed. "Now, just before we head off to this humble little ceremony, we were wondering if perhaps you might be available or interested should other, shall we say, clandestine opportunities arise in the future, all completely unofficial and 'off the books,' as we like to say in the intelligence world. We want to do nothing to impair your perfect cover as a globe-trotting thriller writer, which means you'll need to keep writing. But such a cover might again prove useful, that is, if you're willing."

Once again, I was restrained, calm, coy, and cool . . . until I wasn't.

"Yes, yes, of course, yes!"

I shut up after my third increasingly enthusiastic yes, lest they revoke their offer over concerns for my psychological stability. Anyway, let's just say I eagerly professed my promise to answer on the very first ring should my country call again.

"Excellent," Vivian said. "Now, this makes it even more important that no one know of your role in the Mali operation. The future value of your cover as a famous thriller writer—hiding in plain sight, as it were—plummets if the world learns about your little adventure in Mali. So, tell no one, and do not even consider ever basing a novel on this little adventure."

"I understand and accept that reality completely and unreservedly," I replied.

"This is wonderful news. You've done fine work, lad. Aye, fine work indeed," Angus said. "I reckon we'll keep your file handy in case a future situation warrants a call."

Apparently, I wasn't quite finished yet.

"I've been waiting a long time to work in the field. It was always my dream. And I learned so much from Coop after we got to know each other and figured out that we actually liked each other. She is a great asset to CSIS," I said. "You know, when I was in Mali, for the first time in my adult life, I wasn't living through Hunter Chase's exploits and dreaming about them being mine. I didn't give that smug bastard a moment's thought the whole time I was there. I had my own exploits to worry about. They may not have been quite as exciting and they certainly featured fewer explosions, but I think we got the job done."

"Aye, lad, you got the job done and more, and the nation thanks you," Angus replied. "Now, of course it goes without saying that the nation knows nothing about any of this, and never will. But if they knew, by God, they would surely thank you, that I can promise. So, you have our gratitude on their behalf."

I followed Angus and Vivian out the door and down the corridor feeling a little overwhelmed, not just because I finally knew the reason for my CSIS washout all those years ago but also because I now knew that Coop would go to bat for me, and Vivian and Angus would violate CSIS protocols to share the truth with me. Not to mention their invitation to perhaps serve again if an appropriate situation arose. It was a lot to take in.

I don't remember our route through Centre Block, but eventually, Angus led Vivian and me to the prime minister's office.

"Greetings, Ainsley. You already know Vivian Kent, but we also have a special guest with us for the wee cèilidh the PM is throwing in his office. In fact, this is one of the guests of honour."

"Hello, Minister McLintock. And it's good to see you again, Ms. Kent. Of course, it's also nice to have your special guest here, the man with no name, I've been told." She actually winked at me when she said it.

"Yes, just a standard security protocol. Is the PM ready for us?"

"Yes, Minister, most of the others have already arrived." She nodded to a woman seated at a desk in the corner of the reception area. "My colleague, RCMP Constable Michelle Mitchell, who is part of the PM's security detail, will escort you there, even though you know your way around here, Minister."

"Aye, I surely do, Ainsley. I thank you."

Constable Mitchell rose.

"If you would kindly follow me through."

Just then, a uniformed RCMP officer accompanied by a man carrying a square black suitcase—by his look, he could only have been a plainclothes security officer of some kind—emerged from the corridor leading to what I assumed was the PM's office. The plainclothes officer looked at the minister as he passed.

"Clear, sir."

I looked at Angus.

"Um. Did that guy just sweep the prime minister's office for listening devices?"

"I'm afraid that is classified information," Angus said. "But yes, laddie, he did. I'm told it happens every day."

Constable Mitchell guided us down the corridor and through the open door to the prime minister's office.

The room was stunning—fully and beautifully wood-panelled, with arched windows and, of course, bulletproof glass. All I could think of when we entered was how well I'd be able to write in that space. But alas, the office was already occupied. A long table at one side of the room featured fruit, cheese and crackers, and other hors d'oeuvres. Next to the table, a small bar was staffed by a white-jacketed bartender who undoubtedly enjoyed high-level security clearance. It looked like most of the Canadian expats who had traversed the raging Falémé on a taut rope were there, nearly filling the office to capacity. They nodded and waved but seemed to cling together as a group. The PM had not yet arrived, but another staffer hovered nearby, perhaps to ensure no one stole the lovely Canadian art from the walls.

I suddenly realized that standing next to Coop in a corner of the room was none other than Monique Tardif. She and Coop waved at the same time, and I waved back. I was about to weave my way through the group to join them, but just then, the prime minister entered. Fortunately, he did not seem surprised to see so many people in his office. Never having been in the same room with a prime minister before, I was focused on him. As a consequence, I initially missed the two figures who trailed him into his office. When I did register their presence, I was shocked to see none other than President Adama Camara and his daughter, Amina. Adama caught my eye and smiled in an almost giddy way, as if he'd pulled a fast one on me. And I guess he had. He laughed, pointing at me.

"Ahhh, we got you! You don't think we would miss this, do you?"

I still didn't know exactly what "this" was. Adama had had several opportunities to mention his private little state visit while we were working on his recent Presidential announcement, but he had kept this a secret. And now he seemed to be revelling in his subterfuge.

The room quieted down.

The PM spoke first, welcoming President Camara and his lovely daughter, Amina. He then addressed the rest of us in the room.

"Welcome, everyone. But before we start, I am compelled to remind all of us that nothing that is said within these walls this afternoon can ever be spoken of again. We are bound by the legislation that commits this tale to perpetual secrecy. With that well understood by us all, I invite President Adama Camara of Mali to begin our little secret ceremony," the PM said, stepping back and making room for Adama to come forward.

It was clear that Adama wanted to be involved in this gathering. I doubt a foreign head of state had ever before participated in what turned out to be a secret CSIS commendation ceremony. For each of those being honoured, Adama read the official commendation, editorializing along the way. He started by asking Coop and me to stand with him just in front of the prime minister's desk. He said very nice things about our work together in Mali and how much he loved my novels. He then set his notes aside and spoke from the heart.

He was quite emotional as he closed his remarks.

"These two great Canadians risked their own lives in a faraway land to save their fellow citizens, to save my only child, and, in a way, to save Mali from further descent into corruption and crime. They also saved me from living a lie as a mere marionette, introducing policies and laws, and authorizing actions, against my will and my better judgment. It is not an exaggeration to say that James Norval and Lauren Cooper have changed the course of a nation. And I will dedicate the rest of my useful years to keeping my country on this new path."

While I thought he had grossly exaggerated our contribution, I was touched by his words. He certainly had a flair for the dramatic. When he had finished his remarks, the prime minister presented small medals in red velvet boxes to Coop and me, supposedly for our bravery in rescuing the Tardif Fourteen and spiriting Amina out of Mali. Both Coop and I were surprised and a bit flummoxed by the honour, so we waived an invitation to speak, beyond expressing our heartfelt thanks.

Then Adama asked Monique Tardif to join us at the front. From her shocked reaction, I don't believe she had any idea her role would be recognized as well. After she worked her way to the front to stand next to me, Adama proceeded to tell the story of the day after the escape. This was what I had been waiting to hear. Adama had always put off sharing what had happened that day, and now I knew why. He wanted to tell the tale in this significant setting. You know, again with the flair for the dramatic. He began to speak and quickly warmed to his task.

"I am not a professional actor, but politicians are often required to behave externally in a way that they are not necessarily feeling internally," Adama began. "Without too much exaggeration but not nearly enough humility, I venture to say that the future of Mali rested on my performance when the presidential helicopter landed back in Bamako that night after our day in Kéniéba with Monique Tardif and her team."

There were a few chuckles from the assembled, and Adama laughed, too.

"When we could not find Amina in the helicopter's cabin and then discovered the opened emergency hatch, I'm told my face turned white—and you can imagine how difficult it was for me to achieve that particular look. I then immersed myself in the role of the father terrified and traumatized at the thought that he may have lost his only child. All parents have imagined such a tragic circumstance, and I confess I inhabited it. I embraced it. I wore it like a new suit, and if I do say so myself, that suit fit very well indeed."

More laughter from our little group. But Adama was just getting started.

"I called my old friend the Minister of Defence, and commanded that he amass a force of soldiers and have them transported to Kéniéba at the hint of first light to begin a thorough search of the area. Through tears and a show of great distress and desperation, I implored Demba, my once good friend, to come back with me to Kéniéba to help, reasoning with him that some things transcended national affairs and personal enmity. He readily agreed. I was not surprised he was so willing, as Amina's safety was the leverage he daily used to pull my strings as president. There may have been additional incentive for him to accompany me back to Kéniéba, but you'll hear more about that shortly. So, Demba Dembele came, with four of his burly and surly President's Personal Protection Force soldiers, who were all in his pocket. Now I will invite Monique Tardif to tell the rest of the story."

Monique took a small step forward, smoothed out her dress, and began to speak.

"When the Minister of Defence and three transport choppers filled with soldiers arrived very early the next morning, they started a systematic search of the area, looking for any trace of Amina. Adama—if I may call you that, sir?"

"Of course, Monique, of course. Please proceed. The best part is coming."

"Adama and Demba arrived shortly thereafter in the president's chopper. Adama looked positively stricken and immediately left to join the search team. I should clarify that Demba was so eager to accompany Adama back to the mine site not just because finding Amina was important to him but also because I'd called him the day before to tell him we'd just had a record-breaking diamond haul earlier that week, including the largest diamond we'd yet found. While that information was somewhat less than truthful, I can assure you, nothing would have kept Demba away from the Tardif mine that morning.

"Two of the four PPPF soldiers followed Adama and the other two stayed with Demba, who, by the way, was not at all happy to see me. He wasn't happy because upon landing, he'd been informed that my executive team had somehow escaped the country. The chief security officer at our compound had been scared to tell Demba and hoped the Canadians would be found before he arrived. Alas, James and Lauren had already escorted my team across the river and into Senegal. So, the chief security officer had no choice but to break the bad news to Demba as soon as he landed.

"He was so angry he probably wanted me arrested. But first, he needed me to show him the new diamonds. Finding Amina may have been his top priority but checking out the diamonds was a close second. He took my arm and dragged me over to the secure storage building where we keep the diamonds. The search for Amina would carry on without him, at least for a few minutes."

Monique looked at Amina, who smiled shyly.

"I took my time opening the heavy metal door. I was savouring the moment. He followed me inside, and I immediately opened the safe and pointed to the large drawer holding the latest precious stones we'd recently extracted. In fact, they were lovely diamonds, but they were no larger than any others we'd found. I just needed to distract Demba for a very brief moment. While he was preoccupied, searching for the promised large diamonds, I simply walked back out the main door of the building and swung the heavy door shut, relocking it from the outside and detaining Demba on the inside.

"It took quite some time before he realized he was alone and unable to get out. I'm sure he tried calling his guards on his phone, but no cell signal can penetrate the thick concrete walls of the building. So, he started banging on the door and shouting, though we could barely hear his pounding."

Adama was smiling and obviously enjoying Monique's story. He nodded to her, so she continued.

"A few minutes later, when all was ready, the Minister of Defence stood in front of me as I opened the big door again and quickly stepped back. A furious Demba Dembele burst out to face two dozen soldiers, their automatic weapons trained on him. His two PPPF guards had already been disarmed and cuffed and were locked in the back seat of a Tardif truck parked nearby. His other two guards were arrested shortly thereafter.

"The look on Demba's face was worth all the risk. As he processed what was happening to him, his bravado crumbled before our very eyes. He knew it was over. He was handcuffed, searched, and relieved of a pistol and the stash of diamonds he'd just pocketed. By this time, Adama had arrived on the scene, looking very stern. He nodded to the Minister of Defence, who then stepped forward and officially placed Demba Dembele under arrest for corruption and crimes against Mali. And in my mind, that was the moment the presidency of Adama Camara actually began."

She nodded to Adama while he beamed.

"Oh, and I was never arrested," Monique concluded.

What a story. It had in fact unfolded precisely as we'd drawn it up. Hard to believe, but apparently true.

The PM then stepped forward to present the third medal to Monique Tardif, for, in his words, "courage and resourcefulness in the face of imminent danger and in the service of Canada and her ally, Mali."

She had not expected that.

Angus raised his hand as the applause died away.

"Thank you, Prime Minister," Angus said. "Now, I am filled with regret about what I will next say, but I am not filled with doubt. Let me echo what the prime minister said at the outset, for it bears repeating. I'm afraid only those of us in this room know about this heartfelt but necessarily secret gathering, not to mention the events that prompted it. The nation is in your debt, even if they know nothing of it. So, I must insist that you keep not only this ceremony a secret, but, more importantly, that wee little adventure in which you partook as you left Mali by somewhat unconventional means. It is possible that somehow the story might leak—heaven knows it's happened before—but I trust no one among us today will be the source."

With the ceremony over and the brief reception underway, the PM slipped out for his next engagement. I sidled up to Coop as she looked out one of the windows overlooking the front lawn of Centre Block.

"You're not a very good spy if you can't keep a secret," I said, smiling.

She snapped a quick glance towards Vivian and Angus, who were talking with Monique on the other side of the room.

"Did they find out why? Did they tell you?"

"They did, and I can now put that issue to rest."

"Well, what was the reason?" she asked. "Come on, the suspense is killing me."

"The short answer is that I just wasn't bland enough or average enough for intelligence ops. The long answer would require me to list all the areas in which I am above average and therefore too 'memorable' for field work, and it would veer much too close to bragging . . . actually, it really would be pure, unadulterated bragging, and that's just not who I am."

She was laughing by this stage.

"I guess I can see their point. You do make an impression," she said. "It makes me happy that you now know why you didn't make it through. You have resolved what was such a long-standing and festering mystery for you. I sincerely believe that it, and not your aborted engagement, is what has held you back from, as they say, living your best life. Now you can move on with your future and be happy, fulfilled, satisfied."

"Well, I had been skeptical of your little theory, but based on how I have felt since Vivian and Angus enlightened me, I'm beginning to think you were right all along."

"Of course I was right. So, what now?"

"Well, I have a novel to finish and then another to start. The wheel keeps on turning."

I said nothing of Angus's offer to keep me in mind should future needs arise.

"So, I do want to thank you for caring enough to breach protocol and abuse the chain of command the way you did. It was good of you to ask Vivian and the minister about the baggage I've been lugging around for the better part of three decades."

"That is a long time," Coop said. "But you're carrying those years pretty well for someone as old as you are. I would have only put you at fifty-five, or maybe fifty-six. So, I think you actually look good for your age."

"I'm fifty-three, Coop."

"Oh. I see. Well, I was misinformed, I guess," she said, smirking. "Sorry."

"No matter, Coop, I'm in a forgiving mood. Nothing can dampen my spirits today," I said. "Anyway, thanks again. I know this is not goodbye. In fact, I'm really hoping we'll get the band back together again sometime."

"I'm in."

She gave me a hug and made her way out of the room. Vivian had mentioned that Coop had a new assignment beckoning. Lucky her.

Seeing that I was alone, Monique broke away from her conversation with Angus and Vivian and approached me. We hugged and I kissed her cheek.

"You two certainly deserve the medals you just got, even if you can never pin them on your chests in public," she said.

"Well, I was definitely shocked," I replied.

"Not as shocked as I was when Adama brought me up to the front of the class, too."

"I wasn't surprised in the least, especially after hearing about the day you had with Demba. I love a good sting operation, and you pulled it off! You were very brave," I said. "You earned every ounce of that medal you just received."

"I was so nervous that morning, but the plan was nearly foolproof. Demba's greed was always going to get him into that building. I knew it would work," she replied.

"I'm sorry we never told you about Amina," I said. "We thought you would be safer if you didn't know. We withheld that little part of the plan for your own benefit."

She nodded.

"You don't have to explain. I would have done the same thing," she replied. "'Need-to-know basis,' and all that."

"Well, I'm very glad to see you here."

"And I'm glad to see you," she replied. "The minister called to invite me a week ago. I had to be in Montreal for a regulatory meeting anyway and thought this was important enough to delay my return to Mali until tomorrow."

"Um, listen, do you have time for dinner before you go back?"

She smiled and placed her hand on my arm.

"I think I can squeeze in dinner tonight. I'm staying at the Château Laurier."

"How convenient. So am I. Shall we meet in the lobby at seven?"

"I'll be there."

Then, with the same sense of purpose that always seemed to guide her, she strode out of the room. I had surprised myself by asking her to dinner.

"So, what now?" I asked Adama when most of the others had left.

"Well, we have big plans ahead. There is legislation to draft, and regulations, too, alliances to forge, corruption to staunch, elections to run, and so much more. But I am as happy and optimistic as I have ever been about Mali's future."

"Will you run when the time comes?"

"I do not think so," he said. "There are at least two other candidates who, if I can persuade them to stand, would better serve the nation than I ever could as president. After all, I have a daughter to raise, and I actually miss teaching economics. So, we shall see."

Just then, one of his security guards approached to signal it was time for the president and Amina to leave for the airport. I offered Adama my hand, but he pulled me in for a bear hug, whispering his deep thanks for the umpteenth time. Then he and Amina and their two bodyguards left the room, but not before Amina winked at me.

A few minutes later, as I looked out over the lawns of Parliament Hill, I noticed movement reflected in the glass. I turned around and saw a youngish man in a suit walk into the room. Angus waved to him and started pushing Vivian in her wheelchair towards the door. I figured the newcomer was Angus's famed executive assistant, Daniel something-or-other, who'd come to fetch his minister. Angus stopped at the door, looked my way, and raised himself to his full height of about five foot nine. His beard and hair looked as wild and chaotic as ever. Vivian gave a little wave that had a *we'll see you again* vibe to it. Angus smiled and bowed his head in my direction, before pushing Vivian out the door and down the corridor. To my writerly eye, the whole scene felt like the ending of a novel.

ACKNOWLEDGEMENTS

I may have written this novel, but it would not be in your hands without my wonderful publishing family at McClelland & Stewart/ Penguin Random House Canada. I'm indebted to my amazing editor Joe Lee, our ever-eagle-eyed copyeditor Erin Kern and proofreader Eleanor Gasparik, diligent editorial assistant Rebecca Rocillo, and our talented designer Matthew Flute. And I thank my publisher Stephanie Sinclair, my publicist Ruta Liormonas, and the rest of the team for their efforts. After ten novels, there's still no place I'd rather be.

Of course, I will always be grateful for the years of support from my former editors, Doug Gibson—who I will always think of as my editor emeritus—and Bhavna Chauhan.

Beverley Slopen became my literary agent back in the spring of 2008, and my gratitude for her years of loyalty, expertise, and friendship knows no bounds. She has recently retired after a long and storied (pun intended) career and has earned a well-deserved rest. Looking ahead, I thank Carolyn Forde of Transatlantic Agency for agreeing to be my new literary agent. I look forward to our many new adventures together.

I'm grateful for the support of fellow writers I respect who kindly provided ringing endorsements for this novel. Thank you Wayne Johnston, Rod Carley, Susan Juby, Ali Bryan, Trevor Ferguson (aka John Farrow), and Drew Hayden Taylor.

I also thank my twin brother, Tim, for his "first read" through the manuscript and the sage advice that followed.

As I always will, I give deep and abiding thanks to the Stephen Leacock Associates for miraculously recognizing my debut novel, *The Best Laid Plans*, with the 2008 Stephen Leacock Medal for Humour. My life as a writer changed overnight all those years ago.

Finally, my wife, Nancy Naylor, and our two sons, Calder and Ben, have supported my writing life from its earliest days. I give thanks for their gift daily and will never forget it.

Terry Fallis, Toronto, February 2025

© Tim Fallis

TERRY FALLIS grew up in Toronto and earned an engineering degree from McMaster University. Drawn to politics at an early age, he worked for cabinet ministers in Ottawa and at Queen's Park. His first novel, *The Best Laid Plans*, began as a podcast, then was self-published, won the Stephen Leacock Medal for Humour, and was re-published by McClelland & Stewart to great reviews. It was crowned the 2011 winner of CBC's Canada Reads as "the essential Canadian novel of the decade," and was adapted as a CBC Television series and a stage musical. His next two novels, *The High Road* and *Up and Down*, were finalists for the Leacock Medal, and in 2015, he won the prize a second time, for his fourth book, *No Relation*. His other novels include *Poles Apart*, *One Brother Shy*, *Albatross*, *Operation Angus*, and *A New Season* and were all national best-sellers. A skilled public speaker, he lives in Toronto with his wife, and blogs at www.terryfallis.com. Follow @ TerryFallis on Twitter and subscribe to his newsletter at https://terryfallis.substack.com.

DISCOVER MORE FROM TERRY FALLIS

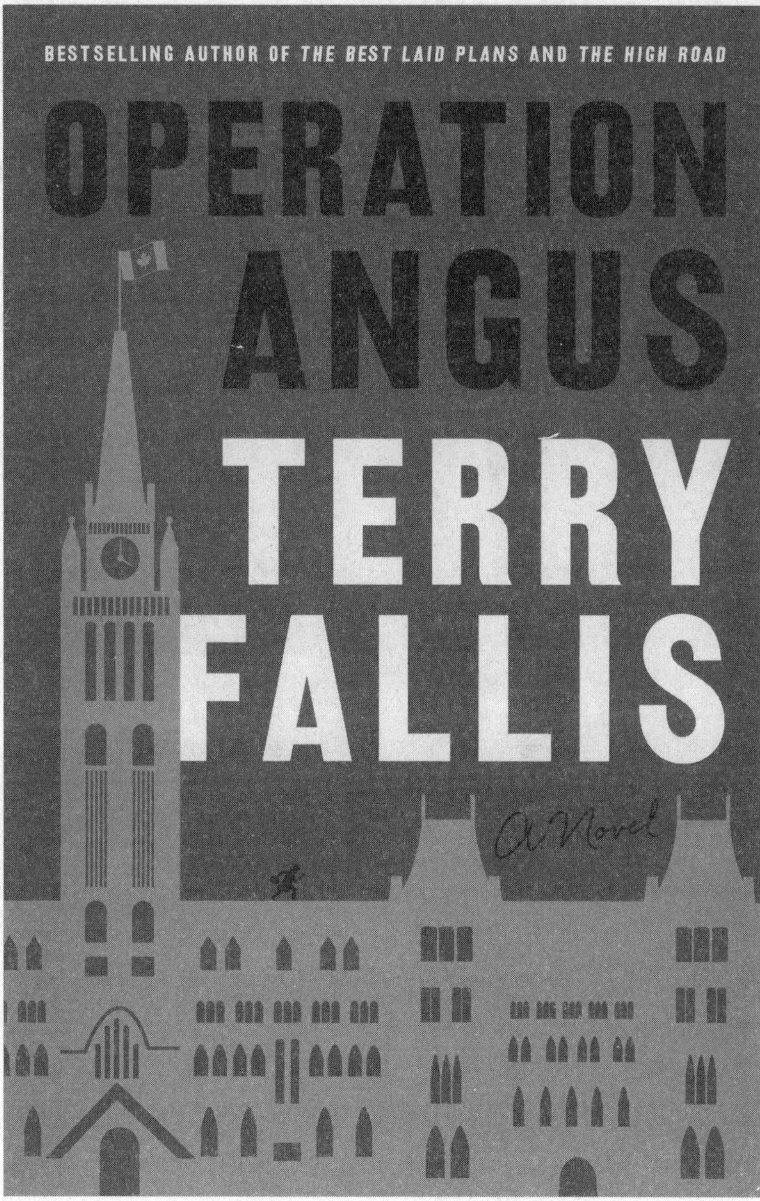

Penguin
Random House
McCLELLAND & STEWART

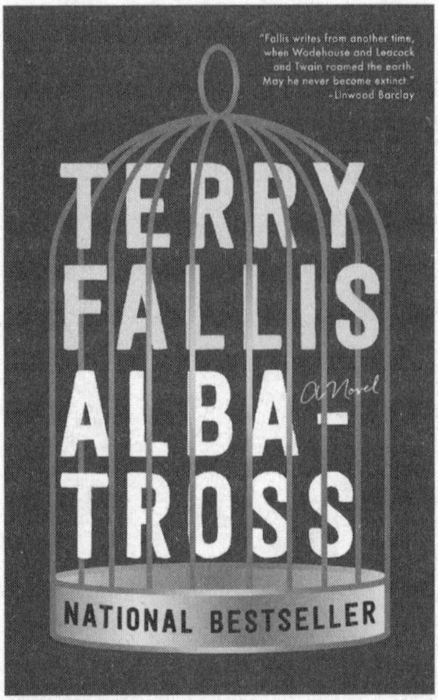
"Fallis writes from another time, when Wodehouse and Leacock and Twain roamed the earth. May he never become extinct."
—Linwood Barclay
TERRY FALLIS
A Novel
ALBA-TROSS
NATIONAL BESTSELLER

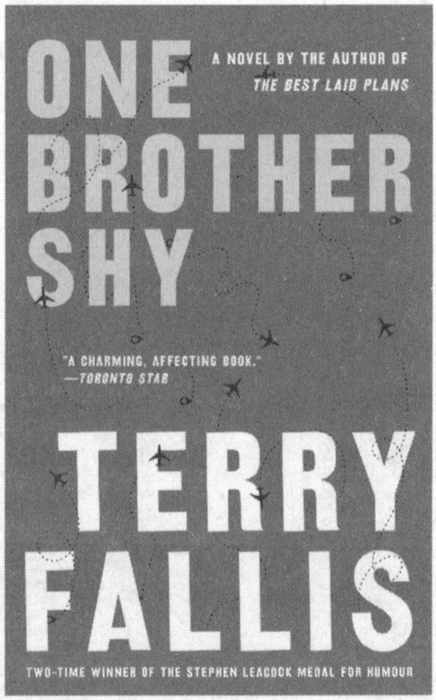
ONE BROTHER SHY
A NOVEL BY THE AUTHOR OF THE BEST LAID PLANS
"A CHARMING, AFFECTING BOOK."
—TORONTO STAR
TERRY FALLIS
TWO-TIME WINNER OF THE STEPHEN LEACOCK MEDAL FOR HUMOUR

TERRY FALLIS
UP AND DOWN
"FALLIS DISPLAYS FORMIDABLE CHOPS WHEN IT COMES TO NARRATIVE PACING, WRANGLING SUBPLOTS, BALANCING COMEDY AND PATHOS."
—GLOBE AND MAIL

THE HIGH ROAD
AUTHOR OF THE BEST LAID PLANS, WINNER OF THE STEPHEN LEACOCK AWARD FOR HUMOUR
A NOVEL
TERRY FALLIS

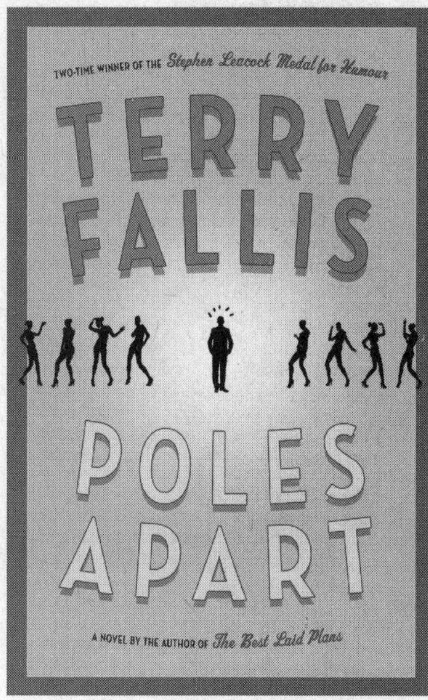
TWO-TIME WINNER OF THE Stephen Leacock Medal for Humour
TERRY FALLIS
POLES APART
A NOVEL BY THE AUTHOR OF The Best Laid Plans

"So what's in a name? When it's Terry Fallis, you know it means a good book." NATIONAL POST
TERRY FALLIS
NO RELATION
WINNER OF THE Stephen Leacock Medal for Humour

THE BEST LAID PLANS
"AMUSING, ENLIGHTENING — AND CANADIAN, AND IT DEFTLY EXPLORES THE MACHIAVELLIAN MACHINATIONS OF OTTAWA'S POLITICAL CULTURE." GLOBE AND MAIL
NOW A MAJOR TV SERIES
CANADA READS 2011 WINNER
CANADA READS
radio one
www.cbc.ca/canadareads
A NOVEL
TERRY FALLIS

Penguin Random House
McCLELLAND & STEWART